Mandate:
THIRTEEN

a novel

Joseph J. Dowling

Manta Press, Ltd.
www.mantapress.com
Cover Design by
Author Photo by Jenny Dowling

First Edition

CHAPTER: ONE

She wasn't eating. Again. His daughter had never possessed a great appetite—just as well, or he'd have even less to eat. But concern should trump greed, right? It was a dead heat. Michael tore his gaze from her plate and instead stared through the grubby twelfth-floor window, where a brisk wind sent granite boulders of cloud scudding across the miserable concrete skyline. A smattering of lit windows glowed back in the autumnal gloom, amber beacons among an ocean of hollow apartments, empty since the exodus.

Hope stopped toying with her food and placed down her knife and fork. "I think I'm finished. Do you want the rest?" Perhaps she'd sensed his hunger, or his eyes had betrayed his complaining stomach.

He swallowed the gathering saliva in his mouth and dragged her plate across the table. Now it was her turn to watch him, yet the innocence in her sweet smile never faltered. Even though he tried to slow himself, the remnants disappeared in a few greedy gulps.

When he glanced across the sparse room, a blurred reflection of his hunched form peered back from the blank television screen. Underneath, a red LED blinked, suggesting the thing might suddenly flick back into life. Lord knew he'd tried to fix it, at least to appease his wife, Allison. What a waste of time that'd been. Modern appliances were no more user serviceable than a discarded tampon. His wife and daughter had never quite forgiven him for owning a car from the previous century—an inefficient lump of metal, according to them—but these crappy modern cars were no different from cheap, flimsy TVs, designed to be driven until they broke, then dumped like thousand kilo piles of garbage. The twentieth-century cars he loved were living, breathing machines, with more personality than half the God-bothering human sheep, squawking their parroted political slogans on the streets below.

He glanced at his watch. Allison would be home from work soon. At least she no longer bothered asking how the job hunts had gone. As usual, the day's efforts had been an epic failure. Potential employers took one look at his criminal record and told him the position had been filled. *Filled my ass.* Soon, they'd force him into a compulsory work detail to keep his meagre state subsistence. It was too ironic. London's work-age population had halved in fifteen years, so why weren't there ample vacancies for men like him? They considered plenty of roles too menial even for the machines, but when the work placement scheme provided an army of unwilling volunteers, even those jobs were beyond reach.

That familiar bile of impotent frustration gathered again, welling in his stomach and rising up his throat. He scratched at the palms of his hands with his fingernails, while an oppressive silence shrouded him, charged with electricity like the air preceding a thunderstorm. His thoughts were getting too bleak, too active; without the distraction of a background hum, they might grow legs of their own.

It was almost time for the late afternoon rerun of *Brain Drain*, one of the more entertaining quiz shows, and he jerked into life for a moment before remembering the bastard appliance was broken. With each passing day, he missed the numbing comfort of television's tit less, but today he needed a surrogate. He raised himself from the table and flicked on the radio. By the time the unwelcome rapid-fire chatter of a news broadcast filled his ear, he'd already collapsed onto the sofa. He and his wife played daily games of ping-pong with the dial. She'd won this round, leaving the radio tuned to a 24-hour news channel, probably that morning while he slept in. The remote-control batteries were dead, of course. If he wanted to spin back to his favourite rock station, he'd have to haul himself upright again, but his last vestiges of strength had turned heel and fled.

He sighed and allowed himself to sink deeper into the couch. *Perhaps they'll report some good news for once.* Not a chance. When had a news channel last mentioned anything uplifting? No, it would be more trouble in Europe—either a right-wing party seizing control, or a left-wing uprising, if anyone was keeping track—or perhaps another historic old seaside town lost to rising water levels. If it was a slow news day, they might report another looming natural disaster on a different continent, but those usually got ignored.

Back when he was a kid, at least they shoe-horned some light amidst the darkness. Now, like a worn vinyl record stuck in the same dismal groove, the endless cycle of bland horror kept repeating. The oppressive tone never wavered, nor did the grand illusion of keeping the masses informed. Other than Allison, whose bizarre interest in keeping up to date had swollen into a morbid obsession, who even bothered to listen anymore?

These days, except for necessity or argument's sake, they rarely even spoke. When they did, it was impossible to converse without touching on the day's news headlines, important for a fleeting moment, then forgotten. They always sculpted their bullshit to fit their ever-shifting narrative, and even five minutes sapped his patience. What did she expect him to do with the information, anyway? But this time, the lead story hooked even his jaded ear.

"*As the population of England and Wales drops below thirty million for the first time in over a century, the government today announced a new mandate to reduce the age of compulsory fertility checks from fourteen to thirteen with immediate effect.*"

A pain stabbed at his chest as he digested the headline. *Thirteen?* Christ, they had to be getting desperate. Hope had recently turned thirteen herself. The poor girl should be out having fun with her friends, not thinking about which hideous option was the least awful: being declared barren or getting hauled off to one of those dreadful schools.

The female announcer's voice, stern and devoid of joy, yielded to a male politician's privately educated tones. The voice, or perhaps the way each word resonated with thinly disguised insincerity, sounded familiar. It belonged not to a concerned man of the people, but to a slimy high-ranking member of the Conservative Christian Alliance—Piers Beauchamp.

"*You, the public, have trusted us to address the issues this great nation faces. This is not a painless process, and the decision to introduce mandate thirteen has not been an easy one. But, in these challenging times, our officially sanctioned birthing schools provide free board and three meals a day for life, alongside the best medical care available. Anyone with a fertile family member should make themselves known immediately. We're offering amnesty to anyone who has avoided their duty thus far. You will not be punished. In addition, we're increasing the annual family stipend to six thousand new pounds. After the amnesty period, we're increasing the penalty for non-compliance...*"

He wished he could travel through the radio waves, only to appear at the other end like some uncaged, malevolent spirit, and rip the bastard's tongue from his throat. The likes of Beauchamp didn't worry about punishments, or a measly six grand a year for giving up their precious daughters. No, it was one rule for the scum in the tower blocks, while the right-wing Christian elite did whatever the hell they liked.

He glanced across at his daughter, now staring out the same window, probably at the grime-encrusted buildings which dominated the landscape. She looked content, with her dimpled chin resting in the crook of her palm. Perhaps she'd found the same stark beauty he'd discovered as a youth, hidden within London's cityscape. Back then, it was full of promise and intrigue. Now, he only saw a bleak reminder of their isolated existence in those impassive grey slabs, rising from the earth like silent sentinels, watching over the idle leftovers of society, those either too scared or too stupid to leave. *So, which are you, Michael?*

The ocean of calm on her perfect face didn't betray whether she'd absorbed the broadcast. Would she understand the implications? After the latest announcement, they could expect an imminent summons to the Medicentre for fertility checks. The odds of a positive result were low, of course. According to the latest stats, which Allison had eagerly sought, only one-in-fifteen.

After hauling himself upright, he trudged across the room and switched to a music station which played non-stop classic rock, mostly from the previous century. It was the station's famed happy hour, a daily dose of uplifting songs, no interruptions, and no bloody news. Free's 'Alright Now,' Journey's 'Don't Stop Believin',' Foo Fighters' 'Times Like These'—hopeful messages whispered through the dense fog of time, beamed from an era when humanity had known true optimism.

He flopped back onto the sofa and allowed the music to envelop him in a fragile cocoon. Maybe the world could be that way again. *Maybe.* If humanity bothered to wake up. Right now, that thought seemed as likely as a time machine whisking him into the early nineties—although what a glorious dream. The past had never seemed more attractive.

A key scraped at the lock, throwing him from the depths of introspection so quickly it was like plunging into icy water. "Hi honey," he said, jumping to his feet, wearing a grin like a circus bear.

Allison flicked her head towards him with barely disguised contempt. His heart raced with a powerful idea that he'd toyed with many times. *What if I tell her about the affair?* In all honesty, their relationship had suffered a downward spiral in the year since his indiscretions. Would she respect him more for coming clean and admitting fault, or was ignorance her way of holding onto those last frayed ribbons of dignity?

"Did you catch the news today?" Her question sounded more like an accusation.

Michael nodded. "Fucking Beauchamp and those Christian Tory bastards. Thirteen? It's insane."

"Have you spoken about it?" Allison flicked her head towards Hope, who was now immersed in her Metaverse, or whatever method of escapism kids used to distract themselves from the horror of reality nowadays. Who could blame her? She must've noticed their deteriorating living standards, but had her parents' subtle digs and passive aggressive exchanges filtered into her subconscious? Probably, but no one could expect to survive childhood unscathed nowadays.

"Uh, not yet."

"I'll talk to her tonight. It's better coming from her mother. What about the car? Have you sold it yet?"

Here we go again. Every evening, they skirted around the real issues in their relationship like two weary boxers in the closing stages of a twelve-round bout. The status of his only valuable possession was the latest substitute battleground. The question hung like an accusation and his internalised response rang out just as clearly. *Course I fucking haven't.*

"Uh, not yet. Bloody time wasters. Had another guy come kicking the tyres and taking the piss with another lowball offer, you know?" How long would the excuses wash? But then, for all he knew, his could be the last Mark III Ford Capri in existence. He'd saved this poor thing—little more than a hunk of metal condemned to rust in a farmer's field—and nurtured it back to life over countless nights, with his own oil-permeated hands, burning and red-raw from the cold. He had little else to look forward to, except thrashing the Capri around a moss-bound racetrack a few times a year. Besides, selling it would never fix their financial worries. The growing stack of bills on their Payscan credit account would instantly absorb the income.

"If we miss another reminder, we'll get C-listed. Hell, Michael, the TV's been broken for weeks, and Hope needs new clothes. Can't you think of anyone but yourself?"

Hope looked up at the mention of her name. "It's OK, Mum. I can manage with what I have."

"We're lucky they don't bother evicting people from this dump anymore." Her protestations lacked their usual intensity. Perhaps she'd resigned herself to their crappy situation.

"Look, the classic car market's going to rebound any day. If I hold on for a few more months—" She cut him off with a snort and stomped into the kitchen. Yes, there was something different about her today, like she'd spent weeks thrashing around in storm-swept seas and they'd finally drained, leaving her exhausted, but alive and breathing on the ocean bed. Her inner turmoil had calmed, as if she'd made peace with a difficult decision.

All at once, the realisation struck. *She's leaving me.* Relief washed over him, cold and shocking, like the brutal honesty of a drunk relative. Who could blame her when he couldn't bring home enough money to feed his family? Without the extra food credits from Allison's part-time *voluntary* work for the local Christian Conservative Women's Group, the three of them would go even hungrier. What a tasteless joke to call it volunteering when the alternative was starvation and a potential shunning by the area parish. Not that he cared what the local bible-bashers thought about his family, but they had far too much sway for their own good.

A hundred questions crowded his brain. Where would he stay and how often would he see Hope? Would she have a new father? He glanced up at Allison, but she tossed her coat onto the hanger and slumped onto the battered old sofa, still warm and indented from his body. It creaked and groaned, but his wife kept silent. If there was to be a genuine confrontation, it wasn't happening now. He sighed and took a seat at the table, resting his glum face on his hands. It wasn't fair to force her to leave. No, he'd take the decision out of her hands and disappear without argument, allowing them both to keep their pride intact.

After nightfall, while his wife and daughter slept, he quietly rolled out of bed and reached underneath for his rucksack. When he'd started keeping a bug-out pack, she'd laughed and called him a paranoid prepper. He'd always imagined it would be the two of them hitting the road together, in search of pastures new, and once Hope arrived, as a family.

He moved into the living room, placed the bag down, and

took a seat. The bag stood upright on the threadbare carpet, glaring back like an accusation. If he walked out now, he could never return. Was pride worth the risk of losing his daughter? Was it worth the self-hatred? He wondered if his old man had been blessed with a similar moment of clarity before evaporating into the ether. If so, he'd chosen to ignore it, or maybe the call had been too strong. *Let's sleep on it, Michael.* Maybe tomorrow, the world would take on a rosier hue.

He rose from the capsized old armchair, dragged himself into the darkened bedroom, and pushed the bag back under the bed. Allison hadn't moved. She lay facing the wall, with her bare back glistening copper from a sliver of moonlight which peeked through the curtains. He undressed and slipped back between the sheets, shivering, then pushed himself towards her, seeking the warmth of her body. She moaned and moved tighter to the wall. *See, even in her sleeping state, she can only recoil from my touch.* Next door, through the paper-thin walls, Hope murmured in her sleep.

Hope awoke with her mother rousing her gently from the swirling depths of an early morning dream. Waves of bitter sadness washed over her, followed by relief when she realised none of it was real. Her father didn't have a new wife and child; he hadn't looked through her like she'd ceased to exist, without the faintest spark of recognition behind a hollow stare.

"Wake up, honey." The moment her eyes unglued, and her mother's concerned face floated into view, the dream's detail faded like a sandcastle, washed away beneath the incoming tide.

"A mail-drone came this morning with a summons for

your hormone check. We better get it over with and see the doctor today, so get ready."

"Already?" she croaked, but her eyelids drooped, shutting off the nascent morning. When her mother shook her again, it seemed like there had been only a nanosecond gap. She stretched and emitted a long, groaning yawn, then sat up and reached for the steaming cup of tea her mother had placed on her little bedside table.

"Thanks, Mum."

With each sip of weak tea, the day loomed closer. With a jolt, she remembered her mother's words, and the previous night's conversation. It was the big one: her first hormone and fertility check. Her parents had never hidden the population's dwindling female fertility rate from her. Ever since she'd learned about sex, she'd been aware this day would come. If she tested positive, they might take her away from her parents, and if she received a negative result, as expected amongst her generation, she'd probably never bear children. But now the moment had arrived. It seemed unreal, like it was happening to somebody else.

With the mug empty, she could delay no further. She hauled herself from between warm sheets, and threw back her dusty and frayed yellow curtains, revealing a wall of misty grey which shrouded the usual panorama. Rivulets of drizzle seeped down her bedroom window, softening the edges. She never grew tired of the view from their apartment. Perhaps it never changed, yet it seemed different every time, an urban kaleidoscope. It was the only redeeming feature about high-rise living, although she'd never known a different life. In her dreams, they lived on huge open lands, with impossible hills and twisting rivers dominating the landscape behind fields filled with an array of animals, stretching as far as the eye could see.

From the living room, the buzz of the radio news channel which her mother never tired of pulsed through her door. She'd learned to filter it out. Her private thoughts provided a far richer canvas than the bleak reality her mother subsisted on. Not that her father's fondness for nostalgia-drenched rock music pleased her ears, either.

What a dreadful irony to have one parent incapable of living in the present, and another obsessed with it. Sometimes, she wondered how they'd even got together. If she concentrated hard, she could recall times when they'd been kinder to each other. At least their rows, after threatening to spill over into the mornings, had eased a little recently. Perhaps the flat's tense atmosphere would improve, but her parents were so distant, almost like strangers who shared living quarters. They'd been in love once, hadn't they? The memory—more sensation than recollection—of combined parental warmth enveloping her contented little soul was so faint, she couldn't have been older than four.

Perhaps she could find ways of being a better daughter and try bringing them closer again. She'd spent far too much time ensconced in the relative safety of her Metaverse avatar recently, ignoring the real world's dwindling appeal. Yes, she'd accumulated hundreds of friends, at least in the virtual world, and more cool tokens and keepsakes than she could ever amass in reality, but it didn't count for much. Not when her generation had so little power to make a positive difference to the world. That opportunity had passed, and now it had become a case of damage limitation. Her generation's duty was to leave as small a footprint as possible, to ensure the sea levels didn't rise any quicker, or the gulf stream didn't get knocked off course any sooner than expected.

Books were a better escape, but it'd been ages since she'd

read one. Now she thought about it, when *had* the Amazon feed on her Metaverse toolbar last promoted a book? Perhaps they didn't even sell them anymore, except at the local mega-store, with its tightly curated selection. And the last few times she'd walked past her favourite little bookshop, it'd been firmly shuttered. What a horrid thought, all those thousands of lovely volumes gathering dust in the quaint old shop, forever frozen in time and inaccessible to inquisitive minds. Hadn't she heard somewhere about a recent political pledge to reduce the breadth of *mind-polluting literature* available to under-eighteens by restricting millions of titles? Maybe they'd sneaked through the law change already. It seemed some news *did* filter into her subconscious, after all.

By the time she'd washed under the shower's weakening stream of lukewarm water, towelled off and dressed, her mother had her scuffed yellow windbreaker laid out. She put it on while her mother waited by the door, tapping her foot.

"Is Dad coming?"

"Nope. You know how rubbish he is with mornings, and he needs to concentrate on finding work. Besides, I figured you'd prefer me to take you alone."

A hazy recollection of the earlier dream had her gripped in feverish panic. Something in her mother's tone failed to offer comfort. "One second, I forgot something."

She dashed back into the narrow hallway in a few bounding steps. The door to her parents' room was open a crack. She peered inside and observed while her father thrashed about in his sleep for a moment before rolling onto his side, quiet. He hadn't vanished in the middle of the night after all—it was just a silly nightmare—but why had he been so miserable lately? Perhaps her father would get back to his old self again once he found work. Yes, she was too young to understand men, but their male pride seemed so easily bruised. *If they had to endure what we women have to… well, let's just say the world would be a different place.*

Her mother held the front door open for her and they descended the stairwell, avoiding the well-worn grooves in the centre. Once they reached the last set of stairs, they had a ritual, one which they'd observed on and off for as long as she could recall. They'd race each other for the door release button. If her mother reached it first, she'd pull away at the last second and let Hope press the big green dome. "Beat ya!" her mother would cry in mock triumph. This time, she made no effort to engage, and Hope buzzed them out unopposed.

They stepped into the damp London morning. Hope stared up at the miserable sky, squinting as water cascaded into her eyes. "Can we get a bus, Mum?"

"Sorry, but you're thirteen now. It's a full price fare. We'll have to walk, but it's only a kilometre."

She'd better get used to being considered an adult now that she'd reached her teens. Free travel and being made a fuss over had been abandoned in the realms of childhood, alongside fairy tales and dolls-houses.

As if to mock her, an empty bus hissed past, splashing the pavement in a mini tsunami, which caught an elderly couple ahead of them. Auto-pilot bus drivers were many things, but considerate towards pedestrians was not one. The couple looked so miserable and cold, and she tried to offer them a sympathetic smile. Now she'd turned thirteen, her parents would surely allow her to volunteer and help some of the older folk left in the block. But did their generation deserve her empathy now? They were offered plenty of chances to reverse global warming before the point of no return. It's not like they hadn't known what needed doing. They just never bothered. And the fifty-plus age group had been instrumental in sweeping the current government, who had shown *zero* interest in environmental matters, into power. But most folk weren't bad people, not deep down.

By the time they arrived at the rundown Medicentre, her old yellow raincoat seemed to have given up the ghost, and the rain had soaked through. Perhaps she *would* need new clothes, but her parents had more important financial considerations than her wardrobe. If only she could earn some money of her own, but if her father couldn't find work, what chance did she have?

They stood underneath the retinal scanner. It flashed green, then the door swept itself open, and they strode inside. Usually, the waiting room, which gleamed in contrast to the building's crumbling exterior, lay deserted. In-person appointments were frowned upon unless unavoidable, but today a sprawl of girls aged roughly between thirteen and fourteen occupied almost every seat. One parent or another accompanied most girls, but some poor things sat alone, and Hope's heart pained for each of them. A buzz of hushed conversation filled the room, with a collective cloud of dread hovering almost visible beneath the harsh white strip lights.

She dampened her own questions as they rose in her throat, and instead cursed herself for not bringing a book, or at least a magazine, especially after her resolution earlier that morning. Maybe it was for the best. She'd received some funny looks from the other kids when she'd last read in public, at least the ones who'd torn themselves from their Head-Up Displays long enough to notice. Her own display glasses had stopped working a few weeks back, relegating her to an old 3D tablet, which performed the job OK. But it lacked many of the most modern features, and the battery life was so bad she couldn't use it without a constant power source.

Eager to strike up a conversation, she glanced across at her mother. She had her earphones in and wouldn't catch her eye—probably to absorb the mid-morning news update. Instead, Hope created a little game to keep herself amused. She gazed around the room, trying to invent a few silly lines of backstory for everyone. A constant stream of comings and goings made the task difficult, but she'd almost finished when an automated voice called her name. *Hope... Randall... Please go to room... Twelve.*

She nudged her mother, who had her eyes firmly shut and jerked at her touch.

"Sorry, Hope, I was just catching the news. Trouble in Europe again. Another uprising, in Austria this time." She stopped speaking to chew her thumbnail while Hope stood and waited. "The socialists have tried another coup and Germany is sending in troops. It's all getting too close for comfort. It'll be on our doorstep soon enough."

"Wouldn't you feel better if you didn't listen to so much? News is always bad, you know."

Her mother rose and flashed a smile. "You sound like your father. It's important to keep current, instead of living in denial about the world we live in, like he does. You don't need to think about these things at your age, not when I do the worrying for you."

Hope followed her mother, weaving through the crowds into a quiet consultation area. Adults sure loved to fret without addressing the planet's genuine problems. But at least she cared. Not like her father, who seemed to have given up on the world.

Her mother knocked on the door marked twelve. After a brief pause, a male voice beckoned them inside and they entered.

"Morning, Hope, have a seat. I'm Doctor Gilligan." He

was short, middle-aged, with thinning hair and a birdlike face. Hope remembered with great fondness her childhood GP, Doctor Laghari, a friendly and patient man with soft, warm hands, always ready with a joke and a smile. By the time she realised all the doctors with cool foreign-sounding names were disappearing one-by-one, she'd not seen him in six months. Nowadays, these centres were a revolving door of faces, and she'd never seen the same doctor twice.

He turned to her mother. "You must be Allison Randall, I assume?" She nodded, and the doctor spun back to Hope. "It's nothing to worry about, just a routine check. The government has decreed we test every young lady of thirteen or older for their AMH hormone levels and ovarian reserve to assess their ability to conceive. I trust your mother has explained what all this means?"

"Yes, she's aware." It was unlike her to be so blunt.

Dr Gilligan's wire-framed glasses sat perched upon the tip of his hooked nose, and he pushed them upwards towards the bridge. "I'm sorry, Mrs Randall, but we require her to answer."

"Um, yes, I know what it means." She wanted to ask the doctor lots of questions, but they all sounded silly in her head. Most of the older girls whom she knew had received a negative result, as expected. But what if she didn't? The glossy brochures about the government birthing schools made them seem like a holiday camp. Perhaps it would be fun, living with girls of similar age twenty-four-seven, but in reality, rather than via the silly Metaverse. Or perhaps that's just what the government *wanted* her to believe.

She shivered at the prospect of being so easily misled. Since her parents had pulled her from the school system, she'd made so few friends. Almost all the kids with whom she'd kept in touch had moved out of London, until now she only had four left: Sally, Karl, Billie and Craig. Billie's dad almost never allowed her out, and Sally's parents were moving to Scotland, once they got permission, although Sally said it could be months. Something about waiting for visas. Who knew?

Most of all, she'd miss Craig. Nothing serious had happened between them, except an awkward kiss or two, and not even with tongues! But, one Saturday, when Craig had kissed Sally in the park, the strength of her jealousy had surprised her. She'd never quite decided whether she wanted to stay just friends, but deep down, she'd always assumed he'd ask her out, eventually. Would she have said yes? Now, she might never discover the purpose of their relationship. Boys were still somewhat of a mystery.

"Would you mind taking off your jacket and rolling up your sleeve so I can take a blood sample?" Her heart rate quickened. Perhaps sensing her worry, her mother flashed a reassuring smile. Of course, the chances were slim. Yes, it was simply a box-checking exercise. She draped her jacket over the chair and folded the sleeve of her damp tee-shirt up to her shoulder. The needle loomed, and she turned her head, grimacing, but after nothing worse than a tiny wasp sting, she cursed herself for being such a baby.

Next, the doctor asked her to lie down and lift her tee-shirt so he could scan her stomach with a plastic device, cold and impersonal against her clammy skin. He'd turned the monitor screen away from view. Not that she'd have known what the images meant. Biology had to be one of her least favourite lessons and her parents had almost given up trying. Chemistry and physics were better subjects. If she progressed well in two out of three sciences, she'd pass just fine.

Doctor Gilligan's narrow mouth opened into a slit of a smile, revealing a set of teeth which seemed too small for an adult. "Brave girl. All done. I'll just put this sample in the analyser. Now, Hope, as you're under sixteen, I'm afraid you'll have to wait outside while I discuss the results with your mother. She'll either explain them herself or you can both come back into my office for a chat about what they mean." She nodded and began chewing on the side of her thumb while her mother stroked her hair.

Hope left Doctor Gilligan's office and took a seat in the secondary waiting room, with a smattering of other girls, all wearing similar anxious expressions. None looked up to meet her attempt at a smile, and she instead settled her gaze upon the TV in the corner of the room. *Television, what a joke. Who watches this rubbish anymore?* She couldn't care less their set had broken, or whether it got replaced.

Why was it taking so long? Had they found something bad? She worked away on the skin around her thumb until it started to bleed, then began picking at a hole in her tights.

Five minutes later, the door to room twelve opened, and her mother stepped out. Doctor Gilligan shuffled around behind her, as if he wanted to be somewhere else. Hope had never been too great at reading people's expressions and her mother's face gave little away.

"Hope, everything is fine. The nice doctor's machine isn't working today, so they'll process the results this evening and call us first thing tomorrow."

"OK, Mum. Can we go home now?"

Her mother nodded and gave her a thin-lipped smile. "On the way back, why don't we stop for coffee and cake at your favourite store? I think you've earned a treat."

"Are you sure, Mum?"

Doctor Gilligan scurried back inside his office and returned seconds later. "Here's something for being such a brave young lady," he said, thrusting a small lolly wrapped in pink and orange foil into her hands.

"Wow, thanks, Doc," she said, fluttering her eyelids.

Under London's dank October skies, the unmarked black van shuttled past rows of identical looking Victorian houses.

"Two-hundred meters, pull in on the left," said Miko. The van slowed to a stop, and he climbed down from the passenger seat to survey the area. It had probably been a desirable place to live, once. Now, these spacious old homes, their market values decimated, cost fortunes to run and bankrupted their owners; probably the exact type of God-fearing people who, desperate to preserve their dwindling wealth, had elected the current government. Too bad for them. Once the foxes were in the pen, they would never leave. While parents were willing to surrender their daughters for financial reward, and while other people were queuing up to purchase them, the foxes of this world needed men like Mikolaj Kozlowski to collect their chickens.

He stabbed a thick index finger towards the target building and strode ahead. His numbers two and three, Wosniak and Hassan, flanked him. Johnson took the rear, accompanied by their newest recruit.

"Johnson, Petersen, get around back." He spun, nearly causing a collision. For a moment, he stood nose-to-nose with Petersen. When Miko crunched his toffee, the man flinched. The kid seemed a little nervous. Perhaps he did not have the stomach for the job. "Covering the rear means covering the fucking rear, not jerking yourself off, understand?"

"Yes sir," said both men in unison, before jogging down

an alley behind the row of semi-detached four-bedroom abodes which, according to the satellite images Miko had pored over on the drive, led to generous but mostly unkempt back gardens.

A mail-drone buzzed overhead, clutching stacks of demand notices in its unfeeling claw. Wosniak took the lead and strode down the target house's cracked front garden path, which once would have seen innocent posties and delivery drivers bringing welcome goods to the family, or at worse, a forlorn salesman hawking miserable wares. He rapped on the door with a fist, rattling the frame. From within came screams and sounds of a struggle and Miko nodded to Wosniak, who took a drill from his black canvas holdall and punched through the lock with minimal fuss. The metal cylinder dropped out with a clunk, and he smashed the door open with a size-fourteen boot.

The three men marched through the dark hallway into a sparse dining room. Inside, both parents sat at a bare table with their lolling heads cradled in their hands. A naked candle cut through the gloom, revealing two upturned chairs on the floor. The mother, shuddering with violent sobs, didn't look up, but the father stood when they entered. In the corner, a girl who looked around twelve, with a round, freckled face framed by long sandy hair, crouched behind her older brother. The boy stood, resolute, with his feet planted and fists raised, spreading his narrow young chest as wide as possible. His face showed no obvious fear, but judging by the fluff on his top lip, he'd barely started shaving.

Miko heaved a deep sigh. The brother hadn't read the script, of course. Often, it was the doctors who tipped off his organisation, affording them an element of surprise, which made their work easier. Sometimes one parent or another family member did the deed alone. It was rare for both parents to make a joint decision about relinquishing their offspring, and this was one such occasion. He did not want to hurt this boy; it was unnecessary. Perhaps he could talk him around with some choice words.

"I'm sorry, son, there is nothing you can do. Your parents should not lose two children today. Life will be hard enough."

The boy said nothing, but his resolve only seemed to deepen, and his lip curled into a snarl. His father coughed and stepped towards Miko, but Hassan drew his pistol and shoved it in his face. The man threw up his hands and inched backwards toward the wall.

Miko held out his arm and pushed the pistol away. "No need for that. Did you have something to say?"

The man swallowed. His mouth sounded dry. "We... we've changed our minds. I'm sorry for wasting your time, but you must go, or we'll call—"

Miko shot out a gloved hand and covered the man's mouth. "Call who? The cops? Sorry, but they have more important things to do. They don't come out for such trivial matters anymore. Perhaps, if we ask them nicely, they might escort your daughter to the government's own school, but then you will not get what you wanted." He eased the glove from his other hand with his teeth and let it drop to the floor, then reached into his pocket and pulled out a mobile Payscan reader. After entering five digits, he held it up for the father.

The mother raised her head and squinted through reddened eyes at the small device. With a crackling, incredulous snort of laughter, she said, "They promised double that! Give us what we're owed, or we'll take her to the government lot."

"My advice is to take what I've offered. Or you could have nothing. We'll still take the girl, and your bills remain unpaid, the rest of your family unfed." He gestured around the modest room. "How does that sound?"

"You bastard." A low rumbling growl rose in the brother's throat, and he charged. Wosniak stepped between them, easily catching the boy's telegraphed haymaker swing, and pushed him to the floor. When he tried to bounce upright, Hassan levelled his pistol in his face.

"Don't be a hero, kid."

The daughter bolted from her new hiding place, behind a beaten old sofa, and dashed for the door, but Miko's arm hooked around her thin neck and swung her off the ground. She squirmed in his grasp, feet dangling, but his grip stayed firm, even when she clamped her teeth onto the exposed flesh of his forearm. He ignored the inconvenience. Let the little scamp taste a man's flesh before they pumped her full of hormones and babies. What did he care?

The brother leapt for him again, but Hassan pistol-whipped him across the temple, and he slumped onto the sofa. A dribble of blood seeped down his cheek. The boy might make a decent soldier one day, but only if he learned to choose his battles.

The mother dashed across the room to comfort her son as he rolled around. She stroked his head, where a maroon welt had started to appear. Her lip quivered, and she hissed, "Rot in hell, all of you. I hope they take *your* kids one day."

An image flashed into Miko's mind. Another innocent little girl, much younger than this pup, and barely weaned from her mother's teat. When had he seen them last? Five years already? Perhaps even longer. He dismissed the unwanted memories in an instant. Past lives were not acceptable for people in his line of work. Besides, family connections provided nothing except easy targets for enemies to exploit.

With the girl flopping in his arms, limp and defeated, he walked from the house and passed her to Wosniak. Then he pulled out his glasses and flicked on his Head-Up Display to call the field office, where his supposed superior, Colin Faulkner, would be sipping tea at his desk in relative comfort and safety.

"Faulkner, target acquired. ETA back to base is forty-five minutes." He stared at his screen, waiting for the expected confirmation, but it did not come. Faulkner's sagging face was easier to read than a horny teenager, and the man looked like he had an unpleasant taste in his mouth. "Spit it out, *boss*."

Faulkner's heavy sigh crackled into the headset. "Kozlowski. The girl's going to the other side. Bertram Eriksson's team is en route."

"Eriksson!? What the fuck, Faulkner?" Miko said, showering one of his men in spittle as he leaned in to eavesdrop. What possible business did the government have with *his* latest acquisition?

"I know it's a shit sandwich, but it's come from the top brass, over our heads. They need to pump their numbers and if we don't roll over, they'll make life uncomfortable. You'll be reimbursed in full, including expenses."

So, they were going to send her into one of those idiotic government schools, and spend thousands on medical care to get, what, two or three babies from her per cycle, at best? Babies who'd end up doing what, exactly? Probably fodder for the military, or brainwashed church minions. "With *respect*, Faulkner, you seem to forget we have buyers lined up around the block."

"I know, Kozlowski, you don't need to tell me. We've already identified a new target, so don't get upset. You'll like this one. She's a promising specimen. Sending the particulars now."

"Lousy cockroach." He disconnected the call and turned to face his men. "Johnson, Hassan, take the girl and wait in the van."

"What's going on, boss?" asked Wosniak.

Miko stood erect but still only reached Wosniak's chin. He glared into the other man's eyes until they dropped to the pavement. Two gleaming, late-model white government-marked SUVs pulled up alongside his vehicle and six men disembarked. At their lead stood a ghostly pale man with a shock of white hair. Eriksson had led the squad—now *his* squad—when Miko joined, but quit soon after, tempted to join the government's own tracking field team and become a glorified child minder. Increased pay and a better benefits package meant more hoops to jump through, for a lot less action.

"Do you need all this muscle to help you pick up a little girl, Bertram?"

"Good to see you too, Kozlowski. What's this, your welcoming committee?" Eriksson jerked his head towards the towering figure of Wosniak. "I've got men who make him look like a child. You're not going to make this difficult for me, are you?"

"Of course not. Do you not think we have professional courtesy in my country?"

"What's left of your country, you mean? I've no idea, but I hear it's full of cheap mercenaries. Where's the girl?"

"Ouch. Wosniak, did you hear that? We are only cheap labour for the British. I guess the accusation is true. Fetch our young charge, will you? Wouldn't want these fine men getting their soft, baby hands dirty, now, would we?" Wosniak stomped off towards the van.

"Look, Kozlowski, I know we've got different methods, but we're on the same side. Suck up your pride and there's room on our team for someone like you."

Miko guffawed from deep in his belly. "And what am I,

exactly?"

"Someone with an edge. Your organisation is just a bunch of thugs and scam artists. The whole clown show will get taken off the road, eventually. Wouldn't you like to land on your feet when it does?" Miko stared at him, saying nothing, and Eriksson added, "Think about it."

The moment his gaze flicked elsewhere, Miko spun and returned to the van. Details of the new target location flashed across his Head-Up Display. It was a mere six miles away. Even in the afternoon traffic, he could be there in under thirty minutes.

CHAPTER: TWO

Michael reached the cabbage-scented landing and took out his key, puffing heavily from climbing twelve sets of stairs. When had the lift last worked? So long ago, he couldn't remember. The lock protested at the metal intrusion. It was a matter of time before it seized up and WD-40 would just delay the inevitable, but for today it clicked open and he stepped inside, shoulders sagging the moment he remembered the letter he'd left sitting on the sideboard. Time had run out. In the morning mail, a week earlier than expected, he'd received his summons for a *Work Placement Suitability Interview*.

If he got lucky, they might send him out to a farm where he'd pick the late season crops, or work as a slaughterhouse operative. At least that one paid a distress bonus, but most farming jobs had vanished. Machines didn't get repetitive strain injuries. A.I. never grew tired of the sight of blood or allowed the screams to penetrate their nightmares. More likely, he'd end up on garbage detail with a sandpaper-rough crew of rubbish men, like last time. It wasn't so bad, not once they realised mocking his lack of dropped consonants in their thick London slur wouldn't get a rise, but they started too damn early in the morning. He'd never been much of a lark.

For once, the room was silent, with no miserable chatter coming from the radio. His wife and daughter, seated at the rickety kitchen table, were playing cards in the fading late afternoon light, bolstered by the meagre glow of an Ultra-Last LED bulb *(we light up your life for life, guaranteed!)* from the solitary lamp in the corner of the room. Who cared if everything else people bought ended up in offshore landfill sites, if the bloody lightbulbs lasted?

A creeping realisation nagged at him. He'd forgotten something important, but what? *Of course!* The note Allison had left him, alongside the bloody letter about the Work Placement Scheme. His wife and daughter had visited the doctor for Hope's compulsory fertility check. How could he have forgotten already? *Too busy wallowing in pity, huh? Worrying about yourself, as usual. What a selfish asshole you are.*

He gulped and dug his fingernails into his palms. "How did it go?" Despite having time to think about it, he hadn't decided which outcome he feared most, and his heart galloped in his throat as he asked the question.

Allison looked up from her cards with a blank expression, but her pink tongue darted from her mouth and moistened her lips. "Uh, the doctor's machine wasn't working, and they have a massive backlog of test results to process. We mightn't hear until tomorrow morning."

Michael stared at his wife while her eyes returned to her cards. She might have thought she was a decent card player, but she had a tell. True, she'd usually got the better of him during their monthly poker nights, back when they *had* friends who still lived in London, but when committed to a serious bluff, she sometimes licked her lips. She was lying or holding back part of the truth—if that didn't amount to the same damn deal.

He chewed the inside of his mouth and pondered the situation. Perhaps Allison didn't want to discuss the matter in front of their daughter. Best to wait until she'd gone to bed to confront her and find out the real story. It would be a long three or four hours.

He joined them at the table, where some empty packaging from Hope's favourite coffee shop suggested Allison had bought her a rare treat. Despite her anaemic appetite, his daughter had a sweet tooth and loved nothing more than coffee and cake. "What are we playing, then?"

"Shithead of course, Dad. OK, let's start a new round." She scooped up the cards and shuffled, beaming while she dealt out three cards face down and three face-up for each of them, followed by three more for their hands. "I can't remember how long it's been since we played together."

He grinned back, but couldn't stop his mind from wandering. After she'd ousted him three games in a row, Hope said, "Triple Shithead, Dad. Are you *trying* to lose?"

"You wait, I'm only getting warmed up."

She seemed calm about her unknown fertility status, but then they'd spent several years getting her used to the idea that she'd most likely never conceive. In a sudden wave, the years of painstaking effort which it'd taken to nurture his daughter hurtled back. The constant worry about her future, which grew as her potential increased. The infinite number of wide-eyed questions, and thousands of bedtime stories, until she'd grasped what the strange hieroglyphs on the page meant and retreated into a vast world of make-believe, which she could control all for herself. Then came the problems with her schooling and, after months of wrestling, the fraught decision to remove her from the system and home-school.

Perhaps they'd not done such a bad job as parents after all. She'd always maintained the ability to float above the buzzing storms of negativity which clouded him and Allison, wearing her youthful innocence like a shield. How he wished he possessed a similar strength, but maybe it was something innate, rather than skilled parenting. But she'd shown signs of their home situation wearing her down recently. She'd never been prone to the bouts of sarcasm and moodiness which had reared its head of late. Or was it teenage hormones playing havoc?

Allison fidgeted and squirmed. She kept checking the clock on the wall. The game wasn't so intense. Something else was on her conscience. Yes, they'd become distant from each other, but he could still read her face. He always could. He didn't like the way she kept glancing at Hope, like she knew something her daughter didn't. The minutes ticked by, and he got lucky, winning two hands in a row, but he couldn't maintain his concentration and soon resumed his losing streak.

His wife kept mopping her brow, but the flat wasn't hot. The heating had been switched off due to late missed utilities payments. Next, all non-essential electric devices would cease working before even the lights went blank, and they'd end up playing cards by candlelight. Was she getting sick or something? There were whispers of another type-four influenza doing the rounds. At least they couldn't send him on a work detail if he had a blazing temperature.

The tiny apartment's door entry system buzzed, ripping his dour thoughts to pieces and startling all three of them. Cards flew across the table as he jumped up and bounded across to the video screen. Allison rose and followed across the threadbare carpet, hands clasped. Hope stayed fastened to her seat.

Three men in hoods and half-masks gazed straight into the camera. A voice barked through the intercom, "Bring her down." It belonged to a bald man with wide, sunken eyes, and a trace of an Eastern European accent, slight but perceptible. He'd never laid eyes on these men, but he knew who they represented. More importantly, he knew who they'd come for.

His fists blinked, and he spun to face his wife. "That

fucking doctor, he's got the results and he's grassed. I'll kill him, I'll…" Allison's face told a different story. He stopped mid-sentence, searching deep into her eyes as they filled with water. "You…?" he said, trying to find the words. "*You* sold her out?"

She crumbled like a decayed ruin in the face of a high magnitude earthquake. "I'm sorry!" she cried. "I had to think of our future, the money. A hundred grand, Michael! She'll be happy there, they promised."

"Not the fucking Baby Farmers, Alison." The words hung in the air while he looked from mother to daughter, still seated at the table with her cards clutched to her breast, the colour draining from her sweet face.

"What's going on?" she asked. Only cloying silence answered. "You're scaring me now. Daddy, what's happening?"

No time for thinking. He had to let instinct take control, or he'd never decide. He willed himself into action, and before he knew it, he'd barged past Allison, through the hallway and into the cramped bedroom. On his knees by the unmade bed, he reached for his bug-out pack. With the bag slung over his shoulder, he grabbed Hope by the arm and hauled her to her feet.

"Let's go, now!"

"Michael!" screamed Alison, "if you run, we won't get anything! They might kill you!" She grasped for her daughter's outstretched hand but could only brush her sleeve as they dashed through the apartment's solitary exit. With her wide, pleading eyes filling with water, Hope cried out and craned her neck for a final look at her mother.

"*I'm sorry!*" Alison's wail followed them down the long corridor past the other flats. Few showed signs of life. Most were boarded up, some burned out. A faint stink still hung in the air—charred possessions on a cruel bonfire of scorched dreams.

They can't have all the exits covered. They can't. Old, mostly empty buildings were prone to blazes. There were several escape routes, and he headed towards the one furthest from the main entrance. He slammed through the fire-exit door and peered over the brown metal staircase snaking down the building's external wall. The quiet street below showed no signs of life.

Hope's voice shook. "What about Mum?"

He ignored the question. "Come on, fast as you can." The metal reverberated as they bounded down the stairs. When they reached street level, nothing stirred in either direction and the streets were still empty, but how long would their luck hold?

He shepherded Hope to the corner of the building and peered around. Opposite the entrance to the underground carpark, where he kept his beloved Ford, stood one of their goons, hunched and talking into his headset. Michael strained to overhear the conversation. "Nothing yet Miko, I've got eyes on his car. It's parked underneath the building." An unintelligible reply hissed through the headset.

He hustled her between two parked cars and motioned for her to squat. "Wait here."

"Dad…" she pleaded, grabbing at his sleeve. How desperately he wanted to comfort her, but he couldn't waste a second. While the gang's lookout remained alone, he stood a chance.

He waited until the man looked the other direction and scuttled across the road to the opposite corner. With his hood pulled up, he doubled back towards the man—an innocent bystander. Alerted by footsteps, the man spun around.

"Everything OK?" Michael said, firming his grip on the extendable former police-issue baton inside his jacket.

"Let's see your hands, mate," ordered the man. Michael

took out his baton, extending it in the same motion, and whipped it like a tennis forehand across the man's jaw, sending him sprawling to the wet pavement. Another sharp slap and blood began leaking from the back of his cracked skull.

He stared at the crumpled figure, blinking and breathing hard. An uninvited memory jumped from the distant past; the last time his hands had inflicted such damage. The looks on the faces of his mother and brother when they found out what he'd done. *Get a grip!* He wrestled himself back to the present and called to his daughter in an urgent half-whisper. She came out from her hiding place, following him underneath the apartment block, into the murky carpark.

Their footsteps cannoned around the dank structure. How long had it been since he'd turned the Capri's ancient engine over? Two weeks? Three? Those first-gen conversion kit batteries were prone to going flat. Thank fuck he'd left petrol in the tank. It wouldn't have degraded yet, would it?

He opened the door and threw his pack into the rear, then slid into the driver's seat. Once he'd leaned across to let Hope inside, he slipped the key into the ignition, twisted it a quarter turn and switched from battery to fuel power. *Will this cranky bastard even start? Here goes!* The glorious roar of a 2.8 litre fuel-injection V6 engine ricocheted off the naked concrete, filling the space like a Philharmonic orchestra playing at *fortissimo*. He spun the car ninety degrees, backwards through a dense black cloud of exhaust fumes, then slammed into first and floored the accelerator. Seconds later, the Capri flew through the flimsy barrier, turned right and scorched down the street.

In the seat next to him, Hope stared through the car's rear window, with tears flowing from her creased face onto the headrest, while the only home she'd ever known faded into the distance.

Miko stopped sucking his boiled sweet and held up a gloved hand. His crew quietened and looked to him for their cue. In the distance, car tyres screeched.

"Let's go." He pulled off his mask and jumped into the van. Wosniak was already seated in the passenger seat, his head scraping the roof. Hassan and Johnson barrelled through the open side door.

The van rolled around a corner. "Miko, stop!" said Wozniak. A motionless heap lay face-down on the pavement. It was their newest recruit, Petersen, with a bloody puddle seeping from the jagged wound across his head. Miko hit the brake and Johnson jumped out to check on their injured comrade. In the distance, the target's green Ford made a sharp turn at speed. The driver was an expert, and Miko didn't think he'd be able to catch him, not straight away, but he would never admit defeat without trying first.

"He's alive, but we gotta get him looked at," Johnson said. "Looks like a fractured skull." Miko rolled his eyes. How many times did he have to tell his men to maintain concentration at all times? Petersen should never have let himself get overpowered so easily, and during a simple cover detail, too. He was obviously not cut out for this line of work, and the man could die for all he cared.

"Leave him. Or keep him company, because I don't give a shit." His subordinate blinked, and his mouth hung open. When he slipped into first gear, ready to pull away, Johnson leapt to his feet and back into the van. The door slammed shut, and Miko stomped the gas, picking up speed and leaving the stricken man behind.

The car sped along a quiet suburban lane, slick with rain and lined with oak trees on both sides. Michael glanced up for a second to check the rearview. The road behind was empty.

"I think we lost them. Are you OK, Hope?"

Her cracked voice, driven beyond breaking point, filled the compartment. "What now? Where are we even going? We've got to go back for Mum."

She turned towards her father, her panicked face pleading for affirmation, but he ignored her, saving every ounce of concentration to negotiate the winding road ahead. The car's tyres weren't exactly brand new. At this speed, with the ancient Ford Capri's tail-happy handling, a tiny mistake could cost them dear. He took his hand off the gearstick long enough to flick the sweat from his brow before it dribbled into his eyes, then shifted down into third, scorched past a car, and swerved back in line before an approaching bend.

Another vehicle rounded the corner, and he hugged the curve with inches to spare. Branches scraped at the side of the car and rattled against the window with a violent clacking sound. A rising and falling blast from the other driver's horn joined the cacophony. Hope screamed and hid her eyes in her hands. When the road straightened, he reached out and patted her shoulder. She jumped at his touch, but her rapid breathing eased when she saw the road, now empty again in both directions.

"We can't go back. It's going to be alright, honey."

She sniffed back the tears. "That man back there, was he… was he dead?"

"No, I just knocked him out. It was him or us." For all he knew, the guy *had* died, but he didn't believe so. What must she think? In all the years, he'd never raised a hand to his daughter, and now she'd witnessed him seriously injure somebody. *Now she knows what kind of man her father really is.*

Once they'd joined the dual carriageway, he peered into the rearview mirror long enough to be certain there was nothing behind except the usual dribble of traffic, mostly electric buses and driverless taxicabs, cruising along the once-crowded highway with their co-pilots in control. He eased off the accelerator until the old analogue speedometer's red needle caressed seventy. Light rain drizzled across the windscreen, slanting from right to left. The skies above were overcast and grey. It was autumn, soon to be winter, and the light was fading fast.

CHAPTER: THREE

Night descended. The Ford rattled past the exit for Swindon. Amber and red lights stretched into the distance, surrounded by tunnel-vision blackness. The monotony of motorway driving made him sleepy at the best of times and, with the adrenaline tapering off, Michael's eyelids drooped. He signalled, took the next exit, and drove for another twenty minutes, searching for somewhere safe to park, until he found a faceless field, pale in the scant moonlight.

He flattened down the rear seats, clambered into the back and located a scratchy old blanket, which he draped over his daughter, now motionless in the front passenger seat. She'd finally stopped murmuring and thrashing around. Now he'd switched off the engine, would the blanket provide enough meagre warmth to keep the cold air from waking her? She looked so vulnerable, with only him shielding her from a life of servitude. Perhaps he wasn't enough, and the girl may never see her mother again. It dawned—their decisions were not his alone to make.

Rain pattered at the window, gathering intensity until it lashed down, pounding on the roof like it was a drum skin. He shivered, but the rain's rhythm helped disengage the spinning-wheel in his mind, and he soon drifted into a few hours' restless, but dream-free, sleep.

When dawn peered through the windshield, his stinging

eyelids unglued. He climbed into the front, awakening Hope. She grimaced and rubbed her neck, sore from the unnatural sleeping position afforded by the Capri's sport seats. When he turned the ignition, the engine sparked into life, but he couldn't summon his usual smile at the sound. Instead, he let it idle and scratched at his palms with his nails. She couldn't find out they had no destination and no plan. He turned to his daughter but couldn't find the words to reassure her. Damn, he couldn't even hide the troubled expression he'd just caught himself wearing in the rearview.

"What's wrong?"

"Honey, you know I love you more than anything in the world, right?" The question bounced off, unacknowledged, and she scowled back. "After what happened back in London, after what your mother did—"

"Why? Why did she do it? Maybe she hates *you*, but I never thought she wanted *me* gone."

He ignored the stabbing in his chest. "I don't know, Hope. I wish I could explain. She'd never hurt you on purpose. She wasn't thinking straight. Look, if you're scared, we could go to one of the government birthing schools. I've heard they're not so bad…" His voice trailed off and his gaze dropped from his daughter's narrowing eyes.

She sat up, snorted, and shook her head. "How could you even suggest that? Christ, you're both as bad as each other."

Did he believe those lies? What a fool. He should've kept his mouth shut. He slumped his shoulders and said, "I'm sorry." The words sounded so inadequate.

Hope leaned back, crossed her arms and hissed, "Fine, take me there, then. I don't want to see either of you again, anyway."

"You're right, and there's no way I'm giving you up." He

killed the engine and smiled at his daughter. Had her frown grown a little shallower at his assertion?

While he tried to figure out the next move, he heated some water on a tiny camping stove from his backpack and made coffee. They leaned against the car in silence, while steam rose from the plastic cups, the boiling liquid warming icy hands and healing bruised hearts.

"Perhaps I could send a message to Ray. I bet he'd put us up for a few weeks if we made it across."

"Uncle Ray? But he lives in Scotland. That's north, and we're going west, aren't we?"

It was hardly a plan. It might take a month to get even a holiday visa to cross the border, and he hadn't spoken with his brother in years. Their relationship had never recovered from the lies and constant disappointment—all his own doing, of course. Most of all, they'd fallen out of touch because of *the incident*, as they'd called it on the few occasions they'd spoken afterwards. He recalled the conversation from a lifetime ago, shortly after he'd been paroled.

"You're a free man again, Mike. Make something of yourself this time."

"I've changed, Ray. Since the incident and being inside… you can't understand what it does to a man unless you've been through it, but I'm not the same person."

The look in his brother's eyes told him everything he needed to know. *Words are cheap.* It might take years before Ray's opinion of him changed. Perhaps it never would.

"Mike, this country's going to shit. I'm moving to Scotland. Andrea wants to live there, and now Mum's gone, I can't see any reason not to."

But he *had* changed. After the yawning chasm of incarceration and the months of crushing depression it'd brought upon him, he discovered a guiding light. Or more honestly, it found him. Without his time inside, he'd never have met Willy and learned to box. But the man had taught him much more. The young Mike, a man moulded in his father's image, quick to raise his fists instead of using his brain, died the moment he first locked eyes with Willy. Michael had been born from the ashes.

Even if Ray rejected him again, Scotland was as good a destination as any. Once across the border, they could surely claim asylum. But the Baby Farmers would expect an immediate move north. He needed time to plan how to reach the border safely and cross into Scotland without getting caught.

"It's too risky heading northwards. We need to lie low somewhere and let you process this madness." A trace of a smile came over his lips and his worry-lines grew shallower, while Hope's scowl deepened. She motioned at him with her hands to reveal more, but how could he explain? "Someone I used to know lives out in Wales. Just trust me, OK?"

So *that's* why he'd subconsciously headed west. It had been more than a thoughtless hunch. Willy had saved him once. Perhaps he could again. His friend's last known address was way across the border, deep in rural Wales.

After Michael had found an abandoned car and jacked the plates, switching them for the marked ones on his Ford, they meandered westward through the early morning. They crossed the Severn Bridge, with the river's vast, turbulent brown waters snaking below, and passed through the open Welsh border just after nine in the morning, pulling into the first available charging station to regenerate the Ford's weakened battery. He still had fuel in the tank, but he'd pushed his luck far enough. Who even knew what the penalty for running a petrol car on a public road was these days? He doubted they'd bother with spot checks out here, but it wasn't worth the risk.

The car passed through the once bustling port cities of Newport and Cardiff, now home to just a hundred-thousand or less. Stark signs of urban decay were visible everywhere on the litter-strewn streets, with tattered posters peeling from boarded-up shops. Many were political. Without exception, they'd been daubed in anti-government graffiti.

Vote Conservative Christian Alliance—A Secular Country is an Unsafe Country proclaimed one poster.

Underneath, the anonymous riposte: *Do you still feel safe?*

They drove onwards, through grey, almost abandoned towns and villages. Soon, they reached countryside so beautiful and stark it made Hope gasp.

"It's so nice out here," she said, staring out of the window, with childlike wonder etched across her flushed face. Since the morning's argument, she seemed to have calmed. Maybe she'd needed to get it out of her system. After what had happened, she had every right to be upset.

"I don't think I've ever taken you over fifty miles outside the city, have I, girl?" There were many things he hadn't done with his daughter. He'd put himself first far too often.

A thick, damp fog formed, obscuring the view as they rose higher into the mountains. When the twisting road reached its apex, the fog cleared, revealing the tips of stout firs like Christmas trees on a carpet of rolling white smoke. They rounded a bend, and another village came into view, shrouded in wispish mist, like a magical location from some long-forgotten fantasy tale.

"Shall we take a look?" Hope nodded, so he pulled into a layby and got out. His daughter joined him, and they both stood, speechless, drinking in the gorgeous vista.

During the descent back into the valley, visibility worsened until he struggled to make out the road twenty feet in front. There was little traffic, but their progress slowed to a crawl.

"I need to find somewhere to take a nap." He signalled for an approaching turn and pulled into an unused National Trust carpark, rolled past a decrepit attendant's booth and onwards down a bumpy stone track.

Hope's nose wrinkled, assaulted by the sickly aroma of fresh manure which drenched the air. "What's that stink?"

"The smell of the countryside, darling. Better get used to it." After another mile, they reached a farm with smoke pouring from a chimney stack. "Someone still lives here. We better turn back."

But before he could spin the car around, the sound of a loud engine turning filled his ears. A giant red tractor loomed in the rearview. He'd not seen one of those since childhood, and it seemed like a relic from a bygone era. Without thinking, he took his baton from the side door tray and slipped it up his jacket sleeve.

The tractor slowed to a halt and a well-built man in his late fifties, tanned with a weathered face and thick grey hair, jumped down. Michael exited the Ford and walked to meet him, hands in pockets, shoulders down. *Please let this guy be alright.* The prospect of using the weapon again filled his stomach with a churning queasiness.

The man's voice boomed, even against the chuntering tractor engine. "Hello there. Don't get many visitors round 'ere, are ya lorst or sommat?" Michael struggled to transpose the man's thick accent. It didn't sound Welsh, perhaps west country, but he couldn't be sure. He seemed friendly enough, though.

"Yes, I'm with my daughter. We're looking for an old friend, but the fog became so thick, and we pulled off the road looking for somewhere to stop for the night. Sorry to trouble you. We'll head back the way we came."

"I see. An' what's your name, little lady?"

Michael rested a hand on his daughter's narrowed shoulder. "Don't be shy." Without looking up from the stony ground, she told the man her name and Michael introduced himself before offering his hand—an antiquated custom, but it seemed appropriate.

A big, calloused paw clasped it. "Jack, nice to meet you. Yeah, the fog comes in pretty fast out 'ere, an' it's a bad one alright. But we can't have you sleep in that car. Come stay with us in the house. We got a spare room an' plenty to eat."

"It's a kind offer, Jack, but…" He hesitated, trying to find a rational excuse.

"But nothin'. Keep followin' the path, I'll come in behind ya." Jack appeared sincere and a proper night's rest would do them a world of good, so he led his daughter back to the car and drove into the farm with the red tractor following close behind. Jagged razor wire topped the old stone walls zigzagging around the property and a set of deep canine barks pierced the otherwise quiet afternoon.

Michael and Hope sat around a sturdy wooden table in a cluttered yet picturesque farmhouse kitchen. Smells of meat and home-grown vegetables cooking on the ancient Aga stove hung in the steam-filled air. Michael fantasied they'd been transported a hundred years into the past, into a scene from an old film.

Jack's wife, Annie, gestured towards a clay jug sitting in the middle of the table. "Would you like some wine? We make it right here on the farm." He nodded, and she dispensed some of the liquid with a proud smile on her face, which was framed by shoulder length reddish-brown hair.

Also seated at the table, their son Oliver, aged in his late teens, was tall and wiry with thick dark hair. The boy stared at his daughter in a way which troubled him, looking at his feet each time he got caught. It rankled at him, but they were visitors, perhaps even viewed as intruders by the boy, and they'd better give him the benefit of the doubt. Perhaps he'd spent little time in the company of women, besides his mother, and Hope looked older than her thirteen years.

After a few glasses of wine, Michael allowed his taut muscles to slacken, and the conversation flowed more naturally. "Jack, why don't more folk move out here to live off the land like you guys?"

Annie answered instead. She had a more neutral accent than her husband, with a modest west-country twang. "It's something learned over decades, Michael. Most of you city-slickers lost contact with your ancestors' skills decades ago and forgot how to work the earth."

"You're not wrong, Annie. I wouldn't know how to grow a decent potato, let alone rear animals."

Jack said, "My family's been farmers for a long time. Owned one near Bristol for many a year, then we came out here because the land was so cheap."

"What happened to your old farm?"

"We sold the land, and they built houses on it, back when there was such demand from people leavin' London in their droves. Probably all sittin' empty now, though."

Michael gazed around the room, finding further clues to suggest keeping their way of life wasn't straightforward. Shotguns and rifles were locked away inside an antique cabinet in the hallway, and the family kept several Rottweilers, which explained the furious barking earlier. They sounded enthusiastic about guarding the property to the best of their ability.

After dinner, they sat around the table for another hour talking about past lives. Jack had always been a farmer, but Annie had worked as a part-time teacher in a tiny local school.

"We always ran small classes, but when the school dropped below twenty children, they shut us down."

"It's handy having an extra pair of hands around the place, now Rhea's gone."

On the wall hung a family picture. Jack and Annie, beaming with smiles, next to Oliver, surly even at a young age. Alongside them in the picture was a red-haired girl with a toothy smile and ruddy cheeks, perhaps two or three years older than Hope.

"Is Rhea your daughter?" Hope asked.

Jack nodded and smiled. "She'll be twenty now." His expression betrayed his belief she remained free. Or at least alive.

"I bet she's fine," Hope said, her tone sincere. Michael bit his lip and kept his opinion to himself.

Annie said, "None of this would've happened if we'd not allowed ourselves to be blinded. I'm ashamed to admit, I even voted for those zealots. Jack warned me not to."

"Maybe we'll get another chance," Michael said. "Don't blame yourself, Annie. It wouldn't have made any difference.

Millions of others like you, like us, voted them in."

"Did you?"

"No, but that isn't the point. We let them spread their bullshit and get it into our heads that science was to blame for the world's ills, all the death and natural disasters."

"I feel so foolish. I always went to church, but I'm not like them. It's shameful how they've turned God into a weapon."

"Always was it so, Annie." Jack said. "Man's been usin' religion as an excuse to fight wars and press its will on others for centuries."

Later, once they'd filled their bellies and emptied themselves of conversation, Annie showed them up the creaking wooden staircase to their rooms. To Hope, she offered Rhea's colourful bedroom, frozen in time, awaiting the unlikely return of its owner. Michael got the guest room.

"I can't thank you enough, Annie. You've been so kind to us."

"It's been nice having company, don't mention it."

The earlier exhaustion flooded back, compounded by the unfamiliar sensation of repleteness. Once he'd managed to pull off his trousers and crawl beneath the covers of the bowed but comfortable old bed, he couldn't remember his head hitting the pillow.

At 5.30am, he awoke with a start when an unfamiliar wail pierced his diffuse early morning dreams, followed by footsteps thudding across the bare wooden floorboards.

"What the hell is that?" he croaked. It took a moment to realise the sound was a cock's crow, the farmer's natural alarm clock for centuries. When his eyes unglued, he discovered Hope peering through the curtains to catch sight of these weird creatures she'd only read about in children's books.

"Dad, come and see." He hauled himself from between the

warm sheets to join her at the window, then draped his arm over her shoulder.

"When I was a kid, your grandparents used to take me to a city farm sometimes. I took you once, but you were only three, so you wouldn't remember." He allowed a wistful smile to creep onto his lips. "As you got older, those places went out of business." Downstairs, the clanging of pots and pans had already begun. He gave her a gentle squeeze on the shoulder and said, "Come on, let's get dressed and go downstairs. I hope you're ready for some proper work." She nodded, while excitement and worry fought to dominate her expression.

At the kitchen table, they tucked into a hearty breakfast. "Sorry, Jack, but I won't take no for an answer. If you're letting us stay, then we're working for the privilege."

They spent a hard morning's graft alongside Jack, helping to prepare the land for winter, exchanging minimal words to save their breath. Hope didn't complain about the labour once, but he could tell she found it tough by the increasing frequency of grunts and sighs as her pace dropped. Despite his more advanced years, the farmer showed no signs of slowing down.

In the afternoon, Oliver returned from working alone across the farm, with an improved demeanour compared to the previous night. Perhaps he'd misjudged the boy, who may've needed some time to warm up to the visitors, or maybe he was shy rather than surly. Hope, eager to know more about the animals, fired question-upon-question, which he seemed happy enough to answer.

"You ever see a cow up close, Hope?" he asked, once she'd exhausted her supply of queries.

Hope shook her head, then wrung her hands and shot him her best puppy-dog eyes. "Can I, Dad, can I please?"

The earlier wariness filtered back, and Michael scratched

his palms. The family had been so kind, but he tried to flash his daughter a look to convey she should keep her guard up.

"I suppose. Don't be too long, mind."

She did a little twirl of excitement, and he offered a smile, which faded as she strode off with Oliver by her side.

He leaned on his spade, jutting from the well-worked soil, and allowed a memory to fight its way into his mind. His daughter had always loved animals as a little kid. Once, she'd returned from school and announced to her parents, with the stubborn and naïve certainty which only young children could show, that when she grew up, she wanted to be a vet. She'd forgotten her new ambition by the following day, of course. He could've done so much more for his daughter if he'd considered her needs before his own. Perhaps she didn't realise it yet, but he had much to make amends for.

Oliver led Hope through the muddy track which ran through the farm's spine, towards a big wooden building. The boy's regular side-eye glances at her made her cheeks burn, but she kept a few feet between them, hoping her signals made it clear she only had friendship in mind. She hadn't needed her father's unsubtle looks to realise Oliver was not used to female company.

Inside the building were large alien creatures which, from her memories of childhood picture books, she knew were cows. One of her absolute favourite possessions had been a thick pop-up book filled with paper farmyard animals. But mere books had transplanted no genuine sense of scale into her five-year-old brain, and the animal's imposing stature came as a surprise.

"They're massive. Can't they hurt people?"

Oliver snorted and said, "They might get a bit aggy if they have a calf, but they're docile, although my dad told me a story once, 'bout a man who got trampled by one."

Hope's hand went to her mouth. "Was he alright?"

"I reckon. Broken arm, maybe?"

She stopped a few feet short and stared at the animal. Its warm breath whistled in and out of its wide nose, while impassive grey eyes stared at nothing. "She's beautiful."

Oliver leaned a little closer and said, "Don't be scared. Touch her." Hope took a step forward and eased her hand out until it rested on the cow's soft flank. She stroked it while the animal continued to ignore her. "You a vegetarian or somethin', girl?"

"Yes, I haven't eaten meat in a year, not that you can buy it in London."

"You can't buy meat there?"

"Well, you can, but it's expensive. At least, anything good is. I don't know how people can eat meat from animals who've been cooped up all day. I bet they can taste the misery. No wonder the world got so messed up in the first place. I don't eat dairy, either."

"Wouldn't know 'bout that. Nothin' miserable 'bout these animals 'ere, though. They're free to roam much as they like. Healthy as anythin'. Would you eat 'em, knowin' where they came from?"

"Maybe, but not this one. Not now I've met her. She's gorgeous, and so gentle."

Oliver laughed and said, "Don't worry, we ain't about to eat old Martha here. She's best damn dairy cow on this farm. C'mon, I'll show ya." Oliver picked up an overturned little three-legged stool and set down a stainless-steel bucket. He motioned for her to sit and knelt on his haunches beside her.

"Are these dangly things, um…" She snapped her fingers, willing the correct word to reveal itself. It slithered around in the depths of her memory, just out of reach, but as Oliver opened his mouth to speak, she found it. "Udders! That's it, they're udders."

"Got it in one. Where the milk comes from. Grab one and I'll show ya how to do it."

He took her hand and guided it towards the cow's undercarriage. She squealed when her palm gripped the fleshy pink appendage, which she'd expected to be much cooler. After they'd coaxed a few gallons of warm milk from Martha, she skipped back to find her father and tell him all about the experience, with Oliver close behind.

"Did you have fun, darling?"

"He showed me how to milk a cow," Hope beamed. "I touched its udders!"

He examined his hands and held them up to show her the blisters. "That's great, honey, but your old man is knackered. I haven't worked that hard in years."

Jack stretched and said, "Aright lad, that's enough for one day. The youngers can do the rest."

"It's gonna rain later," Oliver said, pointing towards the blackening sky. "Hope, would ya mind helpin' me get the pig shed cleaned up?"

Still smiling, she nodded, and they set off for another adventure, while Jack headed back to the kitchen with her concerned looking father in tow. She couldn't wait to meet the pigs, which she'd heard were much more intelligent creatures than people thought. What surprises would the boy show her this time?

"Go make yourself comfortable in the front room. I'll fetch us a drink." Jack said, while Annie pottered around in the kitchen preparing the evening's dinner.

"Sounds great, thank you." Michael flopped into a large armchair with a groan. A moment later, Jack plonked a bottle of whisky on a little mahogany coffee table, along with two pretty crystal glasses.

The big man eased himself onto the vacant chair. "Here's somethin' to wet yer whistle."

"You sure, Jack? That bottle would be worth a fair penny now?"

The farmer blew the dust off the bottle, pulled out the stopper and poured two healthy slugs. "It didn't corst much when I bought it, so don't worry lad."

They made small talk while they sipped the gorgeously smooth whisky, which had a hint of peat smoke, and a thousand other notes which Michael's palate wasn't refined enough to pick out. The conversation flowed from cars to music, and meandered around the subject of family, until an hour had passed, along with nearly half the bottle's glorious contents. Outside, the light had almost faded. Soft raindrops pattered the farmhouse's small windows.

"Hey, Jack, do you reckon the pair of them will be back soon?"

"I'm sure they won't be long."

The minutes ticked by. The conversation ground to a halt, and Michael fidgeted with his glass. "Reckon we could go and check on them, Jack? It's nearly dark."

Before the farmer could answer, a scream tore through the

silence and Michael leapt to his feet, stumbling slightly. Within seconds, he'd shaken off the numbing effects of the booze and barrelled out the door towards the sound.

"Hope!"

"Daddy!" She was close by. He followed the direction of her cries and rounded the chicken coop and sprinted past the pig's shed. In a clearing beyond some trees, his daughter cowered, holding her arms out to ward off the boy, stood a few feet from her. "Stay away from me!"

Oliver barked, "Stupid bitch! I didn't do nothin'."

Michael ran over and grabbed the boy by the throat, slamming him to the floor with adrenaline coursing through his body. He turned to face his daughter. "What happened?"

"He… he touched me and tried to kiss me. When I said back off, he tried to push me down."

"I wasn't gonna do nuffin'. Get off me, man," Oliver spluttered.

"Fucking creep, I'll show you—"

Close to his ear, a metal click cut him off before he could finish his threat. He turned slowly. The antique shotgun was no longer stored in the hallway cabinet. Now Jack held it at chest height, aimed squarely at his head.

In a voice barely above a whisper, the farmer ordered, "Let the boy go."

Michael released his grip from Oliver's throat and backed away, hands raised skyward.

"Easy, easy." He nodded towards Hope. "I'm sure this is all a misunderstanding. No harm done, eh?"

"Yeah, mister. It's OK, let's just forget it," Hope said, but the daggers she sent towards the boy betrayed the passivity of her words.

Oliver stood up, eyeing them both, a snide sideways grin

emerging across his face as he rubbed his bruised neck. "Prick," he spat at Michael. "What we gonna do with these now, Pa?"

"Let me think about dat, boyo. I told ya to keep it in yer pants after last time, eh?" The farmer walked over and clipped his son across the head.

"Look Jack, why don't we just leave? We'll say no more about it."

"You just keep quiet, son. Let's go back to the house." Jack motioned with the shotgun and Michael shepherded his shaking daughter towards the farmhouse. He risked a glance behind. Surely the man wouldn't shoot them in cold blood. "Keep your eyes in front, keep walkin'," said the farmer, ten paces behind.

Oliver shuffled in step beside his father, shoulders narrowed and head down. "Sorry pop," said the boy. The dogs barked, and Michael bit down on the inside of his mouth, drawing blood. Maybe it was past their suppertime.

CHAPTER: FOUR

In a nondescript, dingy little office room in the near-deserted former banking district of Moorgate, City of London, Colin Faulkner's attention lay focused on the flat touchscreen display built into his uncluttered desk. On the other end of the incoming videocall, Piers Beauchamp's huge round head filled the screen.

"Mind you, Colin. If we get to them first, I'm afraid its finders' keepers, old pal," said Piers with a slight lisp. Piers, an old acquaintance from his school days and a high-ranking official in the Christian Conservative Alliance, was a useful person to know, but his fat, colourless face was one even Colin wanted to punch, and he'd never hit anyone in his life.

"She's on your list now, then?"

"As of this morning, I'm afraid so, old buckaroo. The father, Michael Randall, is a person of interest from years back. Did a stretch in prison for something quite unchristian."

"Can you elaborate, Piers? Probably best we know, for the sake of the, um, investigation."

"Sorry, Colin. You know it goes both ways; information is beholden to no one except the beholder!"

He struggled to stop himself from rolling his eyes at Piers' pathetic attempt at profundity. The guy was such a goofball. How'd he ever reached a position of power? Probably slimed and weaselled his way up the greasy pole. Never mind God, the man would worship a stray cat if he thought it would benefit his career.

"Anyway, we have Allison Randall's phone tapped. You have my word that as soon as they try to contact her, you'll be the second to know."

"What about if his ID card shows up?" He allowed his eyebrows to rise in anticipation. "You scratch my back, I scratch yours? I did quite a favour for you the other day, after all."

Piers shook his head, and his jowls wobbled. "No can do, Col-Col. Don't think I'm not appreciative of the gesture, nor have I forgotten, but the house always has an edge. ID hits are ours and ours alone, money cannot buy. Well, not your money anyway. I expect the crypto boys will give *us* the green light for a trace in the next day or so. You lads have got access to the Highways Agency tracking network though, right?"

"Yeah, we got him going westwards, then nothing. Disappeared like a silent fart-dropper in a crowded lift."

So, the government boffins had worked out how to intercept and de-encrypt the independently administered currency servers, had they? No doubt thanks to an immense bribe along the way.

"I'm sure the bastard will show up soon. Can't be many lime-green Ford Capris knocking around the West Country. As soon as we get a hit, I'll be in touch."

"That's helpful, thanks Piers."

"No problemo. Good luck and may the best team win!" Colin prepared to terminate the call, but Piers added, "Oh, what happened to your man who took a bit of a bashing recently? Did he pull through?"

"Just about. Fractured skull and severe concussion. He'll live, for now."

"Right, right. I suppose his *usefulness* to the organisation is compromised, eh? Better make sure the likes of us don't let *our* usefulness expire."

He'd show that stupid greasy turd Beauchamp *useful*. If his perennial ass-kissing finally paid off, he'd be fucking indispensable!

The five sat around the sturdy old table in the kitchen, where only twenty-four hours ago they'd enjoyed a peaceful, cordial dinner together. Like before, Jack sat at the head of the table. This time, instead of a glass of wine, he held his shotgun resting on the worn oak, pointed at Michael. Hope curled up tight next to him with her face buried in his armpit. On either side of Jack, like an angel and devil resting upon his shoulder, sat his wife and son.

Annie knitted her hands. "Jack, this is silly. We must let them go."

Oliver snarled, "Dad, don't lettem. They gonna come back at night and do us in, you'll see."

Michael kept quiet and stared into Jack's hooded eyes. The farmer didn't look like a killer, but people did crazy things when they thought their families were at risk.

The room fell silent, except for the slow tick of a clock on the wall and Jack's heavy breaths. His large pug nose had been flattened. It looked like an old boxing injury, and he sucked air through an open mouth. To Michael, the seconds passed like hours until, at last, Jack took a lungful and prepared to speak. Hope's head lifted; Michael's gaze didn't waver. Annie studied her husband's face, frowning. She'd probably been struggling to grasp Jack's intentions, too.

"Here's what's gonna happen. You two are gonna walk out that door, slowly mind, and back to that nice Ford of yours. You're gonna get in that car and drive away. If I catch you back 'ere, this old gun…" he tapped his weapon, "will be the last thing you ever see."

Jack's finger slipped from the trigger and moved to rest on the shotgun's trigger guard instead. Michael released a long breath and leaned back in the chair.

Oliver banged his fist on the table and cried out, "No, Dad. Don't leddem!" Jack turned and whacked his son around the side of his head. The boy howled and rubbed his ear as it turned purple, while his mother squirmed in her seat.

"You're doing the right thing, Jack." He inched from the chair, keeping his eyes fixed on the farmer while he pulled his pale daughter to her unsteady feet. They backed away towards the door and Jack rose to follow them out.

"Sorry it come to this, Mike," said Jack, ignoring Oliver, who glared at his father with a growing frown on his reddening face, somewhere between hatred and embarrassment, like an offended hound who wanted to bite the hand of its master but couldn't summon the courage.

Michael strode towards the Ford with Hope in tow, and the farmhouse door groaned shut behind them. Raised voices came from within. "Let's get out of here before he changes his mind."

The muffled yet unmistakable blast of a shotgun fired in an enclosed space broke the calm evening air. He flinched, and Hope planted her feet in the mud, throwing her hands over her ears and screaming. Another shot startled him into action. He yanked her arm and dragged her towards the car.

"Stop or you're both dead!" cried Oliver. Michael craned his neck over his shoulder but didn't stop running. They had a decent head start. The boy stepped from the doorway, fumbling fresh shells into the breach of his father's weapon before he broke into a jog. His neck and plaid shirt were spattered with blood.

Michael searched in his pocket for the Ford's keys. He pulled them out, but they slipped from his grasp and plopped into the mud. "Keep running and get around the car," he called to Hope as he dropped to one knee and groped in the half-light. His fingers closed around a chunky piece of plastic, and he pulled the key from the mud a second before buckshot pellets slapped into the finger marks which he'd left in the wet earth.

He reached the car with Oliver thirty paces behind, pulled open the door and slid inside, next to his shaking daughter. *Thank God I left the door unlocked.* He'd parked the car facing a large metal trough, rusted and full of holes, but still far too heavy to ram with the Capri's delicate nose. He needed to reverse out.

A buckshot round peppered the rear driver's side, and Hope screamed again. When he jammed the key into the ignition and fired the petrol engine, the throaty cry sounded better than anything he'd ever heard. He depressed the clutch, scraping into reverse gear with a crunch. The car sped backwards, while he spun the steering wheel ninety degrees and slammed the cranky gearbox into first. But the car wouldn't budge an inch. He pumped the accelerator and burning clutch fumes filled the air. The wheels whined, spinning in the thick gloop beneath. With each step, Oliver gained, and his shadow soon loomed. In seconds, he'd be too close to miss a clear shot at his head—an easy target behind a vulnerable layer of glass.

With one desperate final attempt, he released the accelerator and allowed the car to roll back, then floored it. The tyres found traction and the car shot forward like a wind-up toy at maximum torque. Oliver raised the shotgun, but they were faster. The car winged him before he could fire, spinning the boy into the mud, face first. A howl of pain rose above the engine's high-revved whine, and Michael glanced in the mirror. The collision had thrown the shotgun from his grasp. Oliver rolled gingerly to his feet and started searching for it.

They both bounced in their seats as the Ford burned down the track and past the carpark before skidding onto a country road as Michael performed a flawless muscle-memory handbrake turn. The road straightened out and he peered at the rearview, into the gloom behind. They were not being followed, and he eased his foot off the accelerator while his pounding heart slipped down the gears. Once they reached a main road, with the farm several miles behind, he switched the engine to electric power with a small thump.

Hope's panicked breathing slowed enough to allow her to pant the question he'd been dreading. "Do you think they're OK? Annie and Jack, not that horrid creep."

"Uh, yes honey, he probably—"

"He *killed* them, didn't he? My God!" Her plate-sized eyes bored into him while he glanced back at the empty road ahead.

"He was only scaring them, Hope. Fucking psycho kid! At worst, he wounded them. Didn't you hear Jack's voice? I was closer. I heard Annie screaming too."

He chewed the inside of his lip. She had to believe him. Her face said she wanted to, but maybe she'd also seen the blood spatters on Oliver's twisted, snarling face.

CHAPTER: FIVE

Michael kept craning his neck and trying to glimpse out the window as he drove along the dual carriageway.

"Dad, what are you looking for?"

He tapped the steering wheel with his fingers. "I know it began with an L and sounded a little like Land Rover. Some of these Welsh names are weird."

Hope rubbed her red eyes and said, "What are you talking about?"

"You remember Willy, my old coach, when I used to box? Ah, you were too young."

"Will some guy you've not seen in years help us? How will you even find him, Dad?" She had a point. Her mother had never been able to decide between them who the family's real dreamer was.

"You don't know Willy. He's not just *some guy*, he's a sodding legend and saved my ass once before, when things weren't so great. Before I had your mo... Before I had you. If it's meant to be, we'll find him. He always said the light only reaches us at the darkest of times. Last I heard, he moved to the countryside, a commune or something. No phones, no devices and totally self-sufficient. Perfect for us to lie low and gather information, work out how to cross the border."

But Hope didn't reply. She'd drifted off at some point during his speech. Well, at least he'd convinced himself, anyway. Another fog descended, and he switched the Capri's headlights to full beam. The powerful rods of light sliced through the mist, revealing straight white lines disappearing into the invisible horizon beyond. Once his concentration started waning, he opened the window a crack to freshen the car's supply of air. He had to stay alert.

Thirty minutes later, a road marker flashed past. *Llandovery 18 miles*.

"That's it!" he said, startling Hope out of her fitful sleep. She yawned and began to sniff in small shuddering waves, like when she'd been much smaller, and had been upset by deep emotions which her fragile young brain couldn't yet process. She was close to tears.

"Aw honey, it's gonna be OK, I promise. I know these few days have been crazy."

She nodded in reply and wiped the unbuttoned sleeve of her red and black checked shirt across her nose to catch the escaping drops. He signalled and turned onto a minor road. The fog cleared, and the beautiful but somehow monotonous landscape surrendered to a series of small towns and villages, all carved in an endless palette of greys. Another sign revealed itself. *Llandovery 2 miles*.

He bit down on his bottom lip, drawing a tiny blot of blood, its coppery taste filling his mouth when he licked it. They could drive around for hours and might get lucky, or they might turn up exactly squat. No, he had to remain positive. *We'll find Willy, alright. How big can this place be?*

Perhaps sensing his anxiety, Hope turned to look him in the eyes. With all the authority she could muster, she asked, "Dad, what are we going to do? It's nearly dark."

"We'll drive around a while. If we draw a blank, then we sleep in the car again and search the area properly tomorrow. If *that* doesn't work, we'll play detective. Start asking around." He hadn't convinced her, so he patted her knee and added, "This isn't a big place. We'll find them, eventually. I know it."

She seemed to take some comfort and leaned back, closing her eyes for a moment before sitting up, alert. "What am I looking for, then? You know my vision is loads better than yours. Haven't you got cataracts by now, old timer?"

With exaggerated sweeps, she scanned the landscape, which had turned monochrome in the fading light. He couldn't prevent himself from spluttering at the joke. Once again, her resilience amazed him. Only an hour ago, a maniac kid who had probably just murdered his parents in cold blood had threatened her life.

"Okay kiddo, hope you've been eating your carrots. We're looking for any hidden tracks or tiny roads. Wooden structures, tents, anything to indicate a bunch of hippies out in the sticks."

Hope asked, without a hint of irony, "What's a hippie, Dad?"

You must be fucking kidding me. "You know, peace and love. Save the Earth. That kind of thing."

Suddenly upset, she snarled, "Save the Earth? Why did they let them screw up our entire planet in the first place, then?" Her black curls corkscrewed over her furrowed brow, and he found himself rendered wordless at how beautiful she appeared to him, in the dim light, with dusk shadows dancing across her face.

"I… I don't think it was a fair fight, Hope. Corporations, the elite, all that power and money. The psychotic desire for *more*. Against, well, a bunch of weed-smoking vegans."

"It's crap, Dad! What's left for us now? We might as well…" she paused, groping for a grand enough action, but couldn't seem to find one.

He jabbed his finger at her. "Calm down, Hope—"

"Hope?! I didn't know you and Mum were such comedians. Or is it irony? And what exactly did you do to make the world a better place, huh? You were always perfectly happy driving around in this stupid, polluting old relic instead of getting a modern car."

He took a breath, not wanting to upset his pouting daughter further. One subject which always got his daughter riled was climate change, and who could blame her? "Look, these cars might be inefficient, but they're built to last. Show me one of these silly self-driving cars still running in twenty years' time."

But what good *had* he done for the world? Little, except for his solitary achievement: fathering her. In the face of accelerating global warming, all effort seemed futile, but he'd always kept faith in the basic goodness of humanity. It was still there *somewhere*, underneath all the twisted lies and bullshit, and this wasn't the time to give up.

"Look, Hope. I know the world seems messed up, and it is. But it'll turn around. Things will change. Already have, in some places. Not everywhere has a regressive government like us. What about Scotland? Their birth rates are even growing." He allowed a little of his own anger to creep into his voice as he added, "And that's without goddamn birthing schools and a theocratic government."

Hope sighed and slumped in her seat. "I guess, Dad. Sorry, I just get so upset when I think about what they did to our planet. My generation wasn't given a fair chance."

"It's alright, I understand. We all should've done better." He gesticulated towards the side of the road. "Anyway, let's concentrate on the matter in hand. We've plenty of time to put the world to rights later."

The full darkness of night descended. Their search remained fruitless, so he found a layby on a quiet lane, and parked behind an overgrown hawthorn bush, away from the few streetlights which existed so deep into the Welsh countryside.

"We better be awake at first light. Let's get some sleep." After he'd put down the Ford's rear seats, they huddled in the back. Hope drifted off first, and he listened to her whimper while her breathing became deeper and more rhythmic, until his own thoughts faded, and he fell into a troubled slumber.

Two metres by two metres. One bunkbed and two men. A chipped porcelain sink, and a yawning chrome shitter, with no seat or lid. A window which offered a sliver of daylight and a view of the block opposite's crumbling brickwork, where a man like him sometimes stared back wearing the same frown, an imperfect reflection in a dismal mirror. Every night, in that icy, cloying darkness, he struggled to pull oxygen into his constricted lungs. An hour of blankness, before hurtling back into the world, gasping, clawing, dying. Sometimes he woke the man above. Sometimes, the man had something to say, until Michael put a stop to his complaints. Rinse and repeat until the small hours, then merciful exhaustion, and proper sleep, short but so, so deep, before the blue hue of early morning arrived. Awake, never rested but always grateful to be alive, one step closer to escape, breathing a little easier every time. Eventually, release. Freedom. But never free. How was anyone ever supposed to be free from the spectre of death? Once learned, the knowledge could never be forgotten, and death would always hover above, like a cloud of flies.

How had he ended up back in this stinking place? Hadn't he served his time as a young man? *Anywhere else but here, please Lord.* It seemed even smaller and more cramped, shrinking until the confinement threatened to envelop him like a hundred cotton wool balls jammed into his mouth. His curled fist shot out, struck the low bunk overhead and began clawing at material, not the hard steel springs of a prison-issue mattress as unyielding as winter soil, but familiar and soft plastic…

It was still dark outside when Michael awoke with a sudden jolt, fingers scraping the plastic lining of the Ford's roof. The dream—more like a half-memory—faded quicker than a deflating balloon, but a heavy shadow of displacement lingered behind. He rubbed his face while the events of the past forty-eight hours hurtled back. He reached for a bottle of water and glugged from it, his scorched mouth refusing to ease until it was half-finished. It took considerable effort to stop himself swigging the lot. Hope, still sleeping beside him, would be thirsty too when she woke, and who knew when he'd find a decent water source to refill?

Hit by a sudden and acute need to urinate, he untangled himself from the blanket, opened the driver side rear door and crawled out into the chilly breeze of the extreme early morning. Birds-in-song had awakened, chattering from the trees while the pre-dawn light laid the groundwork for another victory against its time-honoured adversary.

With eyes maladjusted to the gloom, he took faltering steps over to a bush and unzipped, shuddering while a long stream of piss hit the muddy floor, splashing on his boots whenever he lost concentration on his aim.

"Christ, Dad, how can you pee for that long?" Hope's groggy voice growled from inside the car. "You woke me up. I thought it was raining for a minute."

"Sorry," he said sheepishly while he zipped up and stretched his aching arms and legs.

"That's great. Now I need to go. And I'm *so* thirsty. Please tell me there's water in the car." He reached inside, located the remaining half a bottle, and handed it to his daughter. "I hope you washed your hands," she said with a growing grin.

The stark morning light took over, bringing clear skies. Hope sat in the Ford's rear, legs dangling from the open boot. "Dad, can we find somewhere to see the sun rise? It'll be savage." He couldn't turn down such a request from his daughter and expect to keep the fragile peace. Besides, he wanted to witness one for the first time in years. A decent sized hill bulged from the landscape behind them. He squinted past it to the horizon. They didn't have long.

"We need to go now, or we'll miss it." He reached inside the car for his jacket and helped pull Hope upright. She stumbled and groaned, kneading her wooden leg muscles back to life.

"Dead leg," she explained needlessly, and grabbed his arm. Side-by-side, they followed the path upwards, avoiding the muddy puddles which littered the uneven trail.

The terrain rose steeply, the waterlogged low ground giving way to a drier and firmer foothold. They stopped looking at their feet, instead marvelling at their surroundings. When the incline took its toll, their breathing quickened, sending foggy clouds into air so crisp it scorched their lungs. Up ahead, the hill plateaued. A thin treeline which had obscured the view disappeared when they neared the peak, allowing unrestricted access to three sides of the panorama. The early sun came into view, its diffuse glow peaking above the horizon. Hope gasped in awe at the sky, lit with ribbons of bruised purples and pinks. After they'd caught their breath and admired the view, they discovered a decrepit, moss-bound bench facing eastward.

"Risk it?" he asked. She ignored him, skipped across, and flopped down.

"Seems OK, Dad." He moved towards it, but she screamed, "Wait!"

"What?"

"I think your arse might be too fat for it." She chuckled, and he feigned a strangling motion before sitting beside her.

On the return journey, he searched for a water source and soon tracked a mountain stream off the main path. He knelt to sample, and the taste was like nothing he'd encountered—as cool and clear as anything could be in this world. He slurped from his cupped hands before filling up the bottle, drinking half, and refilling it to the top.

"Taste this."

Hope took the bottle, eyeing him with suspicion. "Is it OK?"

"No." He paused for effect before adding, "It's much better than OK." Hope grabbed the bottle and drained it.

"Oh, that's boss. I didn't know water could taste so good!"

He released a long sigh and sauntered back to the stream to refill the bottle. "Alright, we better head back. Could be a long day and we'll need food."

The pair walked in silence. Once they reached the car, he made a quick inventory of their dwindling provisions. They had a few cans of food, along with some energy gel pouches, protein bars, and one slab of synthetic chocolate. He heated some baked beans on the camping stove and slopped it between two scratched plastic plates. They ate fast, without enjoyment.

"We'll have to pick up some supplies if we don't find this place. We should keep the remainder for actual emergencies."

They spent the rest of the morning part driving and part rambling around on foot. Hope found it a pleasant way to spend some hours, but they had no success achieving the principal aim, whatever that was, for she still didn't grasp her father's plan. One of the many vehicle tracks which he led them down ended in a private residence with tall gates and fences topped with black spikes. Cameras whirred and spun, tracking every movement.

"What are they doing out here? Couldn't we knock?"

"We'd better go before we arouse any suspicion," said her father. He grabbed her wrist and guided her onto a footpath, which snaked into dark, foreboding woodland.

"Why?"

"Some people don't want to be disturbed, Hope. Judging by the size of that fence, they have a lot to protect. Either way, best leave them to it."

"If they have so much, why wouldn't they share?"

He sighed in a condescending way which annoyed her, and said, "The world doesn't work like that."

"Maybe it should."

He stopped in his tracks and turned to face her with a thin smile. "Look, Hope, you're not wrong. Actually, you remind me of myself when I was your age. Believe it or not, your boring old father was idealistic once. But you need to understand the reality. It doesn't make it right, but we must accept it."

The path wandered deeper into the woods, where the pale Autumn sunlight struggled to broach the thick canopy. Her mind kept weaving like the path, looping back to the previous day's events, which had taken on a strange, dreamlike quality, one so opaque she hardly knew if they'd happened at all. Her father wouldn't lie about Jack and Annie, would he? They'd been so kind, welcoming two complete strangers into their warm, cosy home. If it hadn't been for that creepy kid ruining everything, she wouldn't be traipsing about in these stupid woods, with her feet turning into a blistered mess. Her father had sensed a wrongness in the boy and tried to warn her. Could she have done more to try warding him off? Perhaps she'd unknowingly given the wrong signal. *Stop being silly.* She'd done nothing of the sort.

A disconcerting rumble soon accompanied an uncomfortable pressure building in her stomach. *Uh-oh.* She bit her lip and tugged on her father's arm. "I gotta go to the toilet."

"A pee?" She shook her head. "Come on, then." He grabbed her by the arm and led her off the track, into a hilly area shrouded in thick fir trees and laden with a carpet of ferns. He turned his back to indicate she should find her spot.

She clambered into the undergrowth in search of a log to use. After locating a serviceable one about fifty yards up a steep embankment, she squatted to relieve herself. A rustling came from her right side, thirty metres further up the slope, and she twisted her neck to investigate. With an electric jolt, she discovered two piercing eyes watching her with intense interest from the undergrowth.

"Oh shit," she said, struggling to tidy herself up as quickly as possible. She hadn't even got her leggings pulled up when a strange grey creature broke cover and prowled towards her, with its undercarriage low to the ground and its tail erect.

CHAPTER: SIX

Colin dropped into his swivel chair and switched on his Head-Up Display. Piers' fish-belly white face loomed on the screen. Despite the video being a recorded message, Colin could almost smell the sweat pouring down his forehead.

"Colin, old chap, I can let you into a little secret about your friend. A camera on the southbound side caught a Ford Capri travelling north on the A470 towards Merthyr last night. Different plates, but I'll wager the sneaky bastard swapped them. The cameras on most of those roads aren't live anymore, or scumbag local vandals have disabled them, so I've no idea where they ended up, but Randall must still be in Wales somewhere. Fucking sheep shagger!"

Piers' face dissolved into a blurry snapshot of Michael Randall's car. Colin zoomed in. He'd be able to make out the new number plate with some digital trickery.

"Dial Kozlowski."

Seconds later, the huge bald head of his lead field agent, Mikolaj Kozlowski, eyeballed him through the screen. Huge piercing blue eyes so fair they were almost white stared out from sunken sockets ringed in black.

"Faulkner, what a pleasant surprise," said Kozlowski, slurping on a candy. Colin's butt clenched at the sound. It was a strange habit. Why couldn't the man smoke or vape like a normal person, or chew gum instead of sucking sweets? Normal person! Who was he kidding? He doubted a man like Kozlowski understood normality any better than Colin knew Ancient Hebrew.

"Randall's in Wales. He's switched plates on the Ford Capri."

"You want me to check it out?"

Colin chewed on the inside of his mouth for a moment. Did he want to send his best man on a wild sheep chase? It was probably better to keep him in situ so he could mop up the area's remaining targets quickly and without fuss. Interest in their services had gone through the roof since the government's recent announcement regarding the reduction in age limit. He had nowhere near enough supply to satisfy demand.

"No, I'll send the other squad. I need you around to check out some new leads. Sending the particulars now. Keep your display on."

"Yes boss," Kozlowski hissed, elongating the double consonant, before muting his microphone. How could anyone fill the word *boss* with such disrespect? While the Pole kept doing his job with such mechanical efficiency, he'd never have to reprimand the man. He shivered at the prospect. How was anyone supposed to line-manage a human wrecking machine like Kozlowski? Might as well try to harness thunder. He longed for the simple days when the likes of Bertram Eriksson worked under him, a man who could be reasoned with and whose motivations were understood. The bastard had long since left for greener pastures, working directly for the government. In other words, less risk and more money.

He wiped a handkerchief across his moist brow. It seemed the office was only ever the temperature of a desert: boiling hot or freezing cold. Things were getting a little too edgy in the IPA for his liking, and a similar move would suit him down to the ground. Piers would hook him up soon enough, right? He just had to remain patient and not make any stupid mistakes. The prospect of a misstep at such a crucial time made him swallow hard. One error too many could mean an unexpectedly early retirement for a man in his position.

A bolt of terror flashed through Michael's chest as the dog stalked towards his daughter, its belly pressed low to the undergrowth. "Don't move, Hope! Stay calm and try not to show fear." The animal was sleek and grey, and none too friendly if appearance was anything to go by. It looked like a mix between a German Shepherd and a Border Collie, with some Husky thrown in for good measure. Its fur was spotted with black, and the tail and legs faded to off-white.

He edged closer, but the dog would reach her first, unless he darted towards it. Once startled, the animal might become aggressive. Its eyes, which shone with fierce intelligence, were fixated on his daughter with unblinking precision. One was blue and the other brown, giving it a strange, fearsome appearance. He held his breath as the dog eased towards her. She reached out, allowing it to smell her hand. *God, she's braver than I realise.*

"There you go, see. Good boy." She pulled up her leggings. The animal nuzzled her leg and licked the exposed skin above her socks, its rough tongue revelling in the salty taste of her sweat.

"Dad, can we give it some food?"

He released his tension with a long, whistling sigh. "We don't have it to spare." She'd already pulled out the remaining half a protein bar from the pocket of her tracksuit top. She ignored his protests, broke it in two, and offered it with an open hand. The dog sniffed once and guzzled it. Tail wagging, the hound licked its lips and looked up, optimistic about more morsels coming its way. Instead, she bent down on her haunches to stroke its long, narrow head. When he approached, the dog turned and growled with a low rumble which made him freeze on the spot.

"It's OK, boy, he's with me." Hope walked towards him, but the dog stayed put, eyeing him with caution. A short bark rang out in the forest, followed by a gentle howl, then it scurried into the thick undergrowth and vanished. Wearing a pout, Hope stared at the spot where it'd melted into the woods.

He said, "Guess he's more of a ladies' dog then."

The rest of the afternoon passed without incident. With an hour of light left, Hope's energy levels started flagging, and his feet were turning into wooden blocks.

"OK kiddo, I think it's time to move onto stage two of the plan."

Hope placed her hands on her hips. "Oh, the masterplan. I forgot about the masterplan. I thought we were just traipsing around the woods for fun."

He parked the Ford at the edge of the tiny Welsh town and walked along the narrow pavement, which reduced to one side as the road tightened. They passed several other cars, including an early model second generation electric vehicle with its wheels missing and the rear window smashed. Safety glass littered the parcel shelf and back seat. Other wrecks sat on bricks with rusted rims, but a newer car, which appeared to be operational, was parked outside a shop. Its hand painted sign read *The General Store*. Every other commercial premises on the tiny high street sat empty, long since abandoned, but this one seemed to be open. Most had been boarded up with cheap plywood, wrapped in bill posters for anti-government rallies and opposition parties, and covered with thick layers of ubiquitous graffiti.

"They don't like the government much in Wales, do they?"

"Exactly why this is the spot for us, Hope. People here are not the establishment's people. You saw how bad it is in the cities. They'll be expecting us to flee northwards and it's harder to blend in where people are better off."

"Do you think they know about Uncle Ray?"

"Hope, they know everything about us there is to know."

"I wish you'd told me more about your brother. I don't remember him."

He took a deep breath and said, "Well, he's bigger than me and four years older, but you can tell we're brothers because our faces are similar. Goes without saying, but he's very handsome."

Hope rolled her eyes. "Obviously."

"His wife is called Andrea. Well, I assume they're still married, but who knows? I only met her once, because Ray and I, we'd… uh, fallen out when they got together."

"What happened?"

"It's a long story, Hope. I'll save it for another day. Anyway, she wanted to move to Scotland, and your grandmother had just passed away, so off they went."

"When did you last see him?"

"Um, it must've been ten years ago when we all went to visit. It was strange. They loved you, of course. But your mother and I weren't made to feel welcome, so we haven't seen each other since. We last spoke on the phone about six or seven years back, but I don't think they wanted much to do with us."

"Do you think they'd take us in now?"

"I reckon. I mean, it's all so long ago. From my side, it's water under the bridge, and blood is thicker than water, as they say. I know they wanted to have kids, but no idea if they managed it. Hey, you might even have some cousins."

Hope squealed in excitement at the prospect. "Ooh, I'd love that."

They approached the store, and they both fell silent. For all the societal changes of recent years, it appeared undisturbed, perhaps identical to how it might've looked twenty or even forty years previously. Out front stood an A-frame, swinging gently in the breeze, advertising the shop's wares—*Provisions, Food & Wine, Ammunition*—bordered by the logo of a local newspaper, probably long since out of print.

When the door, framed with chipped and peeling cherry red paint, swung inwards, an old-fashioned visitor bell rang, disarming his lingering sense of trepidation. At the quaint sound, an old fellow in his mid-seventies, with thick-rimmed glasses and a full head of nicotine-yellow hair, shuffled from behind a partition towards the counter. His face cracked into an amiable smile as he spoke in a gentle Welsh lilt.

"Welcome, welcome," he said, beckoning them further in. "It's always nice to see some fresh faces around here. What can I do you for?"

Michael offered a thin-lipped smile. "Afternoon. My daughter and I are looking for an old friend. Maybe you can help? He lives out this way with a communal group, perhaps a strange mix of accents and ages."

"Hmm, let me have a think." The man paused and stroked his chin. "What does your friend look like?"

"He's a black fella, around sixty, fit looking, greyish hair, quite short and stocky. London accent."

The man's eyes flashed, and he raised a crooked arthritic finger in triumph. "Ah yes! I know who you mean. I haven't seen him in ages, but some of the others stop by occasionally. They brought some fruit only last week, traded it for a few bits and bobs, which is fine with me as it's hard to get good produce these days." He nodded towards a meagre display of withered fruit and veg. "The one good thing to come from a cashless society, I guess. Always loved a healthy bit of bartering. Now, where do they live?"

Deep in thought, he drummed his fingers on the counter, as if coaxing the fragile memory from the darkened recesses of his brain. "Far as I can remember, they rented some land from Old Mr Cargill several years ago. When he died, his daughter offered the land to them for next to nothing. I think she moved to Scotland, when you could travel freely, of course, and left that idiot son Cargill junior in charge. It's quite a way from here on foot. Have you a vehicle?"

He hesitated. Should he trust the old man and tell the truth? The pause threatened to become uncomfortable. "Yes, we have a car outside."

"Good, good. It's easiest if I draw you a little map." The man picked up a notepad and a sharp pencil and began sketching, his pink tongue poking out from the corner of his mouth while he concentrated. "Here you go," he announced, tearing off the page and holding it out for Michael, who glanced at it before folding it into a square and tucking it into the back pocket of his jeans.

"Thank you so much, Mr…?"

"Please, call me John. Can I get you anything while you're here?"

"OK, thank you, John. I'm Michael and this is my daughter, Hope."

She waved. "Hi Mister."

"Well, isn't she a pretty thing? Not so many young'uns out this way no more." A sudden sadness crept into John's eyes as he spoke. Michael turned to peruse the store's wares. He picked up some tins of food and put them on the counter while Hope picked up items at random and examined them. She settled on a dusty snow globe which seemed to fascinate her, but he shook his head when she showed it to him.

He returned to the counter twice more, his pile of goods growing each time, before a small cabinet behind the counter, crammed with weapons and ammunition, caught his attention.

John must have noticed him looking. "Not such a bad idea to own some sort of protection, friend. Even in this area, which is as safe as it gets, we still get the odd gang rolling through every few months, and there's a few ill-tempered folks living out here that'd shoot you in the back before asking questions. I keeps me this bad boy just in case."

He reached underneath the counter, fumbled around, and pulled out an old pump-action shotgun. Michael's eyes widened. John laughed and placed it on the counter with a solid clunk.

"Can't sell you one of these, I'm afraid. Well, not without a bunch of paperwork. We'd need a certificate, countersigned by a weaponry solicitor, and I'd need to call the cops for a background check." John raised his eyebrows, but Michael shook his head. "Didn't think so, but I can sell you this."

John caressed the weapon for a moment, a thoughtful expression frozen on his face, like he'd forgotten what he wanted to do. He jerked back into life and hid the shotgun back under the counter, then reached behind, opened the cabinet, and pulled out a packet the size of a bar of soap, placing it down on the wooden surface.

"*HandyTaze 3000*. Totally legal class B self-defence device, no paperwork required beyond the standard ID card. You do have one of those?"

"Of course."

"Packs a mean punch. You can even charge it in the midi-USB slot in the car. If you've got an old model, don't worry, it comes with a converter. Otherwise, you can use the standard three-pin charger."

"Hmm, my car is an old petrol conversion. No USB at all."

"Hey, if it's that old, it must have a cigarette lighter?"

"Yeah, it's that old."

John chuckled and disappeared into the office. "Give me a minute." His voice came from behind the partition, accompanied by an urgent rustling sound like rats in a dumpster. Michael visualised old jars and tins full of random chargers, cables and nick-nacks, with clutter piled from floor-to-ceiling.

A moment later, John reappeared, holding up an old mobile phone charger with a cigarette lighter socket. "I don't throw much away. You never know when you might need something one day." He held out the charger. "Just use the converter which comes with the zapper, and it should do the trick."

"Thanks, John. We've taken up enough of your time and it's getting dark. It's not a clever idea to rock up unannounced after sundown, so we'd better settle up."

John nodded and reached for an old calculator with an oversized display. He prodded with his index finger and counted aloud. Michael got the impression he made the prices up as he went along, and when John announced the total, his eyebrows shot upwards.

"Are you sure that's enough?" John nodded, so he shrugged and pulled out his ID card, intending to tap it under the Payscan module. Instead, he hovered close to the device, clutching the card in his hand. He had no alternative way to pay for goods and services, and nothing substantial to offer the man as fair barter. Deep down, he realised John would give him the goods for free, if he asked, but the heavy weight of pride stopped him. The old man caught his eye and smiled. He had no reason to worry, the shopkeeper understood.

"All this blockchain encrypto nonsense. Still, it's secure and safe from prying eyes, so they say," John said.

"Yeah, so they say." *But for how much longer?* He brought the card to rest on the Payscan. It bleeped and flashed with a green led to indicate success. *No going back now. I hope the old man's right.* "I can't thank you enough, John. See you next time."

The transaction complete, he raised his arm with a thumb up and turned to leave. Hope waved and twirled her hair.

"Wait one second, young lady." John shuffled towards Hope. Perhaps wary of his intentions, she froze. "There's something on your face there."

Michael relaxed. He'd seen this routine a hundred times before. John inched his hand towards her, then snapped open his palm, revealing the snow globe which she'd earlier been admiring. His faced beamed into a wide grin, displaying a set of teeth befitting of a younger man.

"Don't forget to clean behind those ears, sweet-heart." He handed her the globe and gave her a gentle pat before opening the door and shooing them away.

Michael pulled out the map and examined it as they walked back towards the Ford.

"He was lovely," Hope said, fondling her globe.

"There are still good people in this world, kiddo. Aside from you and me of course."

The drawing was a simple sketch with a few key landmarks highlighted, including a large rendering of a telephone, along with the relevant local roads. When they climbed into the car, he took another moment to memorise the map and handed it to his daughter.

"You OK to navigate?" he asked, cranking the key. Hope nodded and studied the map with a serious expression. While the engine idled, he pulled the taser from his backpack and tore open the plastic packet with some difficulty. He laid out the parts and hooked the taser up to the cigarette lighter. There was a brief delay, and he tutted, thinking it'd failed to work, but then a small LED started blinking amber.

"Alright!"

"Go Dad!" enthused Hope. "Just make sure you don't zap yourself in the balls with that thing."

"Thanks for your concern. I'll try not to." He eased the Ford's cranky old gear box into first and pulled away.

The drive took around fifteen minutes, and they made one wrong turn before finding the old red phone-box, vandalised and probably out of commission for decades, but a welcome sight, nonetheless.

They turned off the road and onto a narrow path. He had to amble along in second gear for three-hundred yards before the track, which was little more than a row of tall weeds between well-worn tyre tracks, ended in a wooden gate, with enough room to turn a small truck. He pulled off the track and killed the engine.

"Here goes nothing," he said. They got out, leaving

everything inside except his pack.

The gate was locked with a combination padlock, but an old-fashioned wooden sty had been built between the gate and a rusty wire fence. He helped his daughter up and over before following with a grunt. The muddy path became a well-maintained surface of gravel and stone. The brow of a hill obscured their view, but once they'd passed it, an encampment revealed itself, spread out below in an undulating valley. Smoke poured from the chimney of the large main building. Several smaller structures and tents were dotted about. He counted six people tending the various animals and crops spread across the farmland, and three vehicles parked at the end of the track. Finally, someone noticed them and strode in their direction, after alerting the nearest other person.

"This is private land. Have you taken a wrong turn?" the man shouted, once in earshot.

With his palms held face up, he said, "I'm looking for somebody. My name is Michael. This is my daughter, Hope."

"Who are you looking for, mate? We're not expecting any visitors."

"A guy called Willy. He's about 60, a boxer—"

"Ah, you're a friend of Willy's. OK then, you better come with me." He motioned for them to follow. "Sorry for the frosty reception. When people show up here, they're usually lost or bad news."

"It's alright, I know how it is. Sorry we had to show up unannounced, but you know Willy, I don't think he's owned a phone since about 2010, let alone another method I could get hold of him by. I didn't catch your name, by the way?"

"It's Bracken," said the man, who was around thirty, average height but strong and fit looking with shoulder-length brown hair and a weathered, expressive face, obscured by long stubble.

They exchanged no further words on the short walk to the main house. Bracken strode a few yards ahead of them and did not look back. He swung the big wooden door open and held it for them to step inside.

"Should we take our shoes off? They're quite muddy?" said Michael.

"Nah, you're good. Just give 'em a wipe. It's all wooden floors, and we sweep 'em every day, anyway. Lots of mud on a farm. Want some tea?"

"That would be nice." The reply came in unison as they wiped their feet on a wiry brown mat in the hallway.

"Just make yourself comfortable in there." Bracken stabbed a finger towards the next room. "Cow's milk or dairy free?"

"Dairy free, please," said Hope.

"Whatever's easiest."

Inside the living room, they found a random configuration of furniture. He chose a beaten looking, faded green armchair, which he found surprisingly comfortable. Hope seated herself on a low wooden stool and held her snow-globe between her legs, staring at it pensively.

They sat in silence until Bracken bought over cups of steaming hot tea, one in a chipped enamel mug, the other in a paisley patterned teacup.

Hope reached for the teacup and examined it. "Cool cup."

"I'll be back in a minute.," Bracken turned and exited the room.

A moment later, he returned accompanied by a tall and serious looking woman with short curls dyed red. Behind her stood a stocky man, tanned an almost caramel colour from the sun, with a receding hairline and thinning, close-cropped hair.

They were both equal height and looked of similar age, perhaps close to Michael's.

"This is Glenda and Pete. Meet Michael and Hope. They're old friends of Willy's."

"Hi there," said Glenda in a soft, husky tone. "We introduced Willy to the community around seven years ago."

"He was my coach for a while. I used to box semi-pro," Pete said.

"Yeah, he's a great fighter and an even better teacher," said Michael. "So, is he off somewhere? I didn't see him outside."

Glenda sighed. She spoke gently and addressed him. "About that. I'm afraid I have some bad news for you." From the sadness in her eyes, he predicted what she'd say next and released a long sigh, letting his head loll forward in dismay. "There's no easy way to break it to you. Willy passed away a few months ago."

CHAPTER: SEVEN

"Sorry you came all this way just to hear bad news," said Glenda.

"How did it happen?"

"Heart attack, we think. He used to love working the crops. We always told him to slow down. One day, we found him collapsed in one of the fields. We were too late, and he'd gone. If someone had been working with him that day, I reckon he'd have pulled through. We've got a defibrillator inside and Siobhan used to be a doctor in a past life. But it wasn't to be," Glenda said.

His eyebrows rose high on his forehead. "A heart attack? But he was always so damn fit. Man ran rings around me when I was half his age."

"Tell me about it," said Pete. "But I think he was far older than he'd admit. Could get away with it too. I think he had his sixtieth birthday four years in a row. My guess is he was around seventy-five." Michael nodded and stared at the floor.

"Look, I don't know your plans, but we can always use extra hands from the right people. You guys seem OK to me and there's always work to do. You can stay as long as you need but…" Glenda paused, as if grasping for the right words, "I won't labour the point, but you'll need to help out."

He managed a half-smile. It would take time for the news

about Willy to sink in, but he had to remain positive somehow. His daughter needed him to stay strong and not descend into his former morose state. He'd done enough wallowing to last a lifetime. "That's great, Glenda. I know you can't carry anyone out here. You don't have to worry about me. I'm fit and willing, and happy to do honest work again. Her, on the other hand…"

He jerked a thumb towards Hope, who looked up with an expression of sheer innocence.

"Me?"

"Just kidding." He patted her on the top of her head in mock condescension. "We left all her bloody devices back in London. It's far easier to get her attention now without the metaverse and whatnot. She'll be happy to help."

"Damn straight. I might be young, but I'm not lazy!"

"Is it OK if I bring the car in? I'd rather not leave it out there, if you don't mind."

"Yeah, no problem. The code for the gate is 1984," replied Pete.

"Nice," said Michael, nodding.

When the car rolled to a stop outside the house and he yanked the handbrake upwards, it seemed like the whole community had gathered in front of the building to welcome him. Their working day must have finished. The daylight had faded quickly, as it always seemed to with winter approaching.

"Wow, cool wheels, man," said an admiring voice as he climbed from the car. "Haven't seen a Capri in years. Mark three as well. Electric conversion?"

"Yeah. Don't tell the feds, but it's dual petrol and electric."

"Nice. I'm Joel, by the way." The man extended his palm, and Michael gripped it, noticing how weathered and rough the other man's hands felt compared to his own. *Time to get those callouses back.*

Another voice, soft and husky, added, "Sorry about him. Joel didn't get the memo about bumping fists and tapping elbows. Monique, nice to meet you." It belonged to a woman with smooth skin with a gorgeous complexion. She offered her fist, which he tapped, holding her gaze for a little longer than he should've. Yet she didn't drop eye contact until he did.

Hope stood chatting with a couple of youngsters of similar age. They looked like brother and sister. The girl was perhaps a year younger than Hope, while the boy looked fourteen or fifteen. The prospect of his daughter spending time with another teenage boy so soon after Oliver filled him with dread, but he tried to tell himself it was good for her to have some age-appropriate company, rather than being surrounded by adults. Besides, she didn't seem worried. Michael wrestled off his apprehension and introduced himself. The boy, Johannes, shook his hand with a firm grip for a teenager. Although he seemed shy, the vibes he gave off were nothing like the farmer's creepy kid.

A deep voice boomed, "Ma's calling. Let's go eat." It belonged to a fit older man of around fifty who appeared to be the group's most senior member. He had a handsome square jaw with short salt and pepper hair. A former military man, surely.

There were twelve people seated around a large, rickety wooden table in the tight kitchen. Despite the clutter, it was cosy and welcoming. Ma wasn't anyone's mother but a short, plump and gentle looking Indian woman who seemed to have taken responsibility for the cooking.

"Her culinary skills are awesome," explained Joel. "I mean, I'm not an awful cook by any means, but she won't let anyone near the kitchen. We stopped arguing, to be honest."

Ma's chest puffed out as she dished up to the two new

visitors, who received their food first. "Don't wait. None of these pigs will."

Eating began once the first morsels of food hit the plates, so Michael followed suit. It was a vegetable stew, spicy and full of flavour, served with fluffy rice. He hadn't realised the strength of his hunger and tried to slow down, but cleared his plate first. Ma jumped up to serve him some more.

"At least finish yours first," he protested, but she slopped another fair-sized portion onto his plate. He offered thanks and resumed eating. After managing half of her meal, Hope slowed, then stopped, offering an apologetic look around the room.

"Don't worry girl, nothing goes to waste here," said Monique as she took the plates and scraped leftovers into a large bucket. "We've got an old mutt called Barney and he'll eat anything. If there's too much for him, we put it in the animal feed. We don't eat *them* mind. None of us eat meat here, save special occasions. It's one of the rules. Luckily, Ma's the best damn veggie cook you'll ever meet."

"Shush, I'm not that good."

Hope wrung her hands. "Can I meet Barney?"

"Well, if you can find him. He's probably on someone's bed, fast asleep, or licking his balls, which is his other favourite pastime." Hope shuttled off to look for the dog and soon returned, animal in tow.

Michael nodded towards his daughter. "Real dog whisperer, this one. We met a mean looking mongrel in the woods yesterday. Terrified me, but she didn't bat an eye. Had it eating out of her palm. Literally."

"Yeah, we got loads of strays out here. Some of their owners died, I guess, but most moved to Scotland, or at least out of Wales. Not much reason for the Welsh to stay after, what is it, nearly a decade of those scumbags in power?"

"Don't mind Joel, he doesn't remember it's rude to talk politics at the dinner table," said Monique. "I wouldn't worry about the strays, anyway. Some of them are indifferent to humans, but most are friendly. I've never known one to attack."

After they ate, they sat around the table for another hour drinking red wine. The bottles had little orange price labels from *The General Store*. He allowed Hope a small glass and she seemed to enjoy the taste.

"Special occasion tonight, but we usually drink the home-made shit. Joel's a pretty mean brewer, you know," the older man, Kevin, explained. Like Michael had suspected, he'd been a sergeant in the Royal Marines. He wanted to learn more about the man's military background, but decided to wait until they knew each other better.

Hope stroked Barney, curled up underneath the tangle of legs. Her face had flushed with the wine. Kevin circled the room, topping up empty glasses, but as he approached his daughter, Michael narrowed his eyes. She must've caught his concerned stare and placed her hand over her glass to refuse.

Pete and Glenda announced they were retiring and made their farewells, while Kevin sent the two kids off to bed. The remaining eight decamped to the living room. Pete fetched some wood and lit a fire. The temperature had plummeted since nightfall and Joel, who seemed to be the resident weather expert, informed everyone it was the coldest night of the year so far.

Once the flames had taken, a warm glow flickered around the room, enveloping Michael with sweet memories from happier times. The familiar smell of burning wood always reminded him of music festivals before they became sanitised affairs. How he'd loved camping out for a few days with friends. Modern bands never excited him, but occasionally the festival organisers had dug up one of the living legends from the nineties whom he revered. Nothing could beat seeing a band playing in their prime, but it'd always been a thrill, nonetheless.

After the group had exhausted the wine supply, Joel brought out some of his home-made brew and poured everyone except Hope a generous glass. The opaque liquid had a thick, foamy, off-white head and a pungent hop aroma.

"This smell reminds me of when I used to smoke weed back in the day," Michael said, sipping his glass with hesitance. The bitter, fruity taste was alien but pleasant.

"Double-hopped unfiltered IPA, my own recipe."

"Yeah, sure Joel, we all know you're amazing. Well done," Ma said, cuddling up to him.

"What a team they make! Think how bland everyone's lives would be with them," Monique enthused.

"Anyone for a little music?" Joel said, switching the subject and blushing from the praise, or perhaps the open acknowledgement of their relationship. They had the awkwardness of a new couple.

"Definitely. What have you got?"

"As our guests, you get to choose." Joel pointed towards the corner of the room, and a vinyl record player sitting on a vintage tea-stained sideboard with a few hundred LPs stored in the shelving underneath.

Michael crossed the room to investigate. "Wow, you've got some awesome records here, man. Reminds me of my mother's collection. Damn, I regretted not hanging on to that stuff." He leafed through the LPs, stopping to pluck out the occasional one and examine it with childlike excitement. "Steely Dan, shit…" He picked another. "Nirvana, Smashing Pumpkins… all this nineties stuff. My mum loved all that. It was her era, so I guess it rubbed off on me. Never got into any music past the turn of the century when I grew up. She loved all this sixties and seventies classic stuff, too."

He picked up Black Sabbath's *Paranoid*, treating it like an ancient holy relic. Once he'd taken the vinyl out of its tattered sleeve and placed it on the turntable, he lifted the stylus and set the record in motion. There was a crackle and slow sirens faded in before the sludgy opening chords of 'War Pigs' sounded.

"Nice choice, man," said Joel. "Not listened to this in forever."

By the time the album's title track jerked into life, conversation had resumed, although Michael remained as close to the speakers as possible, lost in the music. Between songs, he looked up at his daughter and they shared a smile.

"Who woulda thought Ozzy Osbourne would live so fucking long? I thought his goose was cooked, but he nearly made it to 85. Not bad," said Monique.

Joel's eyes widened. "Wait, what? Ozzy's *dead*!" The room erupted into howls of laughter. When side-A ended, Michael asked if he could select another record, which nobody minded. He chose a Fleetwood Mac album, and even Hope sung along to some of the songs.

The next day, Hope put her newfound animal husbandry skills into action and spent a morning with Monique, tending to the animals. There were two cows, three sheep and twenty chickens on the settlement. So many things about country life still puzzled her, but she wanted to learn.

"How do you remember their names?" she asked, as Monique introduced her to the chickens. "They all look the same."

"Ah, but they're not, you'll see. Each one has a personality and unique markings. See Albert's colours, and the way his feathers are speckled? Boris is always quiet, but Henrietta is the noisiest of the bunch."

"What about these two?" She pointed at a pair of identical-looking hens.

"Agreed, they're hard to tell apart, but look…" Monique bent over and rustled beneath the two birds. She held up her hands with an egg in each. "Look, you can tell who's who by the shells."

"And you never eat the animals?" Hope asked, grimacing.

"I'd be lying if I said never, but seldom. There's only three of us who aren't vegetarian, and they can kill one on special occasions, or if their numbers grow too high and we can't look after them. Or if one gets injured. Nothing goes to waste here."

She pursed her lips. "That's fair enough, I suppose."

In the afternoon, Johannes and his sister, Kayleigh, joined them. Hope quietened down, aware of her status as an outsider, but neither of the siblings spoke much. After they'd broken the ice, Monique tasked Hope and Kayleigh with mucking out the chicken coop. She tried to hide her displeasure, knowing she'd better get used to filth if they were staying in the country. It seemed an integral part of farm life. Kayleigh didn't seem to mind the grime one bit. She did most of the ornamental gardening in the flowerbeds around the house, and dirt had caked her fingernails, even before they'd started. She spoke passionately about the subject, but said little else. By the time she left for some other tasks in the afternoon, Hope had learned almost nothing about the girl.

The brother, Johannes, towered over her, yet she got no sense of threat from the boy. Despite an awkward teenage gait, he had his father's strong jawline and haunting eyes. He'd be totally fit once he'd grown into his face. He kept quiet around her, avoiding eye contact, which at first Hope took to be arrogance, but she realised quickly he suffered from genuine shyness. If she wanted to learn more than surface information, she'd be forced to lead the conversation. And, once she'd convinced herself he possessed none of Oliver's creepiness, she quickly found she *did* want to get to know him.

"Do you go to school? Are there even schools around here?"

"Na, not really. I went until I was ten or so. What about you? They must still have plenty of schools in London."

"Of course, same here. My… my dad took me out a few years ago and I've been home schooled." She wanted to say *my parents*, but she couldn't face it, because the word would mean acknowledging her mother's act of betrayal. She would—later, but not yet.

"They allow that? I've never been told if I'm supposed to attend classes."

"Yeah, as long as I go to Sunday school, or at least one specific Christian religion class per week, it's OK."

"Can't say I miss education. Bunch of bullshit."

"I kind of do. Maybe not lessons, and certainly not the teachers, but at least it was easy to make friends. Dad decided they taught way too much religious stuff. I can't remember much, but all that fire and brimstone crap was so overbearing. And they wouldn't teach anything except Christianity. When I joined the school, there were kids from everywhere, all different faiths and we all got along fine. They slowly vanished or stopped wearing their cool outfits or whatnot."

"I wish there were more people our age around here. Do you have loads of friends back home?"

Her heart jumped. *Our age!* The boy was a year or two

older, a proper teenager, and he'd openly referred to her as the same. Perhaps she *was* a proper teenager, but some days she felt like a child. "A few. I miss them."

"A boyfriend?"

Johannes's directness came as a shock, and she felt her cheeks reddening. "Uh, no, not really. I guess I had a crush, but we weren't going out." She leaned on the pitchfork and stared across the undulating land. The scene beneath the low sun wasn't a million miles away from the ones she'd pictured in dreams, and she sighed a long, contented breath which fogged in the afternoon chill.

Johannes stood by her side. Somehow, the extended silence didn't feel awkward, like she expected it to. She thought about her few remaining friends back in London, whom she may never see again: Sally, Karl, Billie, and Craig. Oh, Craig. Perhaps he had been her boyfriend. He and Johannes didn't look dissimilar, either. They both possessed the same endearing awkwardness, with strong, stoic features. Did she have a *type* already? How very adult.

Johannes stopped scanning the landscape and turned to face her. She kept her gaze locked on the horizon, hoping she looked thoughtful. From the corner of her eye, she could tell he was studying her face, and she worried the flush of her cheeks had become noticeable. She could always blame the chilly late afternoon air.

"You'll see them again soon, right?"

"Um, I don't know." Hope prepared herself for the inevitable next question. Why was she here? It would lead to an examination about her mother, no doubt.

"Hope, Johannes, we're done for the day." They both jumped and turned. Bracken laughed. "Are you coming back to the house, or you still got work to do? Not that I see much work happening."

"Uh, no we're done. Come on, Hope, let's head back. It's been nice talking." When the boy turned, she smiled to herself. He was not wrong—it *had* been nice.

Michael didn't mind the early starts and hard physical work, but what he enjoyed most was a couple of lovely evenings spent eating, drinking, and getting to know their hosts. The alcohol made the mornings tough, but the fresh air cleared his head while heavy exertion sweated out the booze. Hope had been distant since the first evening, though. She more than likely needed some space. Besides, they'd have to move on before long. It seemed sensible to let her enjoy some downtime.

After completing the day's main jobs, he usually got roped into helping Joel work on some ancient farmyard machinery abandoned by the former landowner. They'd tinker with the engine of a rusty old digger until the light disappeared, forcing them to work by torchlight. They'd drink glasses of Joel's home-made beer and make small talk, or pass an hour without saying a word, only the clanking of engine parts and wrenches breaking the silence.

After a few glasses of strong beer, Joel always got chattier. Michael caught a glint in the other man's eyes while they shared a cigarette, and stared at him, trying to elicit a response. His patience soon evaporated. "What? Come on, Joel, out with it."

Joel smiled and exhaled a long jet of smoke, then stared back at him, squinting. "You know, Mike. I think Monique has taken a bit of a shine to you. Is she your type?"

"My type? I don't know, but I don't think I have one.

Anyway, don't be silly." He felt his cheeks reddening while Joel's smile widened into a grin. "What, you think so? I mean, she's a very attractive woman and all. To be honest, I've been keeping my head down. I don't know who's with who."

"Fair play, man," Joel said, nodding. "Well, Glenda and Pete are a couple. Kevin's partner, Becky, died a few years ago. He had a thing with Monique months back, but they decided to stay friends. Now he and Siobhan are screwing, but it's nothing serious. They think nobody knows, but literally *everybody* does, even the kids." Michael brayed with laughter and snorted out some beer. "So that leaves Bracken and he's a bit of a quiet type, but I think he's into guys, if I'm honest. If that's his jam, then he's shit out of luck. Not much of a gay scene in rural Wales these days."

"Not much of a scene anywhere now, I guess."

"True. At least they haven't made it *illegal* to be gay. Not *yet* anyway. Fucking God-botherers," Joel spat.

"Tell me about it. I took Hope out of school because of it. Who cares what people believe? They can worship a goddamn purple elephant for all I care. But I don't need religion rammed down my throat with the rest of their bullshit."

"I heard they're trying to make home-schooling an offence."

Michael shook his head and tutted. "Can't say I'm surprised after those dumb anti-literature laws they just brought in. So, are you religious, mate?"

"I'm a Buddhist, believe it or not. Well, at least here I am. Not allowed to be one out there." Joel jabbed a finger towards the setting sun. "I have nothing against God, or what-have-you. But their idea of God isn't loving, or blissful. It's a guilt-trip. All vengeance and power, such shameful shit."

Michael nodded. "I hear you. I'm not atheist either, just

agnostic, I guess. Cheers for the lowdown, man. Hopefully I won't put my foot in it, thanks to you."

"No worries. What about you, Mike? Are you with anyone?"

His eyes dropped downwards as memories of his past life hurtled back. Happy nights stretching out on the sofa, curled up with Allison, when ideas of a quasi-religious authoritarian government were still reserved for dystopian novels and television series. Allison hadn't taken to motherhood easily, but once Hope had passed the baby phase and became a toddler, life had grown easier. Their child had filled every moment of their waking lives, until the day reality came crashing through their world, and the Christian Conservatives took a strong lead in the polls. But they'd been wrong in the past, hadn't they? Of course, the pollsters had messed up, like in 2016 when he was around Hope's age, full of naïve optimism. People wouldn't repeat past mistakes all over again. Finally, election day came, along with the unthinkable. No more denial or blind optimism. Life would change inexorably.

Since then, they'd drifted, like tectonic plates destined to move further and further apart. In truth, their relationship had been messed up for months. He'd been indiscreet. She'd never confronted him, but something in the way she carried herself told him she knew. Why had he done it? His pride, more precisely his ego, battered and bruised by months of failure to find regular work and provide for his kin, needed stroking. What better to rekindle the fire of vanity than the embrace of a woman several years his junior, easily impressed by an experienced older man with a vague degree of intelligence? How pathetic it appeared now, with the hindsight only true distance provided.

Would he ever see Allison again, and if so, could he find forgiveness within himself? Yes, she'd made an awful decision, but his laziness and self-centred actions hadn't left her many obvious choices. He could see that now. But committing such an act of betrayal might yet prove unforgivable. Time would tell, although for the moment the gulf between them looked wider than the River Severn, which separated England from Wales. Any prospect of ever returning to London seemed impossible after what had transpired. Indeed, the M25, snaking around the city like a discarded bracelet, may as well have been a sheer cliff face a mile high. However, one thing was for certain: his days as a self-serving, immature man were finished. Now, he'd put his daughter first, before anyone, even the damn car he'd thought he loved, before discovering what true love meant.

"Long story short, no I'm not."

Joel's gaze didn't waver as he waited for an explanation that Michael was unwilling to give, not yet anyway. He returned his attention to the oily old engine parts spread out on the floor below, and Joel eventually followed suit. The two men reassembled the engine one piece at a time, ignoring calls for dinner. They'd come too far, it had to be completed now. Why, he couldn't say, but when they finished, the full darkness of night had arrived.

"OK man, pull the choke, turn the key and give it some gas."

The engine turned slowly, coughing but failing to spark. He cursed under his breath. Just as he was about to give up for fear of flooding the carburettor, he gave it a final crank and the tractor juddered into life, emitting a thick plume of black smoke from its rear.

"She rides!" Joel said. Seconds later, the engine spluttered and died. "Crap. Well, it's a start, eh?"

Michael sighed and slumped into the hard seat, so worn it

was little more than a skeleton. "We had it for a second there. Always tomorrow, I guess."

Hope and Johannes sat alone in the bedroom he shared with his sister. She rolled her neck, pretending to loosen a crick, but really scanning the room, searching for clues in her quest to understand the boy. But the room was a no-man's-land, a demilitarised zone between boy and girl, on which neither could stamp their personality. Perhaps the time had come for direct questioning, but if she gave, she damn well better expect to receive.

"Where's your mum, Johannes?"

The boy kicked his heels against the bedframe as they dangled, and stared at them like they held answers, until he whispered, "She's gone."

"Oh, I'm sorry, Johannes." Did he mean gone as in gone somewhere else, or dead? The vague answer offered little clue and further explanation didn't seem forthcoming. Should she press him or drop it?

"It's OK. What about yours?"

Here goes. "Mine? You don't even want to know. She's back in London. I think she's alive and well. I hope she is, anyway."

"Do you miss her?" She nodded. "Me too. Look, if you promise to keep quiet, I'll tell you a secret."

She smiled. Perhaps if he shared a real secret with her, she could explain her own situation. "I'd love that."

Johannes leaned over her, reaching towards a drawer at the foot of the bed. She sighed when he withdrew his weight, foreign, yet warm and comforting. In his slender hand, he held out a chunky piece of plastic.

"Is that a mobile phone?"

"Yeah. We're not supposed to have them. It's one of the rules, so keep your mouth shut." She mimed a zipping motion across her lips. "If you wanted, you could call her? While you still can, because you never know when that day passes."

"Are you sure it still makes calls? It looks well ancient. My dad probably had one similar when he was my age. Bet it doesn't even have access to the basic Metaverse, does it?" While her mind battled itself in a futile tug of war, she continued to stare at the device.

"Yeah, it must be at least twenty years old. This thing would survive a nuclear blast."

She caught the boy's eye, and they both looked away. She bit her lip, and he glanced at her. The next time she looked up, their stares locked, and she reached her hand towards his. Their fingers met. His touch was warm and sticky, but she allowed it to linger before plucking the phone from his palm.

As soon as she held it, regret clawed at her. What had she done? The damn thing was a curse. Of course, she wouldn't rat on him, but damn the boy for forcing her into such an impossible choice. He was right, though. Who knew when she'd get another opportunity?

Dad would lose his shit if he found out, but she could hear her mother's voice in a matter of seconds, perhaps even receive the apology she longed for. If she dialed those eleven little digits which she knew by heart, at least she'd know her mother was safe.

CHAPTER: EIGHT

Miko slumped onto the rickety bed with a deep sigh and flicked on the television. He drained the dregs from a half-litre bottle of vodka and tossed it across the room. When he reached for the second, sitting on the worn bedside cabinet, he took a moment to read the label and noticed with a wry smile that the stuff was produced in England. What a joke. His nation had perfected the art of making vodka over centuries and here he was in this crappy country, laid up in a cheap, shabby motel drinking cheap, shabby imitation vodka. Poland had been rough over the past decade, but they always had a decent drink, without spending more than a few *zloty*. This bottle of crap had cost more in hourly wages than the time taken to drink it. Well, it would've if he'd not stuck it on expenses. They always screwed him on the accommodation, so at least they could pay for a nightcap and allow a man to get some rest.

He thumbed through the meagre selection of channels. Nothing held his interest, so he left it tuned to a news broadcast and allowed his mind to wander. Today Birmingham, yesterday London, tomorrow who knew and frankly, who cared? The cities were all the same. One miserable room to the next, one dismal family to another, collecting their daughters like a freakish pied piper. Perhaps he should consider that chump Eriksson's offer. *His* squad sure as hell was not holed up in a dump like this. Their equipment and vehicles were better, honestly their men were better too, but then he would have no power over who he hired. His squad had been hand-picked and assembled by him without meddling from above. No, the likes of Faulkner and Burrows were inept, but they let him do his job.

But he *did* care. Once he'd snared Randall, he'd give it some serious consideration. Normally, he didn't differentiate one target from another—they were all the same—but Michael Randall had burrowed under his skin. They wouldn't need a fucking laboratory to get his precious daughter pregnant. The ease with which the man had dispatched Petersen and escaped in his clown car filled him with an impotent rage. It'd been a long time since a target had outsmarted Miko Kozlowski, and he'd been made to look a fool. He might have hunkered down in Wales, but he'd make a mistake, eventually. A lapse in judgement wasn't merely probable, it was inevitable. Carrying around the lumbering weight of a teenage girl was like having one leg struck in a bear trap.

He twisted the cap from the second vodka bottle, raised it to his dry lips, and pulled deeply.

"*Kurwa,*" he muttered, grimacing and wiping his mouth on his bare forearm. He should have stuck it in the freezer first, but what did it matter? Nicely chilled Polish vodka or nasty paint thinners warmed to room temperature—they did an equal job.

The news broadcast turned its attention to eastern Europe, and he listened impassively. More migrant crises along the Polish borders. First, millions of Iranian refugees fleeing their battered country after the Yanks had bombed it back to the stone age. The Americans didn't get their hands dirty anymore on the ground. Leave it to the Brits and Krauts to mop things up once they'd dropped a billion tonnes of ordinance on the poor raghead fucks. When he'd been in the service, things were simpler. The Polish special forces were little more than a mercenary band of assassins, and that suited him just fine.

Now, the rush of refugees from the former Soviet states had started anew, as their overbearing motherland stretched its legs and widened its borders once more. Even with the American firepower and British-led, German-financed ground forces, the Western allies knew they couldn't afford to get bogged down with the Russian army in a land war, so they let them get on with it. If Russia didn't get too cocky, Poland was safe from re-absorption into the empire. Would his family—no, his ex-family—be safe too? He took another deep glug from the sorry excuse for vodka in his hands. They were no longer his concern. They were better off without him, and that's all he had to remember.

The image on the tiny screen began to waver and separate until it became a carousel of spinning lights. He hurled the second empty bottle towards the television. It clipped the corner and deflected onto a lamp, which exploded with a satisfying crunch, but the undamaged screen kept sending negative proton particles back at him. He rolled onto his feet, stumbled into the room's centre, then ripped off his vest and trousers, losing his balance and crashing to the floor. Tears of laughter rolled down his cheeks as he pulled himself upright and launched himself at the wall. His fist punched through the plaster. What could his knee do? A crevasse the size of a grapefruit appeared when he thrust it into the wall below the first hole and he roared in triumph. In the room next door, a man hollered.

"*Spierdalaj*!" Miko bellowed back and slammed another fist-sized chunk from the wall.

Someone hammered at the door and Miko zigzagged over to it. "Keep it down in there! What the hell is going on?" came the voice from the other side.

Now fully naked, Miko fumbled with the latch and yanked the door open. He leered at the man, who caught his eye for a second, then scurried away.

"Hey, come back and finish our conversation, fuckhead," Miko shouted after him. When no reply came except distant, retreating footsteps, he laughed and slammed the door.

As usual with such thoughts, the sudden image of the young girl and her mother's face, flushed from the autumn winds, blindsided him with its clarity. In his weakened state, he allowed his mind to engage. What were they doing now? Did they have enough to eat, thanks to all the blood money he had provided? Sometimes he imagined interloping on the big moments in her life—her first day of school, her successes in junior sports and the girl scouts. But his chosen path had long since reached the point of irrevocability, and he would find no way back to her now. Men like him weren't released from duty, except by death. It came with the territory. Retirement plans were for bankers and clerks.

He shuffled into the bathroom and turned on the tap, drowning his thirst and allowing water to wash over his burning lips and face. He gripped the sink and peered at the grotesque monster, grinning back from the mirror. Still laughing, his eyes began to water, and he sobbed. Sickened by his own weakness, he slammed a fist into the mirror. Blood dribbled from a cut, and he pulled out a tiny shard of glass before licking the wound. With tears falling from his eyes, he staggered from the bathroom and toppled face-first onto the bed, like a felled oak tree in the Białowieża Forest, the place where he had first learned survival skills as an adolescent. Oblivion claimed him, even before his weeping cut had clotted.

Five days into their time at the settlement, Michael found himself alone with Kevin at last, while the two men harvested the late season potatoes. Of everyone, Kevin intrigued him the most, and strings of questions he wanted to ask jostled for attention in his mind. He forced himself to wait until their conversation flowed to a point where he could start satisfying his curiosity.

"It must have been hard raising two kids alone. What happened to their mother, if you don't mind me asking?"

"No, it's fine. I'm lucky to have the support of what I consider my extended family here, so it's not that hard." He paused, taking in a deep breath. "It was suicide." A silence descended and Kevin stopped working, letting his head loll forward. Michael could almost visualise the dead woman through Kevin's eyes. The poor guy must've found her. Hanging, overdosed, or however she'd chosen to end her life, it didn't matter.

Michael stabbed his pitchfork into the earth and placed his hand on the other man's shoulder. "I am so sorry."

Kevin offered a weak smile. "It was four years ago now. Just after that lot got re-elected with a bigger fucking majority. You could see where things were heading, and she couldn't take it anymore. She was never the same after losing both parents in the first pandemic, but when Johannes was born, she just carried on, you know?"

"Yeah, kids have that effect, don't they? Nothing else you can do but grind on."

"She always wanted to travel around the world once Johannes and Kayleigh grew older, but when they closed all the borders and brought in all those crazy laws, that dream died. I guess it kept her going. Hell, we were lucky to have kids at all. None of our friends managed to. What about you? Hope seems like a lovely girl."

"Yeah, luck doesn't do it justice, does it? I mean, I was 27 when she was born. We'd been trying a year, maybe I'd subconsciously given up. None of my friends managed to have children."

"Have you ever wondered why?"

"Of course. I mean, the official line must be bullshit. Has to be. Maybe their vengeful God has grown tired of us, or the Earth wants rid so it can start again. Who could blame it? You got any theories."

"A few, yeah."

Michael grimaced. "Please tell me you're not into all these vaccine conspiracies, or phone signal nonsense?"

"Well, Becky got pregnant before vaccines became mandatory, so I'm not ruling them out. What about you?"

"Nah, I already had all mine. It's gotta be something else."

"Maybe. But one thing's for sure, there's no way in hell I'm letting them near Jo or Kay. There are still doctors who'll fake that shit if you know where to look."

"Anyway, Kevin, I hear you were in the Marines? Probably would've joined up myself, if I hadn't got into, ah, a spot of trouble when I was younger."

Kevin shot him a look like he was about to press him, then said, "Yeah, I left the service after Iran. Perhaps we justified Iraq and Afghanistan, maybe even Libya. Told ourselves our actions benefited the people. It was easier to pretend we were fighting on the side of good back then. But invading Iran didn't benefit anyone, except *those* bastards in power." Kevin jerked a thumb behind.

Michael sensed the man had more to say and waited for him to resume speaking. "Maybe I'd already racked up enough points for a free pass into hell with the things I did, but after Iran, it wasn't even in doubt. That's why we moved out here, to build a little patch of goodness. I can't believe I was part of that fucking war machine. Do you know who the biggest beneficiary from the birthing schools is?"

He kept silent, doubting Kevin could stop himself now he'd hit full flow. "Damn army, of course. They take them as young as six, for Christ's sake, and leave everyone to rot, yet find the money and manpower to fight multiple wars simultaneously. Where do you think these soldiers come from? There's no conscription, yet we have the sixth biggest standing army in the world. Nothing but guns for hire now, doing America's dirty work since they disbanded half their ground forces." Kevin's shoulders sagged as he finished. The outpour seemed to have exhausted him, leaving nothing but remnants, like a squeezed-out tube of toothpaste.

Michael considered his next words while the late October sun filtered through the treeline warming his skin, and a light breeze caressed his sweaty brow. "Kevin, mate, we can't change any of that shit. Hell, I've done terrible things and I've hurt people. People I love and strangers. All that matters now is them." He stabbed his finger towards the house. "The young ones. They're our hope."

Kevin smiled. "Hope. I wondered why you gave her that name. I'm glad there are optimists like you in this world, Mike. Do you honestly think things will improve? For them, at least."

"They have to, don't they? I mean, you guys can exist out here. They still allow *that*. Realistically, we've got one chance. Next year's election. I think if that lot wins again, it's the end for what's left of our so-called democracy, and there might not be another. But I've got a feeling the tide might be turning. People have to wake up."

Kevin's shoulders remained slumped. "Maybe. I pray you're right, but I can't see them giving up power so easily, election or not."

"Well, you just need Wales to vote for independence and you guys are sorted at least," said Michael. Kevin laughed, but it was a distant sound, and he knew the other man did not believe him. "There's always Scotland though, right?"

"If you can make it across, then yeah."

"You think it's still possible?" he asked, hoping Kevin wouldn't notice how much the question meant. Like a novice poker player, he'd shoved his chips into the centre at the first decent hand. But he had to start trusting these people, eventually.

"I think it's possible, yeah. You're obviously not going to get in via the roads or any other transport links, but they haven't closed the whole border off. Talk to Bracken if you really want to know. He's crossed several times in the last few years."

He took a deep breath. *Here goes nothing.* "My brother lives over there. We don't see eye-to-eye, but I figured if I could get my girl across, maybe she can claim asylum."

Kevin turned and his piercing green eyes seemed to search deep into his. A flicker of understanding passed between them. Kevin let out a long sigh and said, "I've got hope for Kay, too. She's only twelve, so there's still a chance. She takes after her mother. Becky was a gardener too, with a real knack for it. Could grow green shoots in a bloody tundra."

He smiled and nodded, but Kevin stared over his shoulder at someone behind him and he spun around. It was Bracken approaching, a welcome sight indeed. Perhaps luck had come to town, and he could get the information he needed to prepare for a move northward today. The sooner they left, the sooner they would reach a new life of freedom over the border, where they could stop looking over their shoulders.

"You boys need a hand?"

"Mike does, but I gotta get back. See you later."

They watched Kevin trudge towards the house. Hands in pockets and head pointing towards the churned sods of earth, he never looked back.

"He alright? Looked like he had the weight of the world."

"Ah, I think so. Conversation got pretty deep."

Bracken shrugged, pulling the pitchfork from the well-worked soil. "Yeah, that's Kevin. Pretty deep."

They dug silently for what seemed like a long time. He ignored his screaming muscles, waiting for Bracken to pause and take a breather, but it was pointless. The man looked lean and healthy, and showed no signs of tiring. He slammed his fork into the dirt and peeled off his sweat-soaked gloves.

"Sorry man, need five."

"No worries, it takes getting used to. I remember the blisters when I first came here," said Bracken, examining the callouses on his rough hands. Michael held up his palms to show several oozing circular flaps of skin, and the two men laughed.

"Kevin told me you'd been across the border recently."

"Scotland? My family lives there. When I come back, I bring a few bottles of good scotch, so the money I get makes it worth the risk, just about. Welsh whisky is decent, but it's not the same."

"Why do you come back at all?"

"Ah, my home is here, with these amazing people. We need each other. Besides, they're tightening up. With all the bureaucracy, it's difficult to get residency now."

"Even with family?"

"Yup, for a single man, at least. We've all got Scottish ancestry somewhere down the line. Why do you ask, anyway?"

In for a penny, in for a pound. "My brother lives in Glasgow. I plan to take my daughter across, maybe get some papers and live with him, *if* he'll have us, which is a fucking big if."

"Oh, how so?"

Because you killed one of his best friends, perhaps? "Ah, man. When I was much younger, I did something beyond stupid. It was an accident, but I hurt someone close to him."

Michael stopped, hoping Bracken would drop it there. His soft voice had a slight trace of Scottish roots, an Edinburgh accent perhaps.

"Well, it's easier to cross alone, but I'll tell you what I know. There are a few different places. Forget about the River Tweed section way out east. They've defoliated the banks and have them closely watched. And don't cross on the Western side above Solway, although it looks like the best route. Again, it's well-guarded open ground."

The other man paused and ruffled his shaggy locks before continuing. "The section of the border near Berwick is possible, away from the river. It's the more difficult option, mind. They started building the wall there, but they had to stop. You know they're bankrupt, right?"

Michael nodded and said, "I've heard."

"Anyway, around the A1 is out, but near Bailie's Burn, I've crossed there once."

"OK, and the easier option?"

"In my opinion, the best route is via Kielder Forest Park near the Observatory, across Bell's Burn. The English side is clear of trees for a few hundred yards, but once you cross, it's thickly wooded, and you can disappear. There are drones, and the odd foot patrol, but you'd be unlucky to get caught. Of course, they can't follow you once you're across, well not really. They might, but not far."

"What about further east, near Whitelee Moor?"

"If you were alone, that'd be a decent option. But it's too open, too remote. With your daughter, I think you're better off with another route."

"Thanks, Bracken, I really appreciate this." The other man nodded once and Michael yanked his pitchfork back out from the earth, then began digging out potatoes with renewed vigour. All he had to do was break it to Hope. *If only we could stay here. If only. Please let her take the news well.*

Eriksson picked at his fingers, wishing he had a cigarette clasped between them. He'd not smoked for three years, but rarely did a day pass without him longing for a nicotine hit to help maintain his exterior cool. It'd only grow worse during the meeting. From what he remembered, his former commander Burrows was a dedicated forty-a-day woman and would puff on Camels throughout. If anyone dared remind her that smoking indoors had been illegal for decades, she'd offer a dismissive sneer. A second comment invited worse. He'd seen the woman launch a coffee cup at a colleague for repeatedly asking her to extinguish a cigarette. But there would be no histrionics today. Even Burrows would have to behave. Along with the top brass from Eriksson's own organisation, several members of the party would be present. The meeting had already started, and someone of his pay grade would only be invited to join once the serious business had concluded.

On cue, a gentleman in an expensive grey suit opened the meeting room door and beckoned to him. "Mr. Eriksson, they're ready for you now." He entered the room, nodding at a few friendly faces, before seating himself at the large boardroom table. There were fifteen other people present, including a representative from the church. He didn't know many of the religious leaders by name, but his regalia signified a man of importance. He was probably a direct subordinate of the Archbishop himself, perhaps even an envoy of the High Priest.

Piers Beauchamp made the introductions. "Those of you who don't know Bertram Eriksson, he's the senior field investigator for our fertility procurement operation." He raised a hand at the mention of his name, offering a thin-lipped smile around the room. "Bertram used to play for Burrows' team, but he's been on our side for a few years now. Impeccable record, of course. Anyway, let me fill you in, Bertram. You've probably noticed there's some dissent around our fine island. While we're still in a *democracy*—"

Giggles broke out around the room and Beauchamp flashed his greasy yellow teeth before continuing. "While they're still able, the people of our wonderful nation will continue to inform us of their *opinions.* One policy which is not polling so brilliantly right now is our attitude towards fertile young women, particularly our assumed indifference, or some might say encouragement, towards Burrows' IPA crew and their rather vigorous methods."

Burrows wouldn't be able to resist a reply, and it seemed Beauchamp had purposely left her a gap to remonstrate. After a brief pause, his former boss sniggered and said, "We're carrying out the job you've asked us to. It's my organisation getting its hands dirty ninety percent of the time, while *his* lot…" she jerked a nicotine-stained index finger at Eriksson, "… pick all the low-hanging fruit. I've lost two squad members this year. How many men has *he* lost?"

"We've not lost anyone since I moved across."

"Exactly. We do dangerous work. If we must rein it in, fine, but don't expect the same results."

Diplomatic to a fault, Beauchamp said, "Let's agree to monitor the situation. They've baulked at openly suggesting a return to secularism, but the Liberal Alliance are making the end of enforced birthing one of their key policy pledges. Early signs suggest it's a policy which is polling well across the board."

"What do you suggest, letting the masses be in charge of our re-population program?" said another home-counties voice. A murmur of excitement rolled around the table like a Mexican wave.

"Not at all. We're not about to stop doing God's work, but we can't afford to let the Liberal Alliance look like a realistic winner either, or we risk giving people reason to vote for them. Let's ensure the public don't see what we do in an unflattering light, or we'll be left with little alternative but to roll back mandate thirteen, which we only announced a fortnight ago."

"Yes, and you'll appear weak. What has this got to do with my methods, Beauchamp?"

"Look, Burrows, nobody wants to imagine what we do is against parental will. Of course, we all know they need the Lord's guidance, now more than ever. But as His appointed servants we must provide the flock an occasional push in the right direction, to ensure they do the righteous deeds which are their duty."

Her question unanswered, Burrows continued to scowl. Beauchamp allowed a little whistle of a sigh to escape his nose before he added, "Can you please employ a little sensitivity? A light touch, perhaps. Just until we can extinguish this ripple of discontent and renew our unassailable lead in the polls. Once we get past this election cycle, we're going to implement some major changes, anyway."

Burrows drew a huge hit from her vape and blew a heavy cloud of sweetly scented smoke into the middle of the room. "I can be light. Fucking weightless. I'll send the order down as soon as we have Michael and Hope Randall in custody. It's no time for hesitancy amongst my squad while they remain at large."

"Fair enough, Burrows. About that. Any developments?"

"Nothing that isn't in my most recent report, but we're expecting a breakthrough any day. They're still in Wales. We know that much."

Beauchamp turned to Eriksson. "While this situation is ongoing, we want your two operations to keep an open channel and share information. We expect any differences to be put aside." He spun back to address Burrows. "At the end of the day, it doesn't matter who bags the girl. Michael Randall is to be transferred to Eriksson's squad if yours apprehends them first. Atheist scumbags who seek to repel God's work *must* be re-educated."

Eriksson could hardly keep a wry smile from his face while Burrow's scowl burned into him. *Open channel*, that was a funny one. They both knew Michael and Hope Randall had become more than the sum of their parts after such a brazen escape, and now there was a modest ripple of underground support emerging for the pair, at least among the limited groups of people who followed such matters. Their capture would be a giant step towards another promotion, and he certainly wouldn't be sharing any information with the IPA which might offer them an advantage, neither would he expect any favours in return. If Beauchamp was so desperate for everyone to play happy families, he could act as messenger boy himself.

It was another unseasonably warm day, but Michael couldn't shake a strong feeling it would be the last of the good weather. With the sky set fair, he decided to leave the Ford and walk to *The General Store*, with Hope in tow. The conversation with Bracken had yielded enough information to plan the trip northwards. They'd be leaving soon, and the time had come to broach the subject with his daughter. She'd grown attached to the place, especially Kevin's young boy. He wished they could stay put, but the longer they hid, the more likely the baby farmers would pick up their trail.

With the dreaded conversation looming, Michael found it hard to enjoy the walk, which meandered through the quiet country lanes, and across fields left bare after the harvest.

"So, why did you want me to tag along, Dad?"

He gulped. The time had come. "I want to get our hosts a token of appreciation. They've been good to us. Anyway, you've been spending a lot of time with Kevin's boy and not much with your old man."

"You can talk. What about you and Monique?"

Had they been obvious about their feelings? Nothing had happened yet. Perhaps nothing would. "What about it?"

Hope tutted and rolled her eyes. "Have you already forgotten about Mum? She even *looks* like her, for God's sake!"

"Of course, I've not forgotten, but she made her decision when she told those fucking state sponsored criminals about her daughter."

"She's still my mother. She's your wife."

"Not anymore. I chose you, remember? Anyway, we're not talking about me. Watch that Johannes kid. Boys that age only want one thing. I know, believe it or not, I used to be one."

"And what exactly is it they want, Dad?"

"Don't play dumb. Besides, we'll be leaving here soon, anyway." There, he'd said it. *Time to deal with the fallout—here it comes...*

Hope planted her feet and folded her arms across her chest. "Then I'm not going. I love it here."

His patience threatened to evaporate like thin clouds on a blistering hot summer's day, and his voice dropped to a hiss. "This isn't a discussion. You're thirteen and you'll do as you're told."

They hadn't exchanged a word in five minutes when they reached the single road leading into the town. His mood lifted as they approached the general store, but Hope stayed a few paces behind, scowling in silent fury.

"I can't wait to see old John again, you know. I think he took a real shine to you." Hope ignored him.

A notice in the shop window read *back in five minutes.* He laughed and stooped down to perch on the step, content to soak in some last rays of sun. The note might've been placed a minute or an hour ago, but sure enough, he soon caught sight of the old man shuffling along the pavement. John lifted his head up when he was close by and seemed to recognise his onetime former customers.

"So, you found them, I assume?" he said with a growing smile.

"In a manner of speaking, yeah." Michael paused before adding, "Unfortunately, my friend passed away a few months before we arrived. But they let us stay, so it's cool."

John bowed his head. "Oh, I am sorry."

"It's OK, these things happen."

"Nothing to fear but fear itself, I always say. When it's my time, I'll be ready. But if it's not, they'll rue the fucking day," said John, shaking his fist before unlocking the store.

"Kicking and screaming, eh?"

"I'm gonna stay out here and enjoy some sunshine," said Hope. He nodded and followed John inside. *Let her stay outside rather than dragging the mood down.* The ringing bell above gave him a tiny jolt of warmth, and he allowed a smile to creep across his lips.

"Down to business then. To what do I owe the pleasure?"

"I'm after some decent wine. Can you recommend anything?"

The shopkeeper selected some bottles. "I always liked the New Zealand whites the best, but they're so damn expensive now and no-one will pay the premium. Same with the Californian Merlots. At least the Italians still make a decent drop."

"Well, I know about as much about wine as I know about nuclear physics, so I'm happy to defer."

"Oh, and there's some good English stuff these days, if you want to give it a go." He picked out another bottle, which he announced as a white wine made in Cornwall.

Michael held his hands together in a praying motion. "I'll take the lot."

"Maud, get your best dress on, we're closing early today," John shouted behind himself to nobody. Michael laughed at the joke and turned to peruse the store. An old-style carousel with paperback books caught his eye, and he thumbed through some volumes at random. Dust puffed out from their yellowed pages.

"Such few places sell these now."

"Be careful. They'll blacklist you as some kind of subversive if you buy those," John said with a snort of laughter.

"You're not wrong, John." He selected a couple of volumes and placed them on the counter with the wines, then went on a final circuit of the store, picking out a couple of items, including an expensive, but tacky-looking, silver cup. "I think that's the lot. What's the damage?"

Not for the first time, he thanked his past self for at least having the wherewithal to put aside a small fund for emergencies. If he shook off his cloak of sentimentality for a moment, then he wouldn't be spending money on gifts for his hosts. But how could their kindness go unacknowledged? They'd welcomed in two desperate strangers with open arms, and the least he could do was show his gratitude.

John went through the same rigmarole as before, totaling the purchases on his old jumbo calculator before plucking a price from thin air. He'd foreseen this, so instead of arguing, he kept silent and held his ID card under the Payscan. While John was preoccupied bagging up his goods, he took the silver cup and faked to put it in his jacket pocket before placing it back on the shelf.

"Thanks John, always a pleasure. We might not be staying much longer, so it could be farewell."

"Pleasure's all mine. Best of luck on your journey, Michael, and don't drink all that wine at once." John waved and Michael fought off a jolt of sadness as he gazed around the store for what would most likely be the final time.

Outside, in the fading afternoon light, Hope paced the street. When he stepped through the door, and the shop's bell rung out, she turned and grinned at him. Something lay beneath her innocent smile. He'd seen that look many times before. What could she be up to, and was it worth shattering the fragile harmony to find out? He decided not and instead draped his arm around his daughter. She tucked her elbow around his waist, and they walked together in a comfortable silence as the sun slipped below the clouds.

CHAPTER: NINE

After Michael had given his purchases to Ma for safekeeping, one job remained before he could allow himself to relax. With Kayleigh's begrudging permission, he cut some flowers from the ornamental garden, and trotted off across the darkening lands, towards the site of Willy's grave. He reached a picturesque knoll overlooking the whole settlement and stared back across the horizon. The sky had not yet darkened, and the last streaking ribbons of sunset were smeared between the clouds.

A large, rounded stone marked Willy's grave, with a pair of his old boxing gloves draped across. Underneath sat a plastic picture frame containing a photograph of the warm, smiling face which Michael remembered so fondly. He placed his flowers by the frame, pulled out the small metal hipflask which Joel had lent him, and crouched on his haunches, thinking about the first time they'd met.

When he'd noticed the man staring in his direction across the canteen, something in those kind brown eyes had disarmed his usual instinct to glare back and prepare for a confrontation. They showed a complete absence of fear. Even in the eyes of the most violent and terrifying men he'd ever encountered, that primal fear was present somewhere. Michael also sensed waves of knowledge and wisdom, intended for him and nobody else, radiating across the room.

"How did you know?"

"I just get this feeling about some people, Michael. I ain't always had it, but I can look at a roomful of men and I know who is receptive, and who needs it. There ain't no point fighting to help someone who ain't ready or don't wanna change."

Michael raised the flask to the heavens, then lowered it to his mouth, ignoring the burn on his lips and concentrating on the warmth of the whisky flowing into his belly. At that moment, he knew he'd never have found the courage to make the snap decision he'd made back in London, not without Willy's love, carried in his heart all these years. For better or worse, he would've watched them take his daughter away, no doubt about it. Tears pricked at his eyes, and he chased them away with another swig from the flask. It wasn't the time to allow emotion to get the better of him, not yet.

It was another mostly clear night. When he again turned his head upwards and stared at the stars, his mind drifted towards the mistake which landed him under Willy's watch. Usually, he tried to keep the memories buried, but for once he allowed them to show themselves, just for a moment. Ray had never looked at him the same since. His brother's love, often tough and unyielding but always coming from a place of complete benevolence, had been his only grounding as a youngster. Without it, life would've been so much worse. All the times Ray had saved him from getting into serious trouble or rescued him from their father's fists. If his brother would allow it, he'd find a way to make up for his actions. But turning up out of nowhere, uninvited and asking for favours, would his brother even listen?

Later that evening, everyone seemed in fine spirits, encouraged by Michael's purchases. Most of the hard work in preparation for winter was complete. It never truly stopped, but there would be less back-breaking labour for the next few months.

The adults sat on the floor in the living room and passed a joint around. Not only was Joel a decent brewer, but he also tended to a plethora of plants in their poly tunnel, not all for eating. The joint reached him, but he passed it on. Hope had disappeared with Johannes, but he didn't want his daughter to see him stoned when she eventually returned. *Ah, let her have some fun, and stop worrying for one night.* Besides, he had a nice warming buzz from the wine and didn't want to go overboard.

Across the room, Monique's gorgeous brown eyes kept catching his. Something had been building between them over the past few days. This could be his only chance, but knowing she and Kevin had been an item bothered him. Besides, he'd never been the boldest in that respect. But if not now, when? He may never make it back to this wonderful place.

After everyone else in the house had made their excuses and gone to bed, only he and Monique remained in the living room, deep in conversation. With no desire to cut things short, he flipped the Crosby, Stills & Nash record on the turntable to the B-side and returned to his place next to her on the sofa.

She moved closer to him and said, in her irresistible, soft-yet-husky voice, "What about your partner? How come you left London suddenly?" Their thighs were tight against each other. He felt the stirrings of desire and tried to concentrate on the question.

"It's hard to explain. Well, I guess I can tell you. If I can't trust someone who likes Black Sabbath, who can I trust?" Monique responded with a girlish giggle. "Allison, she... she tried to sell Hope to the fucking *Baby Farmers*, for Christ's sake! My daughter is able to conceive."

Monique gasped in shock at the double revelation and her hand went to her mouth. "No way!"

"Honestly, that's what happened. I need to get Hope over the border somehow, into Scotland."

"That's awful. Do you know anyone there? I'm sure you'd be safe with us awhile longer."

"Yeah, my brother. You don't know how much I want to stay. Hope's in love with the place. I don't want to move so soon after the ordeal she's suffered. But we have to try."

"I guess you'll need to leave soon." Monique's hand moved onto his thigh, close to his crotch, and he leaned towards her. She raised her finger and rested it on his lip. "Hold that thought, I need the loo. Be right back." She leapt up and disappeared.

While he waited, he realised his daughter was right. The woman looked quite like Allison. So, he *did* have a type. It was those huge brown eyes and that gorgeous soft brown skin. He'd been attracted to her since the moment they arrived.

Monique came back from the bathroom, but she didn't sit back down next to him. Instead, she held out her hand, beckoning him to follow. He hesitated, and she giggled.

"What, you're not going all coy with me now, are you?"

"No, it's not that. Joel said you and Kevin were an item before."

"Oh, is *that* what's been bothering you? You have my word, there's nothing to worry about. He wouldn't care. We're just friends, honestly."

Her reassurance was enough. He took her still outstretched hand, warm and soft enough, despite all the hard labour. She could still find decent moisturiser, even out here. Together, they walked to her bedroom. The heady, unique, but unmistakably feminine fragrance of her perfumes and lotions mingled together made Michael's head spin, and he was glad he'd passed on the joints earlier. Yes, he was drunk, but not too drunk, by any means.

"Colin, we got a hit from a mobile number in Wales. It's offline again now, but I'm sending you the pin where the call originated from." Piers' excited face filled his screen, the grin spreading from ear-to-ear.

Colin slammed his hand down onto the desk in triumph. "Great news. I owe you a drink, buddy."

"Your boys and our boys, two sides of the same coin, eh? I told you Piers would come through for his old chum, didn't I? Besides, if we get the father, I'm not too fussed about the girl. Michael Randall is our main interest now, after what we discovered at his dump of an apartment in London. It appears he's not been following the scripture, so he's ripe for a re-education camp. Not that I don't think we'll get them both before you get a sniff, but all's fair."

As the call terminated, Colin dialled Kozlowski. A set of GPRS co-ordinates pinged onto his Head-Up Display, followed by a message from Piers titled *Eat a bag of dicks*. It contained one line which simply read *the race is on*...

The agent picked up the call on the third ring. He looked bored, his face dull and tired, with heavy purple bags under his eyes. Colin waved his hands as he spoke. "We've got them. Head west, I'll send the pin. You're still in the Midlands, right?"

"West of Birmingham. I'm on my way."

"The gov team has got a lead on us, Kozlowski. They'll arrive at least an hour before, but you know as well as I do, they adhere to certain rules which we don't. To buy you some time, I'll call in a bomb threat. The area will be sealed off for a while, but it won't take them long to clear it. I mean, who the fuck wants to blow up a place called *Llandovery*? Even the Welsh nationalists wouldn't bother."

The black van hugged the outside lane of the M4, travelling at a steady one-hundred miles an hour. Despite flagging several speed traps, the cops did not give chase. Miko knew their on-board ANPR systems would display the magic code DNP—*Do Not Pursue*.

He stared at the road ahead as his van ate the miles, willing them to vanish even quicker so the real action could start. He pulled a boiled sweet out from the packet in the coin tray and fumbled with his one free hand to unwrap it, getting it into his mouth and sucking while he checked the van's Head-Up Display. They were about seven miles from the Welsh border crossing. Estimated journey time to the target co-ordinates was fifty minutes and counting. He pressed his foot down on the accelerator until it touched the rubber below and the van's engine whined louder. The digital speedometer nudged one-ten, and he crunched down on his sweet, startling Wosniak, snoozing in the passenger seat. The ETA ticked down by three minutes to forty-seven.

"Wosniak, pull your head out of your ass and study the map. I want you to have the town centre grid memorised street-by-street when we arrive."

"*Tak, szefie*," his subordinate said, sitting bolt upright and slipping on his Head-Up Display.

Hope lay on a soft grey blanket, spread out on the floor of an ancient wooden barn, far out towards the edge of the settlement's boundary. Scratchy strands of hay poked through, but she ignored the discomfort. Her loins ached with a strange mixture of pleasure and pain, with the bruised feeling overwhelmed by desires which remained mostly unsatisfied. How it'd transpired, she couldn't explain, but her virginity was gone.

When she'd joined Johannes in the barn, she'd not harboured any intention of sleeping with him. *One thing led to another.* She rolled the phrase around in her mind. How *adult* it sounded. And how apt, now she understood its meaning much more deeply. Perhaps she might even do it again soon. But her dad couldn't find out, under any circumstances. He was so taken with his new friends, especially Joel, who he seemed to be in a whirlwind of a bromance with. He probably wouldn't notice if they did it on the bonnet of that car he loved so much. The car that, in the past, he'd chosen to spend more time with than her. Now, instead of the dumb car, silly Joel had absorbed his attention, along with some abandoned farmyard vehicles, which looked like rusty old junk.

Also, it wasn't her imagination running wild, because something had definitely happened between her father and Monique. All week, their desire for each other had hung in the air like the cloying stink of joss-sticks in the damp church building where she'd attended Sunday school. The previous night, when she'd popped her head into his room, it'd been empty. So had the living room, but she'd heard hushed, excited voices in Monique's bedroom, alright. A wave of sadness washed over her. *It's too soon. What about Mum?* A tear rolled down her cheek, but she wiped it away.

Overhead, a helicopter passed low, the rhythmic pulsing bass of its blades jarring her from private thoughts. How long since she'd last heard that sound? More importantly, what on earth was it doing here? Her heart jumped. Was it because of the call she'd made? *Please God, don't let it be my fault.* It'd been so nice to hear her mother's voice, but what price would she pay? As the alien noise pitched downwards, indicating it was moving away from them at speed, she relaxed a little and clambered to her feet.

A dizziness overwhelmed her, and she bent double, loosening something deep inside, which leaked into her underwear. "Ew, so gross!" she said, with a slight trace of a smile.

Her heart jolted in her chest. Had she been so stupid to forget she'd been diagnosed as fertile? Perhaps she didn't believe it, anyway. Where was the proof that she could conceive? Those harassed, overworked medics made mistakes. On a one-off, what were the chances? Most boys had super low sperm counts, anyway, but they'd better be more careful if it happened again.

"*Bastard*!" Michael screamed, hopping around with his wounded digit clasped between his thighs.

He had almost finished repairing a decrepit old fence when he'd got too casual with his aim and clipped his thumb with his hammer. The fence had fallen in the previous night's wind, at the border between his hosts' land and what remained of the Cargill farm, now owned by Robert Cargill Jr. His poor thumb throbbed, and he cursed the man under his breath. The idiot had complained his sheep would escape through the gap in the fencing. If so, then they were smarter than their owner. Which side of the divide between slow and intellectually backwards did the man occupy, anyway? The pain eased, and he scolded himself for his uncharitable thoughts, then returned to the task.

In the distance, a sound pulsed, so familiar yet out of context he had trouble recognising it. With a jolting flush, he realised. *A helicopter.* In the cloudy grey sky, he saw the unmarked black chopper coming in low and fast. It roared overhead and chuntered towards the town. *This can't be good.* He had to return to the house and find Hope, fast. He dropped a handful of nails to the floor, slipped the hammer into his belt, and broke into a jog.

CHAPTER: TEN

Sirens rose and fell, far in the distance. Deep down in the pit of his stomach, Michael knew their time at this idyllic place was over, and the fragile peace would soon be shattered. He jogged towards the house, where Kevin's young girl, Kayleigh, was kneeling on the ground, weeding her precious ornamental garden.

"Have you seen Hope?" She looked up at him with a blank expression and shook her head. He set off again and rounded the corner of the building, but nearly collided with his daughter. She stopped in her tracks, their eyes locked, and she grinned at him. That sheepish look again. She'd been up to mischief, but there was no time for an inquisition.

"Dad, what are you rushing around for? Did you hear that helicopter?"

"We need to leave."

Her face dropped. "For real? I want to stay. This feels like home now."

"I know, and I wish we could. Maybe I'm worrying about nothing, but we must go immediately." When he marched them into the house to grab their belongings, she offered no further argument. Perhaps she understood the gravity of the situation.

"What's going on, Mike?" Joel asked, a frown etched across his deeply lined forehead.

"Look, I don't have time to explain, but the short version

is, my girl is a breeder. The Baby Farmers came for her back in London, and that's why we skipped town. I think they've tracked us to Wales, and maybe they're on their way here now, so we need to bounce. I'm sorry I didn't tell you guys, really."

"Mate, that's heavy. Let's get you the fuck out of here."

When Miko's van pulled into the quaint little town centre, he found a police cordon across the road at both ends of the narrow high street. Faulkner might be a total gimp, but at least he usually did his job. He stopped fifty feet short of the cordon and switched his Head-Up Display into magnification mode. Halfway down the high street, he made out the target: a little shop called *The General Store*.

He located the government's interception team, parked just outside the cordon in two identical white SUVs, with the unmistakable shock of white-blonde hair belonging to Bertram Eriksson close by. The buffoon shuffled from one foot to another, speaking to a police officer who gestured at his watch. This was no time for another reunion.

"Wosniak, with me. We need to go around," he barked. "Johnson and Hassan, keep your eyes on the gov-crew in the white SUVs, especially that cock with the puffy white hair. As soon as they move past the police block, ping me a code red. Keep the line *open*."

"Understood, sir," Johnson replied. "But do you have to leave me with this raghead fuck?"

Hassan gave him the finger and spat back, "Hey dickhead. You know I'm a bona fide card carrying, god-fearing Christian piece of shit, just like you."

"Sure, sure. Dig on swine, much?"

"*You two, cut this shit out*!" shouted Miko as he disembarked. He spat out his butterscotch candy and turned to Wosniak. "We've got a few minutes at best. We need to reach that shop over there. Once we're outside, I don't care who sees us."

"I've memorised the satellite image. There's an alleyway which runs parallel to the high street," Wosniak said, pointing to a street on their left.

They ducked behind a stone memorial and scurried along the side street until they reached the alley, where the two men vaulted a six-foot slatted fence, landing in a well-coiffured private garden. Three more fences stood between themselves and a stone wall, with the high street beyond. They cleared them in less than thirty seconds while a confused-looking elderly lady watched them with trepidation from behind her yellowed curtains.

Miko peered over the wall, then slid to his haunches next to Wosniak. He jabbed a finger and half-whispered, "Follow me, straight in." Without further pause, he clambered over the wall and arrowed towards *The General Store*.

He barged shoulder first into the door, which splintered inwards despite the resistance of a deadlock. The force sent him sprawling and an old shop bell above rang out. Wosniak followed, helping Miko to his feet. He dusted himself off and took a breath to regain his composure. The old man at the counter let his book fall onto the desk and stared at the two unwelcome visitors. If the sudden intrusion had surprised him, it didn't show.

"Block that door," Miko ordered.

"Yes, boss." Wosniak pulled an old *Coca-Cola* branded drinks refrigerator from the space where it had sat undisturbed for decades, judging by the rising wafts of dust, and inched it with juddering movements towards the shattered door.

"Forgive my entrance, old man, but we need to have a little chat. If you tell me and my friend what we want to know, we'll disappear, just like that." He snapped his fingers.

"No, it's OK. I needed a new door, anyway. Just who are you boys? Ain't the cops are ya? Can I see some ID first?"

Miko brayed with laughter. "No, we're not the cops, friend. We're looking for one of your customers, a Londoner called Michael Randall, and that lovely young daughter of his. She's a breeder, see. She'll make us a lot of money and you're *wasting my fucking time!!*" He screamed the final words, ripping down the flimsy book display carousel and launching it across the room, where it slammed into neatly stacked rows of tinned food, sending them flying through the air and spilling onto the timber floor.

"Don't know anyone by that name, I'm afraid. Can't remember the last time I heard a London accent up here. Sorry I can't be more helpful."

The old man's hands, which had been inching downwards since they'd arrived, made a sudden move, which Miko saw in his peripherals. There was a double-click as the old man worked a round into the weapon's chamber, and Miko ducked, grabbing one of the still rolling cans in one smooth motion. He moved low to his right and launched the can. It struck a glancing blow on the right side of the old man's head, throwing off his aim's intended angle. A deafening blast echoed through the small shop. Buckshot rounds incinerated several bottles of wine on the shelf to Wosniak's right, but a few stray pellets tore through his upper arm and torso, spinning him to the floor. He cried out in pain, clutching his shredded bicep.

Miko leapt over the counter and wrestled the shotgun from

the stunned store owner, chambering a round and pointing it at the now stricken man, whose face contorted in agony and began to turn beetroot. Wrinkled fingers clutched at the left side of his chest, and he tried in vain to ease some air into his lungs. The adrenaline had been too much for the old boy's cardiovascular system, and his heart was going into spasm.

Miko peered at him with cold interest, the same way he had looked at trapped spiders as a bored child, while he pulled their legs off. "Look, you're going to fucking die now, old timer. Why don't you tell me what I want to know, and I can make it quick for you?"

It didn't seem like he could speak even if he wanted to, but his ratcheted fist loosened, and his middle digit eased into an erect position. He was giving Miko the finger and grinning, with white spittle collecting at the sides of his mouth. Then his eyes rolled back into their sockets and his arm flopped to the floor.

"There's a man with real balls," he said, nodding to himself and striding across the debris-strewn shop floor to check on his colleague, now sat up and groaning while he examined his wounds. He'd seen men walk from the battlefield with a ragged stump for a leg, or a missing jaw, and offered a frank assessment: "You'll live. Get up." Wosniak wobbled to his giant feet, grimacing but stoic, and clutched his wounded arm while it seeped blood.

Frantic shouting came from the front of the store as unseen men tried to move the refrigerator. Wosniak had done a decent job of firmly wedging it into the mangled and splintered door frame and it wouldn't budge. He motioned to the rear of the store. They passed the counter and stepped over John's twitching body, but he paused. Where the hunch came from, he couldn't explain, but when he caught the old man's notepad from the corner of his eye, he decided to take a closer look. One page had been torn out and, on an absolute whim, he picked up a pencil from the small desk-tidy beside the till and shaded the page underneath. A crude map revealed itself, and he ripped the page free.

"Let's check this out," he muttered to himself, following Wosniak through the shop's rear exit into a passageway. He glimpsed two men rounding the blind angle leading back to the high street. Before they could spot him, he leapt over a brick wall, close behind his fellow Pole. The pair jogged side-by-side towards the idling van. Johnson helped the wounded Wosniak into the side door. Miko ran around the van and jumped into the passenger seat.

"Turnaround, Hassan, then do a left at the end there."

Hassan performed a hasty three-point turn and burned a hundred yards to an intersection, where the van made a brutal left, causing a sharp screech of tyres. They hurtled past the government team's white vehicles. Eriksson looked up, slack-jawed, as Miko grinned and held out both middle fingers.

"The red phone-box, that's it!" he shouted.

They overshot the turn and the van skidded to a halt. Hassan slammed into reverse and drove backwards at forty miles per hour. Burning clutch fumes filled the cab. When he hit the brakes again, flinging Johnson and Wosniak into the bulkhead behind, the cab reverberated with a mighty clang.

They approached a wooden gate. "Go straight through."

Hassan downshifted, floored the accelerator and the van's bull bars made matchwood of the flimsy old structure.

Kevin, watching from an upstairs bedroom, called down in his booming baritone, "Mike! Go round the back, on foot. There's no way past."

Michael peered through the ground-floor window at the approaching black van. Inside, two heads bounced almost comically as the vehicle sped down the bumpy track. It skidded to a halt fifty yards from the building. Kevin was right: the track sloped into muddy fields on either side. Anything except an off-road vehicle would get stuck. The Capri, with its front-wheel drive and tires built for speed, not traction, wouldn't stand a chance.

"Let's go," said Joel, motioning towards the building's rear. Michael grabbed Hope's arm and followed. Joel unbolted the back door, pushed it open and pointed towards the treeline, fifty yards away. "Take the path into the woods and keep going, far as you can. I'll come for you, once the coast's clear."

As he spoke, Joel pushed something into his hand. It felt strangely familiar. He glanced down, finding an ancient mobile phone, like one he'd owned as a teenager. Most of their features were obsolete, but they could still make and receive calls or text messages.

"Thanks, man."

Joel put his arms around him and they embraced, slapping each other's backs. "We'll hold them off as long as possible, Mike. Don't look back. I'll find you."

Michael gave Hope a gentle shove out the door, and together they sprinted down the muddy path, towards the treeline. Hope skidded and landed on her bottom. He turned to help her up, catching a last sight of the house as Joel disappeared back inside.

#

"Where's the girl?" Miko growled. The man standing across the front door with his arms crossed looked ex-military. His face showed no fear, and he'd not be an easy person to bully around.

"You've no right being here pal, so fuck off."

Without raising his voice, Miko said, "That's not nice. We just want the girl and her father, then we're on our way. We don't give two shits about any of the rest of you. Don't make it hard on yourselves. If you're caught hiding her, you'll all be screwed. It doesn't need to be that way."

The man remained firm. "We've got nothing to say to you."

"Fine, so you won't mind if we have a look around?"

"No chance." He wasn't backing down. Another man, weathered and tanned with long blonde hair, joined his friend at the front door.

"Johnson, get over here." His man rushed to his side and snapped to attention. "These two heroes are not letting us do our job." He jerked his head at the men. Johnson pulled a 9mm pistol from a holster inside his black baseball jacket and levelled it at them. Miko raised an eyebrow. "How about now?"

Finally, the square-jawed man with short salt-and-pepper hair acquiesced. "There are women and kids inside. Do what you gotta do, but they aren't here."

"I told you, we have no interest in anyone else. Johnson, stay out here and keep an eye on these two *wojowniks*, would you?"

Hassan and Miko barged past and bowled into the house. He sent his junior to search the first floor and methodically checked each room at ground level and the cellar. It took less than two minutes to complete the search.

"They're either hiding out there somewhere," he said, flicking his head at the surrounding farmland, "or they ran out the back." He slid open the top bolt and pushed the ancient solid oak door. It swung open with a creaking groan, revealing two pairs of fresh footprints heading towards dense woodland.

"Looks promising, boss," said Hassan. The two men stepped onto the path to examine the prints. One, a large adult shoe, surely belonged to a man. The other was a smaller size, perhaps an average span for a teenage girl.

Near the treeline, they observed a long skid mark. He crouched to inspect, and a glassy glint caught his eye. Half-buried in the dirt, inches from a dainty handprint where the girl had broken her fall, lay a round object. It was a snow-globe smeared with mud. On closer examination, he found an orange price sticker from the dead old man's store on the base. He put the globe in his bomber jacket pocket and broke into a jog, with Hassan following close behind.

Bertram Eriksson and his team pulled up behind a black van, parked at a forty-five-degree angle, blocking the track. He opened the passenger door and dropped onto the gravel to inspect the vehicle. It belonged to Miko's squad alright. He'd followed it for almost a mile before losing it, but fresh tyre marks burned into the asphalt beyond a red phone box had led them to the right place.

He couldn't get Miko's maniacal grin out of his mind. The crazy *Polak* had been flipping him the bird with *both* middle fingers. Kozlowski was an insubordinate swine, but results were hard to argue with. However, after this latest display of disrespect, he'd have to reconsider his offer.

He marched towards the house, with three team members in formation behind. Three men stood outside the house. One, whom he recognised from Miko's squad, appeared to be watching over two residents. "What have we here?"

"Fucking illegal Baby Farmers, that's what," snarled the blonde man. He had a slight trace of an accent, a fellow Scandinavian, probably a Swedish national.

"Johnson, isn't it? Where's your boss?" Eriksson asked. No reply, except a sneer. "You've got no jurisdiction here, now fuck off." Johnson didn't move until he indicated to one of his men. His biggest. Six-and-a-half feet tall, bull-headed, with a bison-like muscular tone bulging out of his too-tight shirt. He strolled past Eriksson and loomed over Johnson, eyeballing him. Miko's man decided against a confrontation and shuffled off to his van.

"I'm sure you know why we're here."

"Nope, try me."

"We're looking for Michael and Hope Randall. Would you care to tell me where they are?"

The man who appeared to be the group's leader said, "We already told this lot and now we're telling you, they ain't here."

"Harbouring a fugitive, eh? We could make life quite uncomfortable. It looks so nice and peaceful out here in this beautiful countryside." He swept his arm a hundred-and-eighty degrees. "We wouldn't want that to change, would we now?"

Another occupant joined them and pleaded with outstretched palms, "Look, he's a friend of a friend who's dead now, anyway. We didn't know the girl was a fucking breeder!"

"It's true. We had no clue," their apparent leader confirmed.

Eriksson rested his fingers on his chin. "I can buy that. But

I want everyone outside, and I'll examine all your ID cards. Then you'll tell me where they went. If everything's in order, we'll leave you alone. But let me tell you this..." he raised a finger for emphasis and wagged it at them, "if there's anything out of order here, anything at all."

He didn't need to finish the threat. Two of the men scurried off to round up their friends, but the Scandinavian remained, leaning against the doorframe, with his arms crossed, glaring.

Moments later, four women, four men and two youngsters were lined up in front of the house. Eriksson inspected their cards but stopped at the young girl. His tongue flicked across his lips as he looked her up and down.

"This one got a non-fertility certificate?"

According to his card, the man bore the name Kevin James Scanlon, the same surname as the girl. His voice cracked as he spoke. "She's not thirteen for a month. She doesn't need it yet."

"I see." Eriksson moved to the next in line but snapped to a stop and turned to address one of his men. "Go get Chandler. Tell her to bring a hormone kit. I want to have this girl examined."

He watched Kevin closely as he chewed his lip. Either he didn't know his daughter's fertility status, or he was trying to hide it. He put his money on the former, but it didn't matter when all would soon be revealed. Kevin approached his daughter, draped a muscular arm around her, and whispered into her ear. While Eriksson checked the remaining ID cards, scanning each one with his remote chip-check unit, Chandler trotted over and snapped to attention by his side.

"Do a hormone test on this girl, please," he ordered. The girl looked terrified. He was not without sympathy; this was an inadequate way to resolve such an important matter.

Chandler put a hand on the girl's shoulder as tears streamed from her eyes. "Hey sweetie, why don't we go inside? This won't take a minute." Her voice hardened as she turned to address Kevin. "You're the father, right?" He nodded. "You can come too, then."

The three of them went inside while Eriksson completed his ID checks.

"Seems all in order. Now is anyone caring to tell me where they went? If you tell me now, I'll make sure my colleagues who I've sent to search the house find nothing they shouldn't."

After a moment of silence, Bracken spoke. "They bolted when they saw the first van. Through the fields, I think. Did anyone see?"

Glenda gestured towards the rear of the house. "They're in the woods." She mouthed an apology while Joel, surname Lindqvist, a Swede like he'd suspected, glowered at her. Eriksson was Norwegian. Their cousins across the Skagerrak always were the more emotional ones. Clearly, the man had grown attached to the two fugitives. He'd have to leave a note on this Lindqvist character's file.

"That wasn't so hard, was it? You've cost valuable time and you've not seen the last of us." He turned to address the rest of his second squad, stood ten yards behind, and barked, "What are you waiting for? *Search those woods, now!*"

They trotted off around the house and disappeared, but they'd never reach the pair before Miko. The top brass would require a thorough explanation once they got wind of the whole shambles. Miko would have to relinquish custody of Michael Randall—they had no business with him anyway—but he suspected the girl was gone. They'd not give up this prize as easily as the other one. She'd become quite the trophy.

Chandler stepped back outside. Eriksson turned towards

her and narrowed his eyes. She shook her head. What a most unfortunate outcome. A positive result would've made the upcoming conversation with his seniors a little easier.

On a final inspection of the house, he paused at the doorway of an upstairs bedroom. To interlope on such a personal moment brought upon him a burning shame, but he couldn't stop himself. On their knees, father and daughter clasped each other like shipwrecked sailors, holding onto driftwood in a vast, featureless ocean. Their wailing sobs followed him all the way outside.

Hope's lungs burned with exertion. Her father, twenty yards ahead, was much fitter. She'd never enjoyed sports and, after her parents removed her from school, she'd never broken sweat where avoidable.

"C'mon, we've got to go faster," he yelled.

"Daddy, I can't keep up." He ran back towards her, hoisted her over his shoulder and set off again.

He grunted, hauling her up a steep embankment. "I can't do this for long. Just… until… you… catch your breath!"

"Sorry," she groaned. Her cheeks burned. Never had she felt more childlike. Behind, two men reached the lip of the escarpment from which Hope and her father had descended moments before. They surveyed the bowl-shaped clearing below. One man was tall and bulky. The sun appeared from behind a thick cloud and glinted off his domed head. He pointed towards them and banked into the valley, gaining ground with each step. The second man picked up too much speed for his short legs, tumbling as he reached the bottom. A sharp howl of pain pierced the calm afternoon air, but the bald man didn't slow to help his colleague.

Her father stopped and let her down, heaving in great gasps of air until he'd recovered enough breath to speak. "You OK to run again?" She nodded, and they set off once more, Hope trying her best to keep up. She risked a peek behind when they reached another incline. The bald man in front had halved the distance between them. By the time her father reached the treeline ahead, she'd fallen another ten paces behind him.

A bizarre moment of recollection washed over her, followed by a heavy feeling of unreality, almost like she'd become an observer. The thick canopy of the woods seemed familiar. *I've been here before.*

A shot echoed out in the forest. Startled birds bolted from the trees. Hope tried to quicken her pace again, but her lactic acid-laden legs had nothing to give. She reached for her father's outstretched hand, and he pulled her alongside him. The second shot whistled above their heads, much closer this time. *It's no good, I'm too slow!*

As if he'd heard his daughter's inner voice, he stopped with his hands in the air and turned. Burning sweat dripped into her eyes, mingling with tears of frustration. With air she didn't know she possessed, she screamed. He could've made it alone, without the burden of *her*. Instead of fear, shame washed over her. Shame like those religious fucks at her old school had made her feel when she'd been caught practicing French-kissing techniques with Molly Carmichael during gym class, and the bastards had hauled them in front of the whole classroom.

"Sorry, Dad," she gasped.

The bald man did not seem out of breath when he reached them. Now she realised he wasn't fat or tall, but stocky with a barrel-shaped chest and powerful-looking shoulders. He wasn't much taller than her, but his violent aura loomed large, making him seem like a giant. Something about the man brought a cold terror seeping from her skin, quashing all the pleasantness of life at the commune in a cruel instant.

He lurched towards her and grinned. Hollow pupils glinted from inside huge white eyeballs, and his gaze seemed to pierce her skull. She shivered. Only once before had she suffered a stare like it: a religious teacher at her old school. Her friend had said the man kissed her one afternoon, when they'd been alone in the classroom, and fondled her bottom. She hadn't believed the girl, who often told silly stories, until the day she'd received that same withering look. It had made her feel powerless. It said: *there's nothing you can do, little girl. Nothing.*

"Hope Randall, I presume?" said the man, his stare still cutting into her. At last, the laser-like heat dissipated, and he turned to address her father. "Which means you must be Michael?"

The other man, shorter than his superior, with narrow eyes and greasy black hair slicked against his scalp, limped towards them. "Don't... fucking... move!" he said, panting hard. In one hand he held a pistol, pointed at her father. The free hand moved towards his ankle, and he rubbed it, grunting but keeping his aim steady. His expression said he wanted to make someone pay.

She tried to catch her father's eyes, to plead with him not to try anything, but his attention lay focused on the gun and nothing else. If he got killed because of her lack of speed, she'd never forgive herself. She sniffed and forced herself to swallow her sobs, until the woods fell silent, except for a gentle humming of the wind in the trees.

CHAPTER: ELEVEN

"We're gonna have fun with you two fuckers. You'll pay for making me run," Hassan said.

Miko tutted and eyed his junior. "Don't be rude to our guests. Would you not have run? Or are you such a tough guy who would stand and fight men with guns, armed only with your charm." He returned his gaze to the man and the girl. "I'm Mikolaj, but they usually call me Miko. That's Michael, in Polish. We share a name, so perhaps we can be civil to each other, at least?"

The father said nothing, but his lip curled into a sneer. The girl buried her face in her hands and sobbed. These silent moments of tension were glorious. He breathed in deeply, absorbing the fear which radiated from them. Now only *he* controlled matters. The man and the girl, even Hassan, were *his* chessmen, the minor pieces on his board, where *he* was king.

From the undergrowth, something flashed in Miko's peripheral vision, a grey and black blur. With a deep growl, the thing leapt and clawed at Hassan. He screamed—a high-pitched girlish noise—and scrabbled in a frantic attempt to ward it off. The gun flew from his grasp, landing in the mulch at the girl's feet with a soft bump. Miko looked at her and she looked at the gun. Their eyes locked. He flinched first, and she scooped it up.

The heavy pistol shook in her hands. At this distance, with it pointed squarely at his chest, she'd be unlikely to miss, but the recoil might throw the shot away from his vital areas. It was worth the chance.

Before he could make his move, a sound like nothing he'd heard before stole his attention from the girl. He'd seen men's flesh burned from their living body, and they didn't scream like that. He turned towards his stricken colleague. With a savage, ripping snarl, the animal tore into Hassan's exposed jugular. Arterial blood spewed out in a thick, pulsing jet, followed by a gurgling rush like water escaping through a sinkhole. The blood slowed to a steady waterfall. The distracted animal—a lean, muscular wolf-like creature—licked at Hassan's neck and Miko moved towards it.

"Give me the gun, honey!" Michael said. Miko spun around. The pistol was again pointed at him, but from Michael's hands. They did not shake like his daughter's. "Move and I shoot, motherfucker!"

He raised his arms, glancing at Hassan from the corner of his eye. It was too late for the man. Would the animal attack him next? He feared almost nothing. But being mauled to death by a dog—if it even *was* one—seemed a dismal way for a soldier to leave this shithole planet. It did not move in his direction, but instead sat in front of the girl and faced him. The beast's different coloured eyes burned with murder, and it emitted a deep, rumbling growl which made his anus clench.

He backed away, an inch at a time. The dog did not move, Michael did not shoot. He looked at Hassan one last time, blood pooled by him like spilled communion wine—he was dead. He kept retreating until he'd reached enough distance to make a shot from a 9mm pistol with a steady hand uncertain, then turned and sprinted into the valley below with every ounce of speed and agility he could muster. Far behind, the dog howled a throaty lament, blasting through the trees like a cry from an upturned conch shell.

Michael tried to process the events of the previous ten minutes, but it was too insane. He tried to summon enough concentration to consider their next move, but his thoughts kept racing backwards. He might never forget the terrible cries of the dead Baby Farmer, even if he lived to be a hundred, and he had to force himself to concentrate on making inventory. They had a few energy bars and no water, transport, or shelter. The light would disappear soon. Once their sweat cooled in the late afternoon chill, they'd start shivering and warmth would be scarce. He rubbed his bare wrist. He'd left his watch back at the house, so he didn't even have access to a rudimentary map. What else could they do except to follow the path and pray it led to shelter?

"We need to keep moving, Hope. Joel gave me an old mobile. If we can get somewhere safe, he'll come for us."

Hope lay among the ferns and moss, entwined with her canine guardian. Its bib was stained with a dark, sticky red. "I'm not going anywhere without him."

Defiant, as always. He sighed and rolled his eyes. "Hope, the animal is dangerous. It just killed a man, for fuck's sake!"

"Fine, you go."

The animal seemed calm and made a satisfied whimpering sound while it licked its front paws clean. It was worthless arguing when they needed the energy for more important matters. Besides, heated words might set it off again, and perhaps it would attack *him* next. If they stayed, others would come, and their brazen luck wouldn't hold a second time.

He examined the Baby Farmer's pistol, which he still held in his hand. After engaging the safety catch, he tucked the weapon into the waistband of his trousers. "Alright, the dog comes, but try not to let the thing rip *my* damn throat out too!"

Hope jumped up. The dog sat with its narrow head pointing upwards, alert and awaiting instructions from its chosen master. "Don't worry, he won't." She stooped to stroke its head, and the dog wagged its scarred tail. "Good boy. Dad's our friend, see." When she walked along the path, it followed gamely.

Look at her, skipping along with that damn creature by her side like something out of a fucking Enid Blyton story! She'd seen a man killed in brutal fashion moments ago, yet seemed unphased. Maybe focusing on the animal had kept her mind off the horror. Still, given the circumstances, her resilience was miraculous. Blind luck or not, he'd raised someone pretty damn special. Perhaps he should listen to her more often.

The men they'd just encountered were the same who'd come knocking back in London. He'd recognised their black van, and their leader, who called himself Miko. Even when he'd pointed the gun at the man's chest, unsure whether he was about to shoot, there had been a total lack of fear in those eyes. They'd burned not with compassion, like Willy's, but with malicious promise.

What about the helicopters and multiple sirens? This wasn't the work of the Baby Farmers alone, who probably just wanted to snare Hope and harboured little interest in him. No, this bore all the hallmarks of multiple agencies, meaning there must be more than just one organisation on their tail. They must have traced him via the purchases he made at *The General Store*.

With a jolt, he realised he'd put John in serious danger, put *everyone* in danger! If they'd hurt the old man, Hope couldn't know.

His fist coiled around the old phone in his pocket—their only realistic chance. Perhaps it had Joel's number stored in its meagre memory, but he'd been told to wait. No option but to hunker down and trust his friend's promise. Who knew what was happening back at the house? *Please let them be safe*. Otherwise, Joel might never call, in which case they were screwed. The Ford was marked; *they* were marked. Were they going to *walk* to Scotland?

They marched through the growing gloom until lights danced in the distance. When they got closer, he realised it was an old pub. It looked warm and welcoming, but far too risky. Most of the locals seemed friendly enough, but it only took one person to notice them covered in dirt, without money to buy a drink. Let alone the wild animal they had with them. It wasn't even an option.

The path, perhaps an old railway track, long since returned to nature, ran underneath the bridge the pub was situated on. The tunnel offered a clear line of sight in both directions and ample shadows to retreat into. They'd hear any vehicles or people passing on the road above.

"Looks as safe as anything we're going to find," he said. Hope needed no further encouragement. She rested her back on the mossy tunnel wall, slid down and onto her bottom with a relieved sigh. The dog stretched out on its front beside her. Michael kept his distance from the animal and sat on his haunches on the opposite side of the tunnel.

"Alright kiddo, let's rest here for a while."

"Sounds good to me. I'm sure your man crush Joel will come through for us." Hope winked. Still cracking jokes, after all she'd been through. He couldn't do anything but laugh.

Under his breath, he said, "That's my girl."

Miko rounded the side of the house as Eriksson's team was climbing back into their transport.

"Nice afternoon stroll in the woods?" offered Eriksson. "No luck, I assume?"

He marched past and clambered into the passenger seat of the black van, ignoring his rival. At the wheel sat Johnson, who turned to stare at him like he deserved answers. Nobody deserved shit in this life, and he'd offer explanations when he felt like it.

"Drive."

Johnson didn't move. "Where's Hassan?"

With a blank face Miko said, "He's dead."

Johnson started the engine and turned the vehicle around. By the time they reached the monolithic old red phone-booth, they were up the ass of Eriksson's white vehicles. How fun it'd be to run them both off the road and watch the fuckers burn.

"How's Wosniak?" Miko asked, in an emotionless drone.

"He's OK, boss. I patched up the arm, fished out the pellets. He won't lose it."

"Good."

Johnson had joined the team the same day as Hassan and they were buddies, despite the constant abuse the guy got about his former religion. He could almost see Johnson's curiosity ticking down like a stopwatch and was not startled when he cried, "What the fuck do you mean he's dead, man?!"

"If I told you, you wouldn't believe me."

"Try me."

He snapped to face his charge, looking down his nose and challenging further insubordination. Johnson took his eyes off the winding country road and the van swerved. A white SUV loomed in his peripheral vision, but he refused to break his stare until Johnson returned his attention to the road and caressed the brake to avoid a collision. The two men sat in silence and Johnson made no further attempt to meet his eyes.

When they hit a straight section of road, Johnson dropped into third gear, burned past the government SUVs, and cut sharply in front of the lead vehicle, drawing a wailing horn blast. With nothing ahead, Johnson finally broke the bubbling cauldron of silence, but he spoke softly and didn't glance up from the road. "Look, boss, he was my friend. At least I gotta know how he bought it. We should go back and get him."

But Miko had already formulated a new plan, and it did not involve heading back to base empty-handed, regardless of what Faulkner's orders might be.

"You're correct. Pull off here and spin around. We'll recover the body now. Then, you'll go back to base with Wosniak. Oh, and I'll need your pistol too." Johnson looked confused, and Miko rested a chunky hand on his shoulder as he drove. "You trust me, don't you?"

"Of course, boss."

He allowed his face to crack into a grin. "Good. They'll pay for Hassan, don't worry about that, my friend. The debt *will be collected.*"

Hope had already fallen asleep, but the dog remained alert,

scanning the familiar landscape for movements. Michael's eyelids drooped. Unable to hold them open, he stuffed the mobile phone into his shirt pocket before drifting off into a merciful doze.

The old phone buzzed against his chest and he jerked awake. Dusk had slipped away, and darkness now cloaked the woods. The pub lights overhead offered a slim reminder of civilisation, projecting strange shadows on the silver path beneath. He pulled out the phone and pressed the keypad, revealing a message. It simply read *'Clear, location?'*

His cold digits struggled to manipulate the tiny buttons. Had he got fat fingers or were these phones smaller than he remembered? *'Under a bridge by a pub.'* Within seconds, the reply came. *'Pub is called...?'* He struggled to his feet, shuffled out into the gloom, and strained his neck to glimpse the old inn. *'Dog & Fox'*, he replied. How apt. *'Stay there, 10 mins.'*

He allowed himself to drift back into a slumber until the light rumbling of a solitary vehicle overhead woke him. A car door opened and slammed shut. Steps echoed out, with an engine turning in the background.

"Mike!" came an urgent whisper, with a slight trace of a Scandinavian accent. *Joel!* He leapt upright and ran out from under the bridge.

"Down here." He waved until Joel spotted him and waved back. Once he'd returned to the tunnel and roused his daughter from a deep slumber, she followed him without searching for the dog. In her groggy state, perhaps she'd forgotten. Hopefully, it had wandered off. This was its territory, after all. Maybe the beast didn't want to leave.

They climbed up the short embankment to the road and Michael hugged his friend. "Fuck, am I glad to see you!"

"Let's not jerk each other off yet. Get in the damn car."

Joel motioned over to a small, dark blue electric powered vehicle, perhaps a decade old. He opened the passenger door and held back the seat so Hope could clamber into the back. Suddenly, the blood-stained hound darted past and curled up next to her in the car's cramped rear.

"What the actual fuck?" Joel said, jaw hanging.

Michael shrugged and slumped into the passenger seat. "Don't ask, man. I *think* it's sound."

Joel danced around to the driver's side. While he drove, he explained what had happened at the house, blow-by-blow. "Your car, it's no good. The plates are hot. They might be back to seize it tomorrow."

Michael's head dropped. His beloved Ford was history. "Fuck it," he muttered.

"But your pal Joel's got a plan, so don't worry. Anyway, what about you guys? How did you slip those Nazi fucks?"

"About that…" How could he explain?

Hope's head snapped up, as if the cold air pouring through the open front passenger window had awoken her senses. "I can tell him if you like, Daddy." He slumped in his seat, relieved he didn't need to try. "My friend here saved us. Killed one of the bad men, and the other ran away when I got his gun."

She sounded like a child trying to explain the plot of a strange movie. The poor girl seemed almost delirious with fatigue. He took over and filled in the blanks.

"That is pretty whacky, man. You sure that thing ain't gonna jump on me?" Joel eyed the hound in his rearview.

"I think anyone who's OK with her is OK with him." He thumbed toward the rear seats.

Without warning, Joel pulled over and stopped. Outside, darkness reigned, except for a sliver of moon between invisible clouds. "Right pal, this is where we part."

Michael's head bowed. "Where are we? Which direction should we walk?"

"Oh no, you guys aren't walking anywhere. Take the car."

"Are you sure?"

"This piece of shit? Man, if I can recover that Ford from the impound and ride it until you get sorted. Even if there's a *chance*, it's worth the trade. If not, then I hardly use this car, so it doesn't matter."

"Fair enough. It's all yours if you can get it. The DVLA log card is stashed in the glove compartment, inside an old Haynes manual."

"Shit, man. I remember trying to understand the manual for my first car, an old Volvo. Thought I'd accidentally bought the Japanese version. Didn't make the remotest bit of sense."

He laughed. "You're a damn fine mechanic now though, Joel."

His friend sighed and slipped out of the driver's seat, leaving the car's low-powered engine idling. Michael shuffled over behind the wheel. Joel leaned in through the open door and flipped something onto the empty passenger seat.

"It's not like we're ringers buddy, but if you grow that hair out a bit and keep that beard, it might, I mean *might,* get you out of a jam. There should be enough on there to get you where you need to go."

Michael fingered his friend's ID card. Before he could speak, the door slammed shut and Joel jogged away, pulling up his hood as he ran. Michael watched until he melted into the darkness, then drove away.

CHAPTER: TWELVE

"So, what you're telling me, Kozlowski, is that one of your guys got shot and wounded by a fucking geriatric, and another was, quite literally, killed by a shitting *dog*?!" Colin Faulkner didn't do angry often. Other people in his organisation did it better. But right now, he'd gone apoplectic.

The agent's tone dripped with ridicule as he repeated his outrageous version of events. "Well, I think it was a dog. Maybe a wolf, who knows? Do they have wolves in Wales?"

"How am I supposed to explain that to Burrows?" The name made his spine tingle, even though he'd spoken it himself.

"That is not my problem. What I've told you is the truth and bad luck, nothing more." He was right, of course. In all his years of service, he'd made few mistakes. If anyone would suffer over this debacle, it'd be him, Colin Horatio Faulkner, not Kozlowski. "One more thing," said the Pole. "I'm taking a few days off."

Colin found himself rendered so incredulous he couldn't even summon a protest and demand the man return to base. Instead, he mumbled, "Super, just, really… really great stuff, Kozlowski!"

The call terminated and Colin allowed his head to loll forward into his hands. He gripped his thinning hair and yanked at it. At least he could assume Eriksson's team hadn't bagged the girl either, as Piers would have sent him a mocking message by now. Such a conclusion offered scant consolation, but while the pair remained at large, at least they might atone for this aberration. He still stood a chance of walking away with his balls intact.

With help from an old *Automobile Association Map of Great Britain*, long since out of print, Michael drove through the night. In the back seat, Hope slept with her canine companion dozing by her side. They would end the journey in Carlisle, rest and lie low for a day before making the short journey north-east. Finally, they'd ditch the vehicle and hike the remaining ten miles to the border.

The car crossed from Wales into England near Chester, at around three in the morning. Half an hour later, several miles east of Liverpool, he stopped to charge the fuel cell. He let the dog out to relieve itself, half-wondering what he was going to tell his daughter if it disappeared. It didn't, so he decided to buy it some food from the petrol station shop and pay for an enhanced speed-charge. The forecourt and shop were deserted. He'd have to use Joel's ID card at some point, and it seemed like a decent chance to test his luck.

The shop door opened with a whisper and the teller didn't look up from her device. Harsh tubes buzzed overhead, bathing him in brittle white light. His mud-caked boots clacked against the tiling while he searched for pet food, leaving a tiny trail of earthy crumbs behind. There were two different brands available. The images on the front of both cans looked equally gross. He doubted the dog was a discerning eater, but one brand had no ring pull, while the other did, so he selected five tins, picked up a bottle of water and some snacks, then approached the counter. When he loaded his provisions onto the surface, the girl lifted her head and offered the faintest acknowledgement to his presence. He flashed his most regular-Joe smile and tried not to look shifty.

"Charge station five. Can you upgrade to a thirty-minute speed-charge, please?"

The teller processed the payment, with nothing but boredom showing on her round young face. He rubbed his sweating palms against his filthy jeans. Thank fuck he'd stopped wearing stone-washed Levi's years ago. Why was it taking so damn long? The girl's oily forehead cracked into a frown, and she looked up at him, seeing him properly this time.

"Uh, everything OK?"

"Connection dropped out. You wanna try again?"

"Sure." He took the ID card out again and flashed it across the scanner.

"If it don't work this time, I'll have to process it manually."

But that would mean handing over the card. She'd see the picture. Would she even care? He stared at the terminal, which remained stuck on a red light. *Not connected.* It turned amber. *Connecting...* Footsteps behind him. He looked outside and noticed the police car parked in the forecourt. His vision blurred as his blood pressure spiked. *Calm down, breathe.* It looked like a regular traffic patrol car. He craned his neck around the store, watching the police officer from the corner of his eye while he perused the snack aisle. The cop looked as bored as the girl.

"Sir?" His head jerked up to meet the teller's eyes. *Here's the part where she says it's not completed, and she'll try to take the card and...* "It's gone through now. Would you like a bag?"

"Uh, no thanks. Goodnight." He scooped up the tins and

snacks, turned, and strolled towards the exit. When he approached the door, the cop glared at him as he passed.

Then the teller cried out, "Sir…? Hey, sir, stop will you?"

Michael became acutely aware of a coldness prickling all over his skin. Time slowed as he spun around, readying himself to launch his armful of tins at the policeman and run. But the teller was holding a bottle of water and waving it overhead. "You forgot your water, sir."

He summoned the best false laugh he could muster, strode back to the counter, and plucked the water bottle from the teller's outstretched hand. "Sorry, been a long night," he said, stuffing the bottle into his back pocket

This time, the cop grinned and held open the door for him. "Thanks officer. Keep up the good work." What an idiot comment! Why on earth had he said that?

In the car, he sipped half the bottle's contents while he waited for the cop to leave the forecourt. Hope murmured in her sleep, but the dog had sat up on its haunches, and was now scanning the road. It seemed fascinated by the cars and lorries rattling past. The cop fired up his patrol car and pulled away. Michael got back out of the vehicle and beckoned the dog to follow, which it did with some reticence.

"Sorry pal, you're gonna have to eat off the floor for now," he said, peeling off the tin's ring-pull and banging the contents onto the asphalt. The animal sniffed the offering before tucking in, its rapid breaths sending clouds of condensation billowing into the cold early morning air while it ate. *I wonder how that tastes after his last meal?*

The speed-charge seemed to take much longer than thirty minutes, but clocks didn't lie. While he waited, he watched the steady dribble of customers. There were taxi drivers, truckers, an ambulance, but mostly there were solitary men in saloon cars,

alone in the vastness of night, on their linear journeys from one
unseen point in time and space to another.

Finally, the charging station beeped twice and flashed, and
they set off again. The dog seemed relaxed and content after
consuming its latest meal and continued to enjoy its new hobby
of watching traffic. Meanwhile, stretched across the rear seats,
Hope slept soundly.

He had to assume their images were already on the
highways agency's tracking database. The plan was to avoid
motorways, which were often the only roads with working face-
recognition cameras. Large service stations would also have
them, as would major urban city centres.

Bathed in amber monotony, the little car scratched a
channel between Liverpool and Manchester. The northern
powerhouses had fared relatively well, thanks in part to mass-
migration from London. The capital's population had halved in
a decade. They hummed through Preston and Lancaster, poor
and forgotten bastions of industry, then sliced an arc through the
wealthy towns on the eastern fringe of the Lake District, past
Kendal, reaching the little town of Penrith around eight in the
morning.

They were still twenty miles short of Carlisle, but after
seven hours and two-hundred-and-fifty miles of road, he could
go no further without risking an amateur driving mistake which
could cost them everything.

Hope's image filled the rear-view mirror, her hair pointing
at unusual angles while she stretched her arms and yawned.
"I'm kinda peckish, Dad."

His own stomach gurgled in agreement. Peckish was her
maximum on the hunger scale, from what he understood. When
had they last eaten a proper meal? "OK, let's find somewhere to
eat." He parked up in the town centre and scanned Joel's ID card

at the meter so they could park without attracting the interest of a Minor Offences Enforcement Drone.

"This town seems to be doing OK compared to Wales, doesn't it?" She wasn't wrong. Most of the shops were open. Perhaps this place hadn't been affected by the social changes of the last decade.

"I guess towns like Penrith never had much other than white folk anyway, so when they kicked out all the other religions, they probably didn't notice much difference."

"Sounds like my old school, Dad. I noticed, though."

They left the dog curled up asleep in the car and entered a quaint looking café called *The Penrith Tea Rooms*, which advertised *Breakfast, Lunch & Dinner—Fine Wines*. They seated themselves at a small circular table. Ornate cutlery had already been placed on the doily patterned white tablecloth and stiff menus stood up in the table's centre, offering numerous delights which got Michael's mouth watering.

"This place is well nice." Hope stared around wide-eyed while he fidgeted with a fork. "Daddy, I've been thinking."

He glanced up at his daughter, hoping she hadn't chosen this moment to have an important conversation. It had become an outright battle to stop himself from falling asleep at the table. "Yes, Hope?"

"The dog needs a name." He smiled. This was a subject he could manage.

An upright, officious looking gentleman approached their table. His glasses were low on his nose and he looked down on them with a mixture of disgust and intrigue. "Are you ready to order?" he said, running a liver-spotted hand through the thin strands of white hair on his pate.

Hope buzzed with excitement, not waiting for the man to get his small waiter's notepad from his breast pocket. "Yes, please! I'll have the belly buster breakfast." He sighed, clicked the end of his ballpoint pen and scribbled down the order. "Wait, are the sausages and bacon *real* meat? And ethically farmed?"

"Of course," he snorted. "Our meat is from farms right here in the town. Certified organic and free range, naturally." Michael raised both eyebrows. His daughter had been veggie for years. Maybe a taste of country life had changed her outlook.

"Wow, real meat, eh? You guys are proper fancy up here."

The man ignored her comment. "Tea or coffee, *madam*?" The elongated *madam* dripped with sarcasm. Who did this guy think he was?

Hope either paid no attention or didn't notice. "Coffee, please. Do you have dairy-free?"

"Soya, almond *and* synthetic cow's milk."

"Oh, synthetic please. I've never tried it, and an orange juice. *Real* orange juice!"

The man turned to him, nose in the air. "And for sir?"

"All sounds great. I'll take the same without milk in the coffee."

"*Real* orange juice as well for sir?"

"Why not?" The man finished writing their order in his notepad, turned, and scurried away, his nose pointing even further toward the ceiling. Michael hunched down to address his daughter. "What a snobbish bastard!"

Hope beamed back at him. "I know right."

"What's with the meat? You're a total hypocrite, with the dairy-free milk as well."

"Oh, I don't know. I just really fancied it. I mean, it's proper and all, not even lab grown! Perhaps being around farm animals has made me reconsider. If they're properly looked after, and you know where they've come from, it's not so bad, right? I'd never eat anything that wasn't cared for."

"Fair argument."

"Thanks. So, what about the dog's name?"

How about killer? "What about Wolfie? I mean, he is basically a wolf."

"It's so obvious, though. But I guess it kinda fits. Oh wait, remember that crappy TV show you loved from like a hundred years ago? The one with all the boobs and slaughtering? *Throne of Games* or something dumb?"

A pleasant jolt of nostalgia flashed through him. "Yeah, of course. Literally my favourite show when I was younger. Thanks for remembering."

"Didn't they all have their own wolf-things?"

"Yeah, the *Direwolves*."

"OK, so what were their names? I'm sure one of them was Grey something."

"Grey Wind," he said, without hesitation.

"Boom!"

"I don't know, darling. I think I prefer Wolfie."

"Well, let's ask him, then."

"Ask the *dog*?" he snorted.

"Well, you know, not *ask* him exactly, but see which one he responds to best."

He released a long sigh of resignation. "Fine, that sounds like a great idea." With the overwhelming tiredness which filled his sagging bones, he would've agreed to almost anything.

Moments later, piled high on their plates and steaming hot, their meals arrived, and they tucked in. Despite his fatigue, he remembered few more enjoyable meals in his life. He soon cleared his plate, but Hope only managed about two-thirds of hers before pushing the food away.

"The eye is bigger than the stomach, eh?" he said. She leaned back in her chair, groaning and holding her midriff. He shoved aside his spotless plate and pulled hers into the newly vacated space.

Replete, they returned to the car to consider their options. Joel had left them a tent and some camping equipment in the trunk, but the weather forecast on the radio earlier that morning had promised nothing but heavy wind and rain for the next forty-eight hours. Besides, camping out might warrant unwelcome attention. Few people did it these days, usually transients and people with a C-listing credit status, meaning they couldn't pass basic landlord worthiness inspections.

"What now then, Dad?"

"I don't know about you, but I'm shattered. If we're to have any chance of making it across the border, we need supplies and rest. Let's find a bed & breakfast which allows dogs and isn't too fussy about ID cards, I guess. Hotels might ask for yours, too, and I'd have to say you're twelve. Reckon you could pass for twelve, honey?" He looked across at his daughter. She didn't look twelve to him. Not anymore.

She peered into the rear-view mirror, checking herself out from several angles. "Nope."

"B&B it is then, if we can find a dog-friendly one."

They spent the rest of the morning schlepping around the town's boarding houses before one kind landlady gave them an address of a pet-friendly establishment out of town. A little after midday, they pulled up outside an old building, painted white and three stories tall. It had the grandiose name *The Belfort Inn—Established in 1996*, according to the proclamation below. They mounted an imposing set of stone steps and rang the bell.

Miko parked his rental car in a disabled bay and got out, ignoring the disgusted mutterings of an elderly couple passing with their shopping. Carlisle wasn't a big city, but it was big enough for a man and his daughter to hide. Randall would never be able to attempt a hike to the border after the drama of their woodland chase, followed by a lengthy drive throughout the night, not with the dead weight of a teenage girl in tow, anyway. If they were foolish enough to try, they would get picked up, and the pair would no longer be his concern. Or at least, he'd require a new, long-term plan to settle Hassan's debt. Every fibre of his experience said that they'd hole up in the nearest place big enough to melt into the background. Nowhere other than Carlisle fitted the brief.

It had taken an hour to reach an old acquaintance at the DVLA and discover the car had stopped at a petrol station near Liverpool during the night. If they were going to cross on the north-eastern side of the border, they would have travelled east, adding three hours to their journey, and he'd pick up the car's trail somewhere on the route. Far more likely, they'd headed north, avoiding motorways. Randall wasn't completely stupid. If he'd taken a major route, the number plate would have popped up again during the early morning. If Randall had triggered facial recognition cameras, Eriksson's squad would surely have the pair in custody by now, and nothing suggested that to be true.

After the previous day's excitement, Johnson had dropped him off in Llandovery. He'd found a nice, comfy tree to watch the commune's comings and goings. The blonde man drove away early evening. Three hours later, in the dead of night, blondie returned on foot, minus his shitty vehicle. Perhaps he had a man crush on Randall. Or maybe he fancied the little girl. Why else would he just *give* them his car, even if it was a piece of crap? People didn't *help each other out*, not in the real world.

The guy probably had his eye on the Ford Capri. Not if Miko Kozlowski had a say in proceedings. Another call to his contact at the DVLA would get that lovely old car seized, crushed into a tiny cube, and posted back to Llandovery with a ribbon wrapped around it. He'd half considered jacking the car himself. What a delight it would've been to see the expression on Randall's face when he came steaming into town in his own fucking Ford. But no, discretion was key here. The black triple-celled Audi hire car might turn a few heads if he gunned its powerful engine, but parked up or driven at the speed limit, such a car would draw no unnecessary attention. Now all he needed was a little slice of luck, along with Faulkner to take the hint and stay off his case for a few days.

CHAPTER: THIRTEEN

Hope scanned the hallway, admiring the thick orange and brown carpet and the striking pink paintwork of the walls. Somebody had great taste.

She nodded and said, "Nice place." Her father's face scrunched up in horror. She doubted he found the décor as impressive, but he liked super boring stuff.

A heavy thumping shook the floor and a lady in her early sixties bounded down the stairs, reaching the bottom out of breath. She grinned at them, baring small yellow teeth. "Hello there, I'm Mrs. Gable. Welcome to the Belfort Inn. Would you be after a room?"

"We would, but there's one slight issue. We have a dog. I heard you might accommodate?" said her father.

Hope grimaced. *Please let them take dogs.*

Mrs. Gable paused for a moment and pursed her lips, as if sizing them up for their worthiness. "Ah yes. Not in the main building, but we have an annexe out back. It's a fully contained apartment, self-catering only I'm afraid, but you're in luck. It's not booked until Friday."

Hope clenched her fist inside her tracksuit top. *More than enough time.*

Her father said, "Excellent, we're only staying until tomorrow. How much will it cost for the night?"

"One-hundred-and-eighty new pounds." He winced. Just

how much money remained on the card Joel had given them? He'd kept tight-lipped, but it seemed they weren't flush.

Time to turn on the charm. She beamed at the woman, letting her teeth show. Hopefully, the old bag would revise her offer. It wasn't like anyone else would take the room now.

"But seeing as you're a first-time customer, we can do it for one fifty…?" Mrs. Gable's mouth widened in expectation, while her new offer hung in the air. Hope sensed the balance of power had shifted, and now she needed to sell the room. "Over seventy percent of our business is repeat customers. We've got a 4.8 out of 5 on *tripstar*, third best in the county." Her voice rose at the end.

"We'll take it," he announced with a grin. Hope did not smile. They'd forced the silly old hag onto the ropes. Perhaps they could've got it even cheaper.

The woman showed them around the side of the building to the annexe. Along the way, they stopped to collect the dog and their belongings. Hope had cleaned its red bib, but still Mrs Gable eyed the animal, fidgeting with her hands. "He's housebroken, isn't he?"

"Oh yes, good as gold, this one," Hope said, patting the animal and summoning her most innocent smile to placate their host.

"Good, good, come with me then." The gravel crunched as they followed. Once inside, she danced around the room. It had fluffy white pillows, with thick duvets, and even a decent sized television, not that it held much interest for her.

Her father slumped down onto the bed in the main bedroom. Less than a minute later, he'd fallen fast asleep with his muddy boots dangling off the end. With great difficulty, she untied the laces, pulled off his boots and hauled her father up the bed into a more natural position. She covered him with a blanket from the smaller bedroom and gave him a gentle kiss on his bearded face, stopping for a second to look at him properly for the first time in ages. The beard kind of suited him.

She flicked through channels on the TV for a few hours while her father slumbered, although his ripping snores sometimes drowned out the program. She'd not watched anything or had access to her Metaverse avatar, or even her social media accounts, for a week now, and didn't miss any of it. But it was nice to switch off from thinking for a while.

When her father stopped snoring for a few minutes, she glanced over. He was lying so still, it gave her a sudden panic and she checked his breathing. He'd reached that age where men needed to start looking after themselves.

After an hour, her enthusiasm for the room started to wane. Nothing on the television engaged her, and she found her mind wandering. Sat in the room's only chair, she stared out the window while the daylight faded. For the first time since they'd fled the commune, she had a chance to think about the place, and what had transpired with Johannes. She missed the boy already. Their moment of desire seemed so distant now, like a dream. But it wasn't.

What if the community had suffered reprisal because of her? Could she forgive herself? There was no way to get in contact with them, unless she could somehow get the number for Johannes's illicit mobile from her mother. At least it was a possibility. Maybe she could return one day. Their little society had been the closest thing to an extended family she'd ever known.

Her father awoke with a start, and she jumped from her seat. His eyes were wide and sweat rolled from his glistening forehead. He seemed disorientated and took a moment to get himself together, then groaned in a horse whisper, "Where are we?"

"Penrith, I believe we are in Penrith."

"Ah yeah, I remember now. Christ, my head hurts. What time is it?" He looked down at where his watch used to be. She had no idea, and switched to a news channel, which displayed the time in the bottom corner.

"Nearly eight, Dad."

They both became drawn into the dismal whirlpool of the news broadcast. Her father chewed his fingers while the presenter delivered his grim commentary.

"The last remaining residents of King's Lynn were forcibly evacuated today. The town is one of many in the region which is almost completely submerged as sea levels continue to rise."

They'd been warned about this for decades. Aged eleven, she'd become obsessed with climate change and read every book she could find on the subject. To her, the whole affair seemed insane. How could humanity not have altered its path as its impact became undeniable?

She couldn't resist commenting. "Perhaps they should've done something about global warming twenty years ago when everyone started telling them we'd screwed the planet."

"I'm sorry, darling. It's your granddad and your great-granddad's generations who messed it up for you. Mine grew up recycling every scrap and not flying anywhere, but I guess it was too late by then."

"Too late? It wasn't too late to stop those religious maniacs taking control of the country. They don't give a crap about the environment."

"I can't argue with you there, Hope."

"But they knew as far back as 1982, Dad. Greedy oil companies paid off the governments to keep it quiet. I hope they're happy now they've killed us all. You just wait until the gulf stream gives up the ghost and we're plunged into an ice bucket, then you'll be sorry."

"Yes, honey, you told me all this during your eco-warrior phase a few years ago."

He was right, it wasn't his fault. Yes, he could've done more, but the chance to avert disaster was missed when he'd been nothing but a child, maybe long before then. She pressed her hands to her temples and tried to focus on her breathing. It wouldn't do to get upset at what she couldn't control. *Time for a change of subject.*

"OK, enough miserable news for today, its name time." She nodded towards the dog and clapped her hands. Its eyes rolled upwards, like it sensed something was afoot. "I'll sit over in one corner while you go over there and shout *Wolfie*. I'll call *Grey Wind*. Oh, then we need to swap, just to make sure." He pouted but did not protest, wobbling to his feet towards the opposite corner of the room. "OK, in three, two, one."

They called simultaneously. The dog tilted its head and looked from one human to another, perhaps unsure. They called again, and this time it ignored her, turned towards her father and approached him tentatively. She sighed. How disappointing. She preferred Grey Wind, but the dog had spoken.

"I guess you win. Wolfie it is." He trotted over to her when he heard his name.

"Looks that way."

"I'm going to take him for a walk around the garden."

"Be quick honey. Be careful and don't leave the grounds."

"Yes, Dad," she said, leaving the room with the newly christened dog close behind.

When she returned, her father hadn't moved. He didn't seem to notice her enter, and the distant look in his eyes made her uneasy. He looked tired and grey, like recent events had aged him beyond his years. For all the craziness that'd happened, he'd protected her to the best of his ability. It didn't erase the past entirely, but close enough.

"I never told you this, Hope, but we used to have one. A long time ago." His voice had a distance, like it was coming from the other end of a long hallway, but it still startled her. Glazed eyes bored into the wall while he spoke, and he seemed to address a ghost rather than her.

"What are you talking about, Daddy, a dog? You mean before I was born?"

Now he turned in her direction, and his eyes sparked back into life, but they retained a watery gloss which she hadn't noticed before. "We got him before you were born. When you came along, he was about three or so. He loved you so much, always by your side if you were sick. God have mercy if you started crying, he'd howl his little face off. You were crazy about him, too."

She frowned. Had her father lost his mind? Was he having some sort of episode, or a false memory, perhaps? Softly, she said, "We've never had a dog, I'd remember. You know I love animals, and I always wanted one, but you said we couldn't afford the bills and licence."

"That's just it. When they brought in the pet licence fee and I lost my job, we had to give him up. I'm so sorry. I wish…" His eyes dropped to the floor, and she thought she noticed an ephemeral tear escape from the corner of his eye. She'd never once seen her father cry, and the possibility unsettled her. A perfect man he was not, but he'd always had the air of someone in tight control of his emotions. Who knew what would come rushing out if the thick walls of his self-constructed dam crumbled?

Conflicting thoughts crowded her young brain, and she dashed into the small second bedroom, flopped onto the bed and buried her head in the soft pillow, bawling gentle, silent tears. She felt a presence and turned to shoo it away; she did not want to be comforted by her father at that moment. But it wasn't him. Wolfie leapt onto the bed and nuzzled her arm until she lifted it and allowed him to curl up by her flank. She smiled through tears and kissed the top of his head. Before she knew it, she'd drifted into the calm oceans of post-cry slumber.

The next morning, Hope awoke refreshed, but with a strange feeling in the pit of her stomach. She sat up in bed and rubbed the sleep from her eyes. Once she'd rolled out of bed and said good morning to Wolfie, she realised her father was absent. An electric charge jumped through her chest as memories of his odd behaviour the previous night returned. Could he have abandoned them during the night, like in her old nightmares? She searched through the apartment, her uneasy feeling growing with each second, but found nothing. *I'm being a baby. He's just gone to buy supplies for the trip… But why hadn't he left a note?*

The minutes ticked by. She paced the room, unsure what to do next. Her mind played out several grim scenarios. At last, a key scraped at the door. All at once, the anxiety flushed from her. She'd been so stupid. He'd never abandon her.

He appeared re-energised, and the horrid grey pallor had vanished from his skin. It was a relief to put the entire episode down to exhaustion. Her resentment might take time to dissipate, but this was no occasion for holding grudges, especially about a pet she couldn't even remember.

"Sleep well, sweet-heart?" She nodded and smiled. "Good. You'll need all your energy today."

"Where were you, Dad? I got scared."

"It's forecast for heavy rain later, so I went to get some waterproof jackets. I've got a walking guide to the area, so we don't get completely lost. You needed new boots too. Those shoes of yours will let in water now the soles have started to come away."

She picked up one of her shoes and pulled at a flap. "What, these things? They've got hundreds of kilometres left in them."

He pulled out a cardboard box and threw it onto the bed. "Try those on."

She opened the box, yanked out a hiking boot, removed the paper from inside and slipped it onto her bare foot. "A little big, but should be fine with an extra pair of socks."

He prodded at the toe. "Damn it, I can never remember your bloody shoe size. Anyway, we should leave soon. Do you need a shower?"

She sniffed her armpits and recoiled. "Definitely."

"Me too. You first?" She nodded and dashed into the bathroom.

When she got out ten minutes later, with a thick white bath towel wrapped around her waist, and her hair wet and dripping, she felt even fresher, ready for whatever the day might bring. He'd prepared tea for her. She grabbed it and went into the second bedroom, closing the door behind her while he made breakfast.

After they ate, he showered while she got her things together. Once he'd dried and dressed, they left the apartment. She took a last look around. It'd been a nice place to spend the night.

Weird old Mrs. Gable met them in the lobby of the Belfort Inn to receive the keys. Hands clasped, and with an unnerving smile, she said, "Did you enjoy your stay?"

"Everything was great, thank you."

Her smile widened. "Don't forget to leave us a rating on *tripstar*."

An obscure memory flashed through Hope's mind. An old music video, a band her father had loved from a million years ago. The grotesque amplified gurn of their smiles had intrigued her, even if the music hadn't. 'Black Hole Sun.' The woman looked like she'd stepped straight from that bizarre video.

Once they'd settled the bill and returned to the car, it was past ten in the morning. She'd grown rather fond of Penrith, and the stylish interior of the Belfort Inn, but she wouldn't miss that strange woman one bit.

Mrs. Gable sat in her small office-cum-lounge, watching her beloved late morning quiz shows. She liked them even more since so few of the contestants were dark-skinned with foreign-sounding names nowadays. They'd mostly been sent back to whatever grubby little hellholes they crawled from. Or made to take good *Christian* names and discard their silly little faiths. *A secular Britain is an unsafe Britain*, is what she always said. Look where science had got everyone. Nearly wiped out, for goodness' sake. *Where science fails, God saves.* That's what the party said, and by golly they were spot on. God held no place within the gates of heaven for scientists, any more than for paedophiles and murderers.

When her husband had been alive, they sometimes felt like the last two good *Christian* folk in Britain. Throughout her lifetime, she'd watched the country slip deeper into godlessness. First, those damn mobile phones, or smart phones, as the silly devices were known. *Smart, my bottom.* They'd turned Britain's once proud youth into stupid narcissists who worshipped only at the altar of self-obsession. The Conservative Christians had turned that around, too. *May they rule for a hundred years!* Lord have mercy if those Liberal scum ever seized back power.

She'd let herself get all lathered up, and she'd better calm down, or her blood pressure would go through the roof. *Focus on the quiz shows.* Perhaps she could beat her personal best record for the number of questions answered correctly in one session.

Her absolute favourite quiz of all time was *Brain Drain.* The show required contestants to answer questions in an enclosed bubble. As the prize money increased, their oxygen levels dropped lower with each passing round. If the contestant made it to the end and beat the final round without falling unconscious, they won the grand prize. *Brain Drain* started at midday—still forty-five cruel minutes away.

Yet another commercial break began, and she groaned and rolled her eyes. She wanted to get up and make a fresh pot of tea, but her body felt weighted down, as if some malevolent goblin had festooned her with invisible sandbags. *Grin and bear it. You can resist them.* But there were so many adverts, and they were so awfully invasive nowadays. They always knew what she wanted, even if she didn't. One moment she'd be tutting to herself at yet another interruption, only to be suckered in to purchasing some worthless piece of junk in the blink of an eye. Two-hour drone-drop delivery, one touch ordering, instant credit. It was relentless and far too easy. *Well, not today.* She switched over to a news channel, the one place she could avoid those bothersome commercials.

The news anchor droned on, but she ignored him, until an Arabic looking man flashed onto the screen. "*Detectives have issued the identity of the man they want to speak to in connection with the death on Monday of Martin Hassan, original first name Mohammed.*"

"Martin, that's a fresh one. Wouldn't fool me. Good riddance to bad rubbish, that's what I say," scoffed Mrs Gable to the empty room. She unpeeled a nice, ripe banana, her regular lunchtime sweet treat since the diabetes diagnosis two years ago. She'd been forced to cut out her favourite midday reward of two *Fry's Turkish Delight* candies, but the doctor said a banana was fine. The photo of the dirty Arabic man faded into a different image, and she paused, the pale fruit inches from her open lips and expectant tongue.

"*Michael Randall is believed to be armed and dangerous. He should not be approached.*"

The *direct connect* icon flashed at the bottom of the screen. Her mouth widened. Free of the supportive structure of its skin, the top half of her precious banana capsized and rolled onto the carpet. She recognised that degenerate, but from where? Yes, of course! The grubby fellow who'd only just checked out an hour ago with the sweet-faced young girl and frankly *horrid* looking mutt in tow.

She fumbled with her Head-Up Display, powering it on and jabbing at the *direct connect* button on her control pad. A ringing sound replaced the dial tone, then an automated voice came on the line.

"*Your call is important to us, please hold. You are… fourth… in the queue.*" She tapped her foot and muttered to herself. Didn't they know she had vital information about a murderer? A minute later, a voice came on the line.

"Hello," she said, her voice rising beyond its usual pitch. "I have information about Michael…" she grasped for the surname. "Ah yes, Michael Hardall."

A pause, before the voice replied, "Michael Randall?"

"Yes, that's the one. Mitchell Randall. He was right here at my hotel, with his young daughter. They only left about an hour ago." What if it *wasn't* his daughter? Maybe he'd taken an underage lover. She shuddered at the prospect, and a sickness swilled in her stomach.

"You're sure it was him, madam?"

"I may be getting old, but I'm not *blind!*"

"OK, we'll send someone. They'll arrive shortly."

"Do you need my address?"

"Belfort Inn," said the voice.

"Oh, yes, that's the one. Is there a rewa—" The line disconnected.

The helicopter flashed north at a hundred and eighty miles per hour. Eriksson eavesdropped on the two police detectives while they discussed their strategy, shouting to be heard over the roar of the blades. With a potential murder enquiry on their hands, Michael Randall was wanted by the police, but they would release the girl to Eriksson's team, after questioning, of course.

It would take another hour to reach the Scottish border. The cops had a mobile dog unit on standby and three fast response patrol units stationed across the county, whom the detectives had assured him were ready to move at a second's notice. They had Randall's number plate and had tracked its route leaving Penrith, but no further cameras had picked it up.

The car they'd escaped in belonged to one Joel Lindqvist. He'd warned those damn hippies back in Wales to sharpen up their act, and he'd be returning before long to teach them a proper lesson, not that he wanted to go back to Llandovery in a hurry. He didn't think of himself as a man who held grudges, but Lindqvist's choice to actively help a fugitive could not be ignored.

Eriksson sighed and allowed his mind to drift. From up here, England looked quite beautiful. The small mountains of the Peak District and the undulating valleys of the Yorkshire Dales were nice enough for an afternoon stroll, but nothing like the breathless landscapes back home in Norway. How long would it be until he tasted its crisp, unblemished air again? The Highlands of Scotland had some serious peaks, but the true sense of isolation one encountered in the north-western region of his homeland was a different proposition.

Two members of his own squad were also on board. Schofield's shrill voice invaded his thoughts. "Hey Chandler, where do you think they'll cross?"

Chandler rested her finger on her lips. "There are a few obvious places travelling from Penrith, but my money is on Solway, across the Esk near Gretna."

"That's exactly where I would choose. If I didn't know better," Schofield said.

"Want to put a hundred on it and make things interesting?" Chandler said. Schofield laughed but didn't reply.

While they idly speculated, Eriksson studied the border region on his Head-Up Display. The Super-HD satellite images scrolled in tandem with each movement of his eyes as they darted across the map. He hoped they would attempt a crossing near Gretna, because they'd be caught quickly and the whole sorry episode would be finished. A more probable scenario was they'd try somewhere between Kershopefoot and Whitelee, which represented a lot of ground to cover. Past Whitelee lay open countryside, while the land to the west offered miles of thick forest. That's where he would try, if it were him down below, trying to escape.

"Can you believe that cluster-fuck back in Llandovery?" said Schofield. "That's the end of those Baby Farmers, I swear. Heard we're gonna absorb them into our unit. Their leader Burrows quit this morning. They say she's coming to work for *us* now."

"So I hear," said Eriksson, smiling to himself.

Miko could quit horsing around now. He'd soon be back where he belonged, under the command of someone who understood how to deal with such a force of nature. Eriksson had tamed the highest and most feared mountains around Europe before he joined the most elite branch of his country's military. He could break a wild horse like Kozlowski, but the Pole's current senior, some flabby dope who probably finished bang average in his private school exam tables and had never seen a day's action in his life, didn't stand a chance. No doubt he'd earned the job through nepotism rather than performance. He'd be first out the door in the shakeup, and it didn't mean a golden handshake and a carriage clock. Oh no. The guy's predecessor, and his own former manager, would attest. If he could speak from his resting place at the bottom of the fucking River Thames.

The little blue car flashed past a sign which proclaimed, *Welcome to Brampton*. Michael eased his foot off the accelerator as they passed through the small town. They'd skirted the city of Carlisle half an hour ago. Now it lay twenty miles to the east.

"We'll park at the visitor centre for Hadrian's Wall and hike from there. It's about nine miles. Any closer and we might have border guards coming to check us out."

"Always with the miles, Dad. You know us kids are fully metric now, right? What's Adrian's wall, anyway?"

"Hadrian's Wall, honey," he corrected.

She rolled her eyes. "Duh, what I said."

"Back in the day, when the Romans ruled England, they built a wall to keep out the marauding Scottish brutes."

"That's ironic. Now they're trying desperately to keep us out of Scotland."

He attempted his best Scottish accent, and roared, *"You'll neeva tek euur freed'm!"*

Hope spluttered with laughter and held her hand to cover her mouth as her last bite of muesli bar threatened to leap out. "What the hell is that supposed to be, Russian?"

"Was it that bad?"

They turned off the A69 towards Lanercost, passing through another tiny village. He admired the straight and narrow road ahead of him, offering an unobstructed view of any oncoming traffic. If he were still in the Ford, he'd not be able to resist gunning it. Just as well this feeble car had nothing under the bonnet—far less likely to draw attention.

Ten minutes later, they passed the visitor centre, called Birdoswald Roman Fort. According to the handy pocket-sized *Northumberland Guide,* which he'd perused over breakfast, it housed a museum which had been closed for a few years. However, many people still came to view the attraction, and they could surely leave the car in its ample car park without arousing suspicion. The road bent around sharply. He braked, turned right into the car park, and killed the engine, pleased to note there was only one other car present, with nobody lurking around.

"OK, Hope, are you ready for a little hike now?" She did not reply, but unbuckled her seat belt, clambered out, and walked around to release Wolfie from the rear seat. The dog jumped down and stretched before emitting a long yawn.

They might need to camp on the other side of the border. If they made it. He corrected himself. No, *when* they made it. He hauled the little tent out from the boot. It fit neatly in the large rucksack Joel had left them, along with their food supplies, a tiny camping stove, some waterproofs, and bottled water. Tucked down the side was the hefty bulk of the dead man's pistol. He hoped he'd never need to use the thing. It'd been many years since he'd fired a weapon.

Hope knelt to lace up the new boots he'd bought for her that morning. They might be too big, but they were far more suitable than her tired old footwear, which she abandoned in a nearby rubbish bin. She slipped on his smaller old backpack with her waterproofs and a few other belongings inside.

He looked up at the sky, laden with wet promise. The cold and humid air swirled around their heads, but it remained rainless, for now. The wind picked up further while they walked out of the car park and followed the road up towards Harrow's Beck, to join the trail to Kielder Observatory, the nearest landmark to where they would cross the border, less than a mile further to the west.

A pair of hikers dressed in colourful jackets with walking sticks and mud-caked boots appeared from a bend in the trail ahead. He nodded as they passed, but kept his head as low as possible without risking rudeness.

The powerful engine of his sleek hire car idled. Miko gripped the steering wheel and listened in to the police radio chatter while he clenched a butterscotch between his teeth and poked at it with his tongue. From his position, parked close to a busy five-way junction, he could head north, east or west at a moment's notice. He'd driven to Carlisle assuming that was where they would go, but he'd lost them because they'd never got that far. Now he knew for sure they were trying to cross the border in the northwest, just like he had always suspected they would.

His headset buzzed with another call, and he cancelled it. "*Kurwa!* Stupid idiot."

Whatever Faulkner wanted could wait, or the dumb cunt could leave a message. Didn't the idiot realise he was going to set the record straight, once and for all? He released the steering wheel, picked up the snow globe from inside the car's drinks holder and fondled it absentmindedly.

Randall had a good head start, but Eriksson's lot should catch them up. *Should.* Eriksson and his bungling clowns would fail, because they would have to stop at most a few miles inside Scotland, or maybe even at the border. *He* would not. He would go any distance necessary, for as long as it took, to make Michael Randall pay.

Faulkner slammed his fist down on his desk, causing his array of pens to leap up and roll towards the edge.

"Goddamn you, Koslowski, answer your damn phone."

He scanned the earlier email from Piers one final time.

The feeling, like a toilet plunger sucking his vital organs from his chest, deepened with each word.

> *Colin,*
>
> *I'm sorry my old buckeroo, but it's only fair I warn you. I've just been told the IPA is being wound up with immediate effect. Your field unit will be absorbed into Bertram Eriksson's team. I'll do everything I can to make sure you land on your feet, but this is coming from way over my head. Our voters don't want such a hardline approach to foetal procurement anymore, so it's softly-softly-catchee-monkey in future. The metrics and pollsters don't lie, unless we tell them to, of course. With the election coming up in the spring, we just can't accept the fallout from the whole mess in Wales, so the decision has been made to disband the unit. Your licence to trade is revoked forthwith.*

So, the market was closed off, a one team deal. Piers *would do everything he could.* Reading between the lines, that meant fuck all. Only the likes of Burrows at the top and the most valued field agents like Kozlowski would land on their feet. Those in the middle of this giant shit sandwich were buggered. He'd be ground to dust, wedged between top and bottom like miniscule grains of wheat inside two massive millstones.

A cold acceptance washed over him. He opened the top drawer of his desk and stared at his gleaming pistol. He'd not fired the thing since training, and he'd never discharged a weapon in active service. Perhaps Piers would come through for him. But if not, there was no retirement plan for men in a clandestine quasi-legal operation like the IPA, or the Baby Farmers, or whatever you chose to call it. Burrows would need a scapegoat, and that person would be strung up by the testicles for the media to devour, then quietly disappear in the furore of an inevitable scorched earth approach. If they chose Colin Faulkner as their spring lamb, perhaps he'd surprise a few people and go down swinging.

CHAPTER: FOURTEEN

The chopper buzzed over the city of Sheffield, spread out below like a shattered clay pot. The pilot announced they were about forty-five minutes away from Carlisle. An update came over the detectives' radio and Eriksson's Head-Up Display simultaneously, causing an echo.

The car had taken the A69 east of Carlisle, which ruled out a crossing at Gretna. Further details would follow. Things were happening fast on the ground now, but was it fast enough? Eriksson leaned forward and shouted over the roar of the blades, detailing the latest route to the pilot.

"Told you, didn't I?" Schofield said, grinning and chewing his gum.

"Shoulda taken the bet then, ya dumbass."

Twenty minutes later, there was another incoming call from control. The car had turned off near Brampton, so that ruled out crossing near Whitelee Moor. There were no more cameras they could check to narrow it down further.

He suspected they'd driven north to cross near Kershopefoot. There was a border guard outpost a few miles to the west, but most of the troops were out on manoeuvres.

Schofield scuttled over on his haunches and said, "The coppers have dispatched a patrol and try to intercept them,

Guv'nor."

"That leaves around ten miles of border to the east. Tell the pilot we need to search the area around Kielder Forest from the air while the cop units close in below."

Schofield nodded and went to deliver his message, while he stared into the gloom. It was getting rough. Visibility would start declining the moment they hit the thick clouds up ahead. He'd spent many days battling such weather up in the mountains and knew only too well how quickly conditions could deteriorate. The plan would only work if the weather held.

Hope stared at her father while he peered up at the sky, his face a picture of worry. "We better put the waterproofs on," he said. "It's going to bucket down soon."

They stopped and took out the equipment from their packs. The jackets offered welcome wind protection as it howled. The skies still held back on their promise. In the first hour, they'd covered around three miles on well-marked trails with good footing, but now they were heading into a thick, foreboding forest.

Wolfie jogged along beside them, his ears and tail erect as he scanned the trail from side to side. They'd seen nobody since the pair of hikers whom they'd passed not long after leaving the carpark.

It started to shower, lightly at first, but with an increasing intensity so gradual it seemed almost imperceptible. Before long, it grew to a deluge of driving rain, which even penetrated the dense woodland canopy. Despite the valiant efforts of her raincoat, water began dripping down her neck and rising up her legs. Wolfie stopped and shook himself vigorously, but it made little difference. It seemed even he'd begun to find the trek tiresome.

"It'd really help if they had some fucking signs out here."

"Are we lost, Dad?" She'd not seen a sign for the Observatory in ages. Perhaps they'd made a wrong turn.

"No, we're not lost." He turned towards her and smiled as she lagged ten yards behind. "You're doing great, honey. I don't think it's so far now." She hadn't complained once yet. Her father *should* be impressed.

"C'mon!"

"I'm *tryyiing!*" she whined. It wasn't fair. His legs were longer.

"Not you, Hope, the sign…" he pointed at the wooden marker, which read *Kielder Observatory—5 miles*. He didn't *think* it was far? Five bloody miles, barely halfway.

She muttered under her breath, "Way to go."

The pilot's strained voice came over the Helicopter's in-flight radio channel. "It's no good. We can't stay up in the air any longer. It's becoming too dangerous with this declining visibility. I'll reroute to Carlisle Lake District Airport. Prepare for landing, eight minutes."

Eriksson cursed under his breath and turned to the two detectives with a scowl riding his face. "Make sure there's a fast response vehicle waiting when we land." When the detectives failed to reply, he added, "Do I need to remind you what'll happen if you hamper our operations?"

"Yes sir, I'll make the arrangements," said one of the

detectives.

"And get me an update right away." The other detective nodded and hunched into his radio.

"Sir, we have sent the other two response units to pick up the trail towards Kielder Forest Park." There were few roads traversing those remote areas. They were running out of time.

The chopper touched down with a shuddering bump at the windswept airfield. It'd been a hairy approach, but his stomach had quickly settled once they'd disembarked. Schofield and the fatter of the two detectives, however, were competing for who could throw up the loudest. His man looked set to win.

At least the requested response car was parked on the airfield. A fresh-faced young police officer approached and snapped to attention. "Eriksson? Sergeant Glass, sir. There's been a development, a piece of luck actually," said the copper in a thick northern accent. "One of our units questioned a couple of hikers near the museum. Birdoswald, I think it's called. They reported seeing an older guy and a younger girl, possibly related, heading north into Kielder Forest. It *could* be them, although they weren't sure about the descriptions."

"Sounds promising. Get the dog unit across to meet us and get a move on!"

"One thing, sir. The hikers said the pair had a dog with them."

"A dog? Are you sure?" Glass nodded. "We've got nothing else to go on right now."

Glass drove the police vehicle expertly, sirens screaming all the way, and they reached Birdoswald before the dog unit, less than ten minutes since setting off from the airfield.

A two-man response car was already waiting in the car park by a small, dark blue, old-model electric car which had been hurriedly parked, judging by the angle. Eriksson got out to examine it. The plates matched Lundqvist's vehicle. *So, it was them.* Perhaps the hikers had been picking mushrooms and hallucinated the fucking dog.

The police dog unit came screeching around the corner and pulled up. The handler introduced himself as Wallis. He already had the target's pillowcases from *The Belfort Inn*, but the scent permeating the car's seats would be fresher.

Eriksson tapped his feet while Sergeant Glass took out his police-issue baton and shattered the driver's side window, safety glass spilling inside. Wallis had a German Shepherd, and his colleague had a Doberman bitch. The Doberman strained at the leash, spit drooling from its snarling black lips.

"I didn't think you used Dobermans anymore," said Eriksson.

"Sally's the last one, real tough girl this. The other shep is off duty," said Wallis.

"Is it on holiday?" Eriksson said, sandpaper dry.

Wallis missed the joke. "Vaccinations."

The two dogs scampered at the car seats, barking incessantly. Once they had the scent, the group consisting of Eriksson, Chandler, Schofield, and Glass, along with the two dog handlers and two detectives, set off northwards, leaving the police response unit behind to continue examining the scene and question any passers-by.

Miko's Head-Up Display flashed with an incoming video message. No prizes for guessing who—he'd already received multiple missed call alerts from the field office. Faulkner's stupid fat face and greasy ginger hair sprung to grim life in front of his eyes. There were hollow bags under his eyes that he had never noticed before. The guy had aged a decade in the past week.

"Kozlowski, answer your damn calls, man. It's over, the whole shitting thing. I'm afraid the agency has been disbanded. You're to report to Bertram Eriksson as soon as you get off leave, Monday morning at the latest. He's your new superior. Your unit is now under his command."

"Go fuck yourself," Miko snarled, depressing the accelerator as he passed a sign for *Brampton - 2 miles.* The car responded effortlessly, and the speedometer pushed past eighty.

Ahead, a ramrod straight road offered faultless lines of sight, and he bulleted past a slow-moving vehicle, drawing a furious horn from its startled driver. The museum approached, and he eased up on the pedal. He rounded a corner and slowed further, craning his neck around to see the police vehicles parked close to a little blue car with a shattered window. Two uniformed officers leaned against it, chatting away to each other, but there was no sign of Eriksson.

He scanned the landscape until, in the distance, he located the Norwegian, heading towards dense woodland with a load of coppers, mostly in plain clothes. He passed the car park, pulled into a layby, and killed the engine. The time had come for another pleasant afternoon stroll in the woods. After getting out of the car, he leant on the roof and watched Eriksson vanish into the forest, with his dumb hair billowing in the wind.

In a pinched, mocking squeal, he said, "Hey boss, I'm early."

Michael finally had to admit they were lost. He'd last spotted a sign half an hour ago, and they'd made several more turns through the twisting forest since, making it hard to work out which direction they were now heading.

He banged his fist against his head, trying to visualise the route and their rough location along it. The paths had been well marked for the first few miles, but now there was little indication whether they were still on the right track, and the rain had soaked the little pocket guide he'd purchased earlier. In any case, its tiny map of the area offered minimal help, so he might have to rely on memory alone.

Up ahead, he spotted a large, colourful wooden map. *What a stroke of luck*! He ran towards it, Hope trailing behind with Wolfie at her side, and studied it while they caught up.

"This is no good. We've taken a wrong turn, so we need to go back about three-hundred-yards and make a right."

She let out an exasperated sigh. He pulled off his rucksack and dug out the old phone Joel had given them. It still held a little charge, enough to switch on camera mode, but not for the flash. Although the light was poor, it hadn't yet completely darkened. He took a picture of the map, gloomy but decipherable, re-shouldered his pack and jogged back the way they'd came, stopping to encourage Hope, who had planted her feet and crossed her arms. She set off after him with a modest huff.

Rain fell incessantly from the pregnant skies above. His daughter kept up, although their pace had slowed down significantly, and she appeared to be tiring. He thought they were about four miles from the observatory, but they needed to turn west before they reached it.

"We have to stay alert for border guard patrols, especially

when we get close to the border. It would be *much* better if we saw the guards before they saw us."

"I know, Dad."

"What's our story if anyone stops us?"

She parroted the words he'd taught her. "Hey mister, we're hiking Adrian's wall and we've taken a detour to see the Observatory. I just *love* astronomy!" She beamed at him, her beautiful white teeth showing, the bottom set slightly crooked.

He didn't bother to correct her small error as it sounded more authentic, anyway. "Spot on, Hope. When all this is over, you should consider a career in the theatre."

"Wow, thanks. Maybe I will."

"And if we've turned west when they stop us, I'll say we took a wrong turn. Act surprised and annoyed."

Her smile dropped. "The second part will be easy."

Except for the ceaseless rain, and the wind whistling as it swirled through the trees, the forest kept silent. Somehow, the silence seemed ominous.

The group of seven trotted through the woodlands. Eriksson thought it was a shame they didn't use horses much in the modern age because this hunt was tailor made for horseback. Nothing provoked fear like the thundering hooves of horses in pursuit. He couldn't imagine what it was like to be chased, but in his mind, he saw frightened foxes cowering from barking, snapping hounds, with red-coated huntsmen on horseback, their bugles blowing, sending strange songs across the wind.

Their dogs strained to go faster, but Schofield was struggling to keep up after losing his lunch earlier, while the detective with the ample gut had already dropped back after suffering a stitch. His colleague looked ready to throw in the towel, too.

Chandler, Glass, Wallis and the other dog handler were all lean and fit. Eriksson himself regularly ran half-marathon distances of thirteen miles, and it couldn't be more than another five miles to the border. They'd covered around four so far at a good speed, but how much of a head start did the target have? The footprints looked fresh, and the dogs had no trouble following the scent. They must be closing the distance with each step, but would they be fast enough?

The thought of having to return empty-handed needled him. It would be a lonely place, having to explain himself to his superiors, if they missed out again. All they needed was a little luck, but a man such as he shouldn't be relying on luck, not with reputations at stake. There were sure to be changes within his organisation, and change brought opportunity for advancement. If the pair managed to cross, should he pursue into sovereign Scottish territory, and risk the diplomatic consequences? Or be damned with the rules, victory at all costs? If it somehow got out that the targets had been apprehended on foreign soil, it could be the end of his career, but then an agent was only as successful as their last mission.

At last, they reached the fork in the path Michael had been expecting. "Let's stop here for a quick breather, before the final push across."

Hope puffed up her cheeks, let out a long breath, and dropped to her haunches. He pulled out an energy bar and demolished half in one giant bite, then offered the rest to her. She shook her head, but Wolfie stared at the food, his long tongue flicking his lips. Michael shrugged, broke the rest in two, and dropped a piece by his feet. Wolfie needed no second invitation and guzzled it up, then stared up at him, mistakenly optimistic of more.

A few more minutes passed, with only the driving wind and rain breaking the silence, before Michael said, "OK, let's go." One way was sign-posted *Observatory - 1 mile.* They headed in the other direction, which was not signed at all. Unlike the well-maintained paths before, the track was muddy and narrow, with thick nettles and thistles crowding in at the sides. They could only travel single file, and their pace slowed to a crawl. Between them, Wolfie's paws *pitter-pattered* in the mud.

"We're so close now. Keep going, Hope." His jacket caught a thick bramble, which bent forward, then whipped back viciously, snapping across her breast.

"Oww!" she cried out in pain, startling him before he realised what he'd done.

"Sorry, honey." Carried on the wind, far behind them, came a noise. It sounded like a dog barking. *Get a grip. It's probably just your imagination.* But then Wolfie stopped in his tracks, turned, and sniffed the ripe air.

"Shit, did you hear that?" said Hope, also stopping.

"What? I didn't hear anything."

Her voice rose in worry. "It sounded like a dog. Wolfie's heard something too."

"It's probably someone out walking their own dog, sweetheart. People live up here, surely."

Her voice returned to its usual pitch. "I guess they do."

He patted her on the shoulder, and they resumed their

march onwards. Once Hope could no longer see his face, he dropped his strained expression of calm and resumed clawing at his wet palms with his nails.

Eriksson halted the group to examine clear footprints in the fresh mud, heading towards the border around a mile away; one large adult pair and a smaller shoe a few steps behind. Step-by-step next to the girl's prints, he noticed large paw markings. "How strange," he said to nobody in particular.

Wallis and the other handler could hardly restrain their hounds. The swirling gale kept changing direction, occasionally carrying a clear scent of the fleeing pair and, by the looks of it, an intriguing smell of another of their kind. His heart rate crept upwards. He could almost feel the moment approaching where he'd take the pair down. Their devastation at coming so near and falling at the final moment would taste exquisite.

"They're close," Wallis shouted over the din. "Let them off!" He stuttered to a struggling stop, the dogs pulling even harder, and reached down to release the German Shepherd. Sally followed a second later, snarling and snapping with her breath fogging behind. The two dogs accelerated out of sight, and by silent consensus, the group slowed to catch their breath.

Eriksson frowned. Had Sally the Doberman seemed a little *too* excitable? "That rabid hound of yours better leave us something alive to question," he said.

"Relax, she's a professional," Wallis replied, before turning to his colleague. "But I definitely wouldn't want to be in the shoes of those two right now." The second dog handler laughed as much as his burning lungs allowed, but Eriksson did not find it funny.

He picked up the pace again and jabbed a finger ahead. "Stop slacking and get a march on. We've got a job to finish."

Michael thought they were almost at the border. To fail now was unthinkable, but how far would they be chased on the other side? Wolfie kept sniffing the air and growling intermittently as they ran. The gruff barking from behind had become unmistakable—not just one canine, but two distinct tones.

He spotted a clearing in the distance, the English side of the border. Beyond, on the Scottish side, they'd find more thick forest, with a fast-flowing stream between the two countries.

"The border's up ahead, Hope. We're so close."

The air was heavy with mist, the sky a sheer wall of grey. Water dripped into his eyes, distorting his lenses. Hope panted a few steps behind him, doing her best to keep pace, but lumbering in the new boots which were not worn in. The mud grew slipperier with each step. He considered ditching his backpack, but it was pointless. He could force the pace, but she looked maxed out.

By the time he approached the stream, Bell's Burn, Hope had just reached the clearing, a hundred yards behind. On the far bank there was nothing except freedom, so close he could taste it. The barking grew closer and louder. He turned and moved back towards his daughter, ready to carry her the final distance if necessary.

"C'mon Hope! You can do it! We've made it," he urged as she bounded towards him. Seventy-five yards, then fifty.

Behind her, the two dogs honed into view, tearing out of the
treeline. He sprinted towards her without a second thought,
clawing for the taser in his pocket while he ran.

CHAPTER: FIFTEEN

Miko stalked a hundred yards behind Eriksson and the others, easily keeping pace in the driving rain. Johnson's gun, now *his* gun, rattled around in its holster by his ribcage.

If Eriksson's lot caught the pair, he would see or at least hear the fracas, and they would have to come back past him. They'd have Michael Randall handcuffed, and he'd pop a couple of rounds in the bastard's face at close range before melting into the forest. If they sent police dogs after him, they too would die. The thought of dogs sent a shiver down him, and images of Hassan's mutilated throat and haunting screams flashed through his mind. He shook them off. Miko Kozlowski was afraid of *nada*, least of all some stupid hounds. Yes, he owed the canine race a measure of revenge for Hassan, but such considerations were secondary. The primary objective was Michael Randall, who would pay his debt with his life. Eriksson could keep the fucking girl, for all he cared.

If the pair got across the border, then even better—he could stalk them at his leisure. He would follow until Eriksson's crew had to turn back, dodge them, and pick up the trail. If fact, he hoped Michael and the girl *did* make it, because a showdown would be far more interesting. He could take his sweet time with them. There would be no damn wolf-creature to save the day.

\#

The dogs were close. Hope knew it from her father's terrified expression, but she dared not look behind. Between them, Wolfie skidded to a halt. In one smooth motion, he dug in his heels and turned, almost like a cartoon character. A raking snarl rose in his throat as he stalked towards her. Razor-sharp incisors glinted in the fading light. Behind, the other dogs barked and snapped. She could almost feel their rancid breath on her back. Visions of the dead man's shredded throat pumping thick blood flashed through her mind. She wanted to scream, but every ounce of available oxygen pushed her burning muscles to run faster.

She reached Wolfie, his lithe body coiled, low to the ground, sprung like an archer's bow. Every sinew strained as he waited for the right moment. Then he was gone, darting towards the police dogs in a flash of fur. *Grey Wind after all.*

She reached for the relative safety of her father's outstretched arm, finally daring to turn her head as she clasped onto it. The dog in the lead was moving at pace, its eyes fixated on them. Wolfie snaked around from the right and blindsided it. With a surprised squeal, the animal tumbled as its legs vanished from underneath. Wolfie was on top in a flash, savaging the stunned creature, forcing it out of the hunt with brutal efficiency. Before he could strike a mortal blow, the other dog, a vicious looking beast, approached and stopped to size him up. No element of surprise for Wolfie this time. Both dogs growled and snarled, eyeing each other. The pair looked evenly matched in weight and size. They reared up on their hind legs to attack and met with a colossal screech.

"Wolfie!" She found the air to shout his name.

"He's gone! We have to cross now!" But, all at once, her remaining strength deserted her, like the last remnants of air rushing from a deflating balloon, and she dropped to her knees. He hoisted her up on his shoulder in a fireman's lift and waded into the fast-flowing stream, gasping as the brutally cold water reached waist height. Some of it splashed the exposed skin of her midriff as he flailed and struggled to keep his balance on the rocks beneath. Once they'd reached the far bank, he laid her down with a bump. Still, she couldn't find the strength to stand, and he dragged her by her arm, up the steep earth embankment, wheezing with exertion until they reached flat ground.

"Move it, soldier!" he commanded, while she lay on her back, spread out on the wet grass. "We have to get into the treeline before the rest of them show up."

With his help, she clambered to her feet. When she craned her neck to glimpse the fracas, all she could make out were brief flashes of fur, with canine howls and screeches, carried on the breeze. *Poor Wolfie.* She knew she'd never see him again, but would these men ever stop chasing them? Everything she'd lost hurtled through her mind like a rushing train: her mother, her friends, Johannes, and most of all, her innocence. Now, even Wolfie was gone. It had to count for something. Those sacrifices could not be in vain. The realisation gave her fresh impetus and they set off again, marching as fast as her starved lungs would allow.

Eriksson reached the clearing first, with Wallis by his side. The dog handler cried out when he saw his beloved hound, motionless on the floor except for his fur, buffeted by the wind. Sally had disappeared, but in the distance, the wind carried sounds of frantic barking.

Glass arrived behind them, heaving for air. "What the fuck happened?" Wallis ignored him and ran to check on his dog. It had a ragged wound across his flank. Blood oozed out, but it appeared to be breathing.

"First aid kit!" Wallis screamed, before turning back to the stricken animal. He stroked its head. "Poor Alfie. You're gonna be OK." The dog whimpered a little as it regained consciousness. Perhaps the thing might live if they got it to a vet soon enough, but Eriksson did not care. He'd made his decision. One failure on an otherwise spotless record was better than being known as a rule-breaker.

"Just like that and they're smoke," he said to no-one.

Chandler arrived beside him and put her hand on his shoulder, patting it gently. "Sorry, boss."

"Shit happens. If the Jocks turn him up, we can apply for extradition, but I doubt they'll grant it. The girl's gone for sure. They'll never send her back."

The other dog handler called out for Sally. Eriksson doubted it would be the end of the world if the dog had vanished. It seemed like more of a liability than anything.

"Sir, the weather is improving. I'm calling for a pickup," said Glass. "We can look out for Sally once we're airborne too."

He shrugged. Whatever. Let these wet kids wait an hour for their stupid chopper. He had a sudden urge to be left alone. Besides, he needed time to think and get his story straight. The report would be an important one.

"I'll meet you back at the car. I feel like walking."

Glass peered into his eyes with a quizzical expression, before a flicker of understanding flashed across his smooth, almost hairless face. "OK boss. Take my car and I'll wait for you at the airfield." Glass launched a set of keys. He caught them, stuffed them into his pocket and turned, ready for the nine-mile return hike to the car park.

Miko crouched motionless and watched from the treeline. Eriksson and the rest of the group were turning back empty-handed. The pair had crossed the border, after all. They probably thought they'd made it to safety. Not a chance. He could almost taste Michael Randall's fresh pain while he witnessed his daughter's suffering. He would be forced to watch. Left to wonder what Miko had in store for *him*—the main meal after the girl had provided a pleasant little *przekąski*.

Somehow, the guy had disabled one of the police dogs. Impressive, but *he* would not underestimate the man. But hadn't there been two police canines? Yes, that's right. He could hear the handler off in the distance downstream, shouting the missing dog's name. He giggled to himself. What a bungling fool Eriksson was. And the man wanted to command *him*, Mikolaj Kozlowski! It would be a long walk, taking turns carrying the wounded hound. Hopefully, it would die anyway.

One of the men stood hunched, talking into his headset. From the radio, he heard the tinny reply. "Stand by for pick up in forty minutes. Over."

So, they had a chopper coming. But where was Eriksson? He scanned the trees and caught sight of the familiar blonde shock of hair flapping across his idiotic skull. He had to blink several times. The Norwegian was walking into the forest alone. Had he gone insane?

He smiled to himself. If Eriksson wanted to present one to him, he would not shirk such a gift. No, he would graciously accept. Once he'd skirted past the others, he came out from the tree line and broke into a trot, following the same path Eriksson had taken.

His hand caressed the smooth metal of Hassan's pistol. He'd much rather use the knife he usually carried in his inside pocket, but he had lost it during the woodland chase back in Wales. It would've been quieter and far more personal. More enjoyable, too.

Miko stalked twenty paces behind the Norwegian, who marched onwards at a fair pace. He didn't once look behind until a branch snapped beneath Miko's boot. When he spun around, Miko grinned, registering the exquisite look of shock on the other man's face.

"Kozlowski, what the fuck are you doing in the woods? You're too late. They made it across before we could get to them."

"Ah, that's a shame. I knew you'd screw it up. I suppose you haven't got the balls to follow them."

"That's your problem, Miko. You need to start playing by the rules if you want a future in my organisation. Hasn't Faulkner told you?"

"Told me what?" The two men stood ten feet apart, eyeing each other. Miko continued to smile.

"You're under my command now. Your unit is history. Just like I told you it would be. You didn't listen then, so you better start listening now."

"Ah, that. Yes, he mentioned it, but I chose to ignore him."

Eriksson sighed and said, "Stop being a belligerent shit and get with the program. There's still a place for you if you buck up your ideas, but you're really trying my patience with this nonsense."

He pulled out his pistol and levelled it at Eriksson's face. "Do you think I'd work for a clown like you? I killed better men for fun back in Poland." But the man did not show the surprise and fear he expected, no, *demanded*, to see.

"You're making a big mistake, Kozlowski," Eriksson said, but now some delicious fear had crept into his voice.

Despite this, he grew bored with the exchange. If time had allowed, he'd have put down the gun and done it properly, man-to-man, with hands and nothing else, but Eriksson didn't deserve such theatre and reverence. He was nothing but an entrée. Each second spent in this futile dance, which could only end one way, was allowing Michael Randall and his little cunt daughter to waltz further into Scottish territory, and closer to freedom.

"It wouldn't be my first mistake, old friend. But for you, walking off in the forest all alone is going to be your last. Goodbye Bertram."

He stared down the pistol sights, tensing his index finger in readiness. Eriksson's face twisted, and he flung his pale forearms up in a futile attempt to protect himself. *Now* the man understood the hopelessness of his situation.

"No, don't do it. What do you want?" Eriksson cried. Miko's ecstasy deepened as he watched the pathetic display, then the smile drained from his face like the blood gushing from the slashed neck of a pig, hung upside down on a butcher's hook.

His finger caressed the trigger before squeezing once. The round slipped through the Norwegian's outstretched hands and slammed into his long forehead, sending shards of skull and brain fragments upwards, streaking his white hair with crimson spatters. He toppled backwards, with a look of infinite shock written into his face.

Miko took one last look at his former boss, spread-eagled on the forest floor, with a leaking pool of blood painting the leaves beneath, and sprinted back the way he'd come.

Michael and Hope marched through the woodland on the Scottish side of the border. They'd made it across, but who knew how far, if at all, they'd be pursued? Safety seemed light years away. The plan was to keep heading north-west, cross country, until they hit the A7. From there, they could hitchhike to Edinburgh and then take a bus or train across to Glasgow. Hope's tears flowed anew, and she soon ground to a halt. He stopped and put his arm around her.

"Honey, you know we can't go back, right?"

She nodded.

"And we can't stay here and wait, either?" She said nothing and followed him. Slowly, her tears dried to a sniffle. The rain had stopped, but he shivered now the adrenaline had worn off, and Hope's teeth chattered with the cold.

"I need to pee," she announced, walking off the track and into the dense forest. He stopped and leaned against a tree. While he waited for his daughter to relieve herself, he tapped his boot on the soft forest floor. What was taking so bloody long?

A muffled scream came from the woods, and he spun around. Hope inched out from behind a large pine tree, but something wasn't right. A bald head with sunken, fearless eyes loomed beside her face. A wide hand covered her jaw, with thick, meaty fingers spread over her mouth. *It was the man who'd chased them in the forest—the Baby Farmer! The one I let go.* He should have shot him when he had the chance, and now they'd pay for it with their freedom.

"Hello again," Miko said, his eastern European accent only slight.

Michael's stomach somersaulted in cold terror as he saw the pistol resting against his daughter's temple. He stood tall and tried to sound bold, but his voice came out weak and strained. "You've got no authority here. We're in Scotland now."

"What you say is true. But I am not here to bring you in. Maybe the girl, maybe not. After I've taught her a lesson, that is."

The words dripped with malicious intent. With cold certainty, he understood the Baby Farmer intended to murder him right here and would probably rape his daughter, or even worse, it would be the other way around and he would be forced to watch first. Something had pushed this man past the limits of his sanity and sent him teetering beyond the edge of reasoning.

His thoughts raced. Inside his backpack was the pistol. *What good was it there, instead of in my fucking jacket?!* The taser was there too. He'd put it away once they'd begun their march through Scottish territory. *What a fool.*

He eyed the distance between them—around forty feet. Once Miko had closed it, he was finished. He had only one chance. Time slowed to a thick soup as Michael launched himself and sprinted away from the line of fire. The surprise worked, and Miko took a few valuable seconds to lift his pistol and squeeze off two rounds in response. The jolt of adrenaline pushed his body the vital extra inch, and the bullets zipped past his head, slamming into a nearby tree with two dull thuds.

Once he'd opened enough distance, he dived down a small embankment and into the heavy undergrowth, rolling and struggling to pull off his rucksack at the same time. *Thank fuck I didn't do up the safety straps!* When he came to rest, he ripped the pack open and scrabbled around inside for the pistol. His fingers closed around the cold, oily metal of the gun barrel and he wrenched it out of the bag.

With his back at the base of a thick tree, he sat with his knees drawn up towards his chest. He risked a peek, and his reward was to witness Miko pistol-whipping his daughter across her temple. The blinding white shards of pain she must've felt from the blow hit him like he'd been struck himself, and he winced. When she crumpled, Miko pushed her limp body to the floor and loomed towards him.

His voice boomed through the forest. "Michael, you surprise me. I did not think you'd be a coward and run away. Are you sure you want to leave your beautiful daughter's fate in my hands?"

He checked the safety catch. Who knew how many bullets were inside? He was certainly no gun expert. If he took the magazine out, his shaking hands might not get the weapon ready again. For a second time, he peered around the tree. Miko moved with surprising grace for such a heavyset man and had already cut the distance in half.

A bullet grazed the side of the trunk, inches from his retreating head. He returned fire, but the pistol bucked, jerking his aim off-centre, and his shots sailed wide of his target, where they got eaten by the foliage. Miko dropped to the ground into a prone firing position. He'd missed his best chance, but at least now they were on an almost equal footing. *Equal? Sure, except for the other man's years of training and obvious penchant for violence.*

"That's the spirit!" Miko cried, a crackling madness present in his voice. Michael readied himself to transition cover. The man would have a deadly bead on him now. He levered himself to a standing position with his back firm against the tree-trunk, which was wide enough to completely shield his

body, then flung himself away and rolled outwards. Something grazed him, leaving a burning trail of pain down his side. He couldn't tell if it was a bullet, or he'd caught a sharp branch, but he spun around and landed on his back, crashing against a wide rock, leaving him winded, gasping for air and momentarily helpless.

Miko roared in triumph and bounded through the woods, but he somehow summoned the strength to roll out of the way just as two more bullets thudded into the earth where his face had been. The other man's eyes widened in surprise, like a dead certainty had been ripped from his grasp, and Michael raised the pistol, firing twice. One round missed, but the other found its target, gouging a little red hole above Miko's right breast. The Pole let out a strange *oohmph* noise as the round thudded into him. He clutched his collarbone but remained upright. The gun dropped by his boot, and he clawed for it, while Michael took careful aim and fired again. This bullet struck square in the stomach and doubled him up like a collapsing ironing board.

He dragged himself upright, wincing with each step towards the stricken man, until he reached close enough to administer a fatal round. When he pulled the trigger, nothing greeted him but the hollow *click* of the firing pin as it struck metal. Miko heard the empty sound and his head snapped up. His arm rose, shaking and unsteady from the wounds, with the pistol held in his weakened grip. Otherwise, Michael never would've had a chance to dive to his left. Miko fired three times and a zinging agony like a fierce hornet sting ripped through him as a bullet dug deep into his buttock. The others sailed through the space he had just vacated. There was no fourth— Miko's gun clicked empty, too.

Ignoring the pain pulsing through his wounds, he knelt and launched his empty pistol, barrel-first, like a boomerang. It struck Miko square on the top of his head as he crouched, bent over, fumbling inside his jacket pocket for a spare magazine. He toppled backwards onto his ass, his stout legs lifting skywards as he landed. The weapon flew from his grasp and vanished into the undergrowth.

While Miko was on his knees, scrabbling around in the dirt, Michael pounded towards him like a linebacker, careering headfirst into his torso. They wrestled and rolled on the forest floor. Michael had a brief advantage over his winded adversary and attempted to lock a firm chokehold around his thick, sinewy neck. Miko was wounded but possessed a madman's strength. At the last second, as the crook of his elbow closed around his windpipe, Miko got his wide forearm inside the hold and broke it, pushing him away and using the momentum to roll him.

Once the other man was on top, Michael could do little against the crushing weight. He flailed and jabbed, but his hands bounced harmlessly off the top of Miko's bulbous head. He tried to push his thumbs into the other man's eyes, but powerful arms pushed him away and began to pin his shoulders under his knees, from where there would be no escape.

Still, Michael fought and struggled, squirming in vain until an iron grip closed around his throat and started choking the life from him. His eyes bulged and, as his oxygen starved brain began to shut down, he peered into the manic, twisted face that would be the last thing he ever saw. Blackness invaded his peripherals until only tunnel vision remained, distorted like a fisheye lens. The whistle of one squealing, high-pitched note drowned out all other sounds.

The pain softened. Oblivion beckoned, and he sensed a dark shadow looming above. Death, arriving to claim him, just as he'd always pictured. But the grip around his neck loosened. Another bassy thud, booming as if it had travelled underwater, reverberated through Miko's arms and into his own numb body.

With his last remaining strength, he ripped free from the brutal hands clamped around his throat and sucked sweet, cordite-filled oxygen into his screaming lungs. He turned his face upwards to Hope, an avenging angel with her arms raised high above her head. In her trembling grasp, she held a jagged, bloody rock. Miko's twitching face glazed over as she brought it down with every ounce of might she could possibly possess in those delicate hands, once, twice, three times. Etched with grim shock, like the victim of an epic grift, his eyes rolled, and he slumped over to his left, a leaden weight, his skull caved in like a cracked egg. His fingers spasmed and his arm jerked upwards as Hope delivered one last, crushing blow.

CHAPTER: SIXTEEN

When they spoke about it, neither could remember much. The blurred hours it took to stumble out of the wilderness, in complete darkness, were forever lost. Michael, delirious and covered in blood, recalled little except clinging onto Hope, who herself had double-vision from the concussion. When they'd reached the quiet, single-lane rural route, rather than the busy A-road which he'd intended, they must've looked like a walking nightmare. It was a miracle anyone stopped at all. How long they'd waited or who picked them up neither could say, but *somebody* drove them to an Edinburgh hospital, and to that person he wished he could offer his sincerest thanks.

He planned to discharge them both as soon as he could move well enough. The doctors had fished out Miko's bullet from his ass and stitched him up. They'd assured him he'd not suffered any lasting physical damage, although his body held a different opinion: one which said he'd gone twelve rounds with a heavyweight boxer. Hope seemed OK after the head injury, but they wanted to keep her one more night for observation.

"Talk me through the events of two nights ago one more time, sir, if you'd be so kind," said the young policeman, in a guttural Glaswegian drawl.

"Like I said, two men in masks attacked us in the woods. They took everything we had and gave me a right beating. They hit my daughter with the gun, and they shot me twice and left me for dead. I have no idea how she got away."

"And your name is Mr. Craig Smith, correct? And your daughter is Jess?" Michael nodded, wincing at the shooting ache in his neck. "It's only the doctor swears you called her by a different name."

"Don't be ridiculous. I could barely remember my *own* name when I got here, and she was delirious with concussion."

"We'll need you to verify your identity as soon as possible, Mr. *Smith*." The detective accented the name, making sure Michael understood he did not buy it. The pretence wouldn't work for long, but he had to deflect their questions until he could find Ray. "And you have no ID at all?"

"None. They took my wallet and my bag. Once I've been home and got my stuff together, I'll be over to the station to straighten everything out."

"Yes, that reminds me. The home address you gave. I can't find any record of a *Smith* there." The cop raised one sandy eyebrow at a skeptical angle.

Michael shrugged. What could they do? He'd caught sight of himself in the mirror that morning and still looked like an extra from a post-apocalyptic horror movie. Hope looked OK except for the huge, purple welt on the side of her head, but she remained quite disorientated from the concussion. Still, she'd kept tight-lipped and refused to speak to them. Clever girl. At her age, they couldn't question her without a parent or guardian present, at least over the border in *this* fine country.

They hobbled the half-mile from the hospital and boarded the first available train to Scotland's biggest city, Glasgow. The two cites lay less than eighty miles apart, but the differences between them were stark. Edinburgh had always been the richer of the two, but the divide had widened in the years since independence. Most folk with money chose the capital. Glasgow's metropolitan area population had nearly doubled, and many of those new residents had started from scratch.

Michael stared out the window while the gleaming train rattled through the outskirts of the city, where swathes of land had been given over to buildings for all the new residents. Imposing high-rise structures rose from the ground; concrete monoliths, surrounded by the rusted remnants of industry.

While the train moved deeper into Glasgow's heart, he stared into the vaults of his own. He'd always forced his inner gaze away from the stark, horrible events of that night—the night of *the incident*—as if he could somehow erase history by refusing to remember the details. Since almost meeting his end, his outlook had changed. Denial had never worked, and it never would.

The argument had been the usual petty nonsense between young men, brimming with pride and bravado. The boy, Sheridan, was one of a group of his brother's friends whom Mike had been drinking with. Sheridan had been ribbing him all evening, like the way his own brother did. But Ray held that privilege, nobody else. Young Mike wasn't afraid of this uppity shit who wanted to look tough in front of his mates.

The verbal exchange became more and more personal until Mike said something from which there was no going back. The boy knew he couldn't back down after that, and his mates gathered round, eager for the inevitable confrontation, convinced their boy would triumph. Ray was probably chatting up some tail at the bar, otherwise he'd have snuffed out the brewing fight in a heartbeat.

Sheridan swung; an angry right hook, which Mike saw coming a mile off. He swerved out of the way and, while the boy was off balance, Mike struck him with an uppercut so sweet he saw the lights go out the moment it landed.

He remembered examining his fist as the first signs of swelling appeared, waiting for the boy to get up and either dust himself off and leave, tail between his legs, or get ready to go again. Both were fine with Mike. His mates urged him to get up, but Sheridan didn't move. Blood began seeping from the back of his head, almost black against the dark wood of the pub floor, and everyone suddenly looked serious.

"Sheri, you alright mate?"

"Wake up, man."

"Call a fucking ambulance!"

"You've killed him!"

Then Ray came running over. The ambulance arrived soon after, while Mike sat, numb, staring at the pool of blood smeared across the floor. No fear, no remorse. Nothing. When the police arrived, cuffed him and dragged him towards the waiting wagon, he craned his neck for a last glance over his shoulder at Ray. He wanted his brother to tell him it would be OK, and it wasn't his fault. He wanted him to promise to protect him like he'd protected him so many times from their father's rage and his own stupidity. But he didn't. He just stood there, head in his hands, and watched them take him away.

Michael and Hope clung to each other as they walked down a quiet street close to the city centre. Hope took an occasional misstep and nearly toppling the pair of them. Ray's last known address was six years old. He might have moved on several times since then, but where else could he start?

"Times must've changed. This used to be quite a rough area, if my memory serves."

Now it seemed to be one of Glasgow's more desirable parts. They arrived outside an immaculate looking three-story Georgian townhouse and stopped to admire it before climbing the towering steps. He reached out and rang the buzzer. Above it, written in neat lettering, was the name Randall. *They were still here!* A moment later, the smooth, shiny black door opened a crack and a woman's face peered at them, trepidation etched across it. She was in her late forties with well-coiffured brown hair.

"Yes, can I help you?"

"Hi. I'm Michael, Ray's brother." The door closed and he heard the woman's voice calling to her husband. Moments later, it reopened.

"Michael, what the hell are you doing here?" Ray asked, before looking him up and down. "Christ, what happened to you? You'd better come in."

"Thanks. You remember my daughter, Hope?" Ray's face broke from a look of deep concern to a smile as he cast eyes on her for the first time in a decade.

"My Lord, Hope! Last time I saw you, you were just a little child." In the ample hallway, he hugged them in turn. They both winced in pain.

"This is my wife, Andrea," Ray said, introducing the woman who had opened the door. Perhaps he'd forgotten they'd met all those years ago, or maybe it was their way of offering a new start.

Andrea led them into the drawing room and offered them tea. They sat on the rigid sofa and Michael poured out their unlikely story, with assistance from Hope, while Ray perched on the edge of an uncomfortable-looking armchair, wearing an expression which revealed little about his thoughts. Would his brother listen to him now, after he'd lied so many times as a boy? He had no choice but to tell it liked it happened, and whether Ray chose to believe it was out of his hands.

In the morning half-light, Michael became an observer, maybe even a ghost. Through fogged windows, he watched Hope and her new family. Outside, everything was colourless, like in the heart of a snowstorm. Inside, where she was, it looked like a Christmas card come to life: warm, brimming with colour and so, so beautiful. Her cheeks glowed, her face radiating pure innocence, like it had before they'd been forced to flee London. On either side of her sat Ray and Andrea, with Wolfie curled between their feet, licking his paws. She looked so happy. They all did. She didn't need him; she had everything she could ever want.

His daughter tore herself from her family's loving embrace, as if she'd realised someone was watching from outside, invading their precious privacy. He waved and banged frantically on the window. It made no sound. When she looked in his direction, her smile dropped for a moment, but she stared right through him. When she turned her gaze back to them, the television-advert-smiles returned. The picture zoomed out until they were nothing but a scene inside a snow-globe. Michael held the orb in his hands, turning it in all directions, searching for a way inside. There was none, and the more he looked, the more he disturbed the snow inside, until it was nothing but white static on a detuned television.

Days passed while Michael's strength slowly returned, at least enough for conversations to turn towards the future. "What's our move, Ray?"

"It should be straightforward to claim asylum, for her at least. There's a very clear policy on fertile women," said his brother. "She's in danger of being forced into a birthing school against her will, and should automatically be granted residency here, once they've confirmed her identity and status."

Michael stared around the room, his eye passing an ornate wooden crucifix and settling over a picture on the wall. In the photograph, Ray and his wife stood on either side of a grinning teenage boy, around Hope's age. The boy was black, perhaps Somalian. Underneath hung a framed certificate, which proclaimed *East Glasgow Foster Parents of the Year.*

Ray caught him staring at it. "We always wanted children of our own…" his voice trailed off and he turned to his wife, taking her hand.

She smiled softy and said, "We're in the process of trying to adopt, but it will take another year, at least."

"We've tried everything," Ray added. He didn't need to finish. Like millions of women, Andrea was most likely barren. If not, then like the majority of men, Ray would have a miniscule sperm count.

Andrea clasped her hands together. "We considered paying a surrogate to come from Poland or somewhere else in Europe, but it felt too exploitative."

Michael cynically wondered if they'd ever considered buying a child on the black market, perhaps even from the Baby Farmers themselves. From what he knew, there was a brisk trade in both practices, even north of the border.

Once Andrea had left, he beckoned his brother to the far corner of the room. It was a long shot, but what options did he have left? "Ray, is there anyone you know who could get me papers for a new ID card?" His brother stared at him blankly. "You know, under a different name?"

Ray shook his head. "I'm sorry, Mike, I just don't know those sorts of people."

His head lowered and he stared at the floor. "It's alright, Ray, you've been a real saviour already." Did his brother believe their story? If he hadn't bought it, they'd be out on the streets by now.

"Look, I've already started the process for Hope's asylum claim, and they're going to put two and two together once I take her along to the Robert Office in a few days." Michael flashed him a confused expression, and he added, "That's an official Scottish government building, a bit like the Home Office in London."

"OK, Ray. And thank you."

The cops must have realised the Smith name was bunk, but how much else did they know? His brother would see they didn't come for him, not yet, but they'd come knocking soon. He'd have a lot of questions to answer.

The next day, Hope was ready to go in her new outfit, which Ray had bought for her, including a brand-new rain jacket and properly fitting shoes. It never seemed to stop bloody raining in the city.

"You'll get used to it," Andrea joked as Ray and Hope stepped out into the drizzle. She smiled up at her uncle, linking her arm with his, and they strolled off. Ten minutes later, the rain ceased, temporarily at least, and weak sunlight glinted through, bouncing off the pavement. Even the cracked concrete glistened, displaying a thousand different shades of grey. Everything looked so much nicer in the sunshine.

"It's so clean and tidy here," she said, looking in all directions at once.

"I guess so. It's really that bad in England, huh?"

Hope nodded. "I won't miss it." *Well, maybe I'll miss Johannes.*

"Let's get everything signed and sealed before we count chickens."

Hope stopped walking and chewed her lip. "They won't send me back, will they?"

"Of course not, sorry, darling. I wouldn't allow it. So, what do you want to do with your life, Hope? You'll have to go back to school first, of course."

They resumed walking. Why had he changed the subject? His answer was far from convincing, and adults seemed to lie an awful lot, but what options did she have but to place her faith in this man? "I don't mind school, uncle. I think I want to work with animals. I love them all, especially dogs."

"One of Andrea's friends runs a veterinary practice. I'll find out what the career path looks like, if you're interested?"

She squealed and put her hands over her mouth. "A vet! You think one day I could be a vet?"

"You could do anything you put your mind to, Hope."

She smiled and gripped Ray's arm tighter, her heart swelling with pride. Perhaps she *could* do it, and she wasn't as dumb as those horrible Christian teachers had told her. Now she thought about it, her reports from little school had always been quite good.

An annoying question kept needling her while they walked. Ever since Ray had come back into their lives, it had bothered her, and she could hold it no longer. "Ray, can I ask you something?"

Now it was his turn to look worried, and they stopped to

face each other. "Yes, of course."

"Um… what did you and my dad fall out over?"

Ray exhaled a long breath, while a concerned look edged onto his face. "He's never spoken to you about it?" She shook her head. "That's for him to explain, in his own time, Hope."

What on earth could it be? "Must be something terrible."

"Your dad did something regrettable, which I found it hard to reconcile, at the time. But he was a different person then. People change. He always had so much energy as a kid, tired the hell out of me, trying to keep up with him. He was a great sportsman, smart but impulsive, you know? Michael never had a proper male role model. Our father, your granddad, of course, vanished. He'd have been…" he paused, perhaps pulling unwanted memories from a deep pit, "… well, your age, I guess. It's such an important time. I'm four years older. I was angry, too, but it didn't affect me the same way it affected Michael."

Hope pouted and her head dropped to the floor. She'd rarely thought of her father as a young man. Deep down, she knew so little about him. But what act had he carried out which was so terrible that his brother hardly spoke to him again? She had to know.

"Can't you tell me the whole story? I'd never rat you out."

Ray shook his head and gave her a tight-lipped smile. "Sorry kiddo. It has to come from him."

She shivered and buried her hands deep into her pockets. They walked in silence for another five minutes, their breaths fogging in the crisp winter air. Ahead, the streets got busier, the buildings grander, until finally they stopped outside a fine-looking old building. A shiny plaque announced it was *The Robert Office*.

"OK, Hope. This is the place. Are you ready?" She nodded, and they climbed the steep steps. "Remember what we spoke about, and what to answer. If they ask any questions you don't like, tell them you need me present."

"Yes, Uncle Ray. I know." But did she? They might be smarter than her. Would they try to trick her? Elicit a confession?

At the desk, a woman with immaculate hair and makeup tapped ferociously at her keyboard. Her head snapped up and she flashed a toothy smile.

"Hope Randall?" They'd obviously been expecting her. She couldn't decide if she felt important, intimidated, or a mixture of both. The receptionist turned to Ray, all-business again. "You're her uncle, correct?"

"Yes, I'm Raymond Randall. The father, Michael, is still in bad shape, so I am acting as her guardian. I have a signed letter."

"We have all the details, thank you. Please take a seat and someone will be with you shortly."

Hope fidgeted while they sat in a vast oak-paneled waiting room. A sprinkling of other people, mixed in their ages and attires sat, dotted amongst the sea of mostly empty seats. What business could they have here? There was no discernible link between them to explain. There were minimal signs of the building's purpose, and she had only a vague understanding of what the place was: the Scottish equivalent of the Home Office.

A white-robed man with a stethoscope briskly strode past, while another fellow in an impeccable dark blue suit descended a stone staircase in the hallway, accompanied by an attractive, raven-haired woman, bespectacled, and wearing informal clothing. The man stopped and surveyed the room. His eyes locked on her, his face wearing what he probably hoped was a disarming smile, but it did nothing to assuage her fear.

"Hope, I'm Simon Collins. I'll be looking at your case

today." She remained seated, flexing her wrists, her gaze fixed to the floor. "Don't worry, we're here to help." His smile widened, and she stood, but couldn't meet his eye.

"Am I in trouble?" She looked up from her bowed head.

The man laughed. "No, you're not in trouble of any kind. My colleague here, Dr Glanville," he swept his arm to his left, "is going to take you for a few tests. Nothing painful, I promise. Then she'll get you a nice hot cup of tea, and some lunch if you're hungry."

The woman beamed at her and said, "Call me Linda."

She seemed friendly, and it didn't sound so bad. "Can my uncle come too?"

"He'll be along in no time, but Simon needs to have a few words with him alone, if that's alright with you, young lady?"

Ray rubbed her shoulder and said, "Nothing to worry about, Hope, just formalities. You go along with this nice woman. They have to examine you and check your well-being after the horrible ordeals you've suffered."

Linda led her to another floor of the vast building and Hope had the impression of being in the bowels of a giant, swaying ocean liner. It seemed like a hospital ward, and they entered a brightly lit room filled with medical equipment. A raised blue bed dominated the middle of the room. She changed into a gown and the doctor asked her a never-ending stream of questions before asking her to lie down and taking a blood sample. This time, she didn't even flinch. She was a big, strong girl now, and no doctor would dare give her a stupid lollipop.

The doctor examined the wound on her temple, checked her pupils and her mouth, then examined her breasts and abdomen, stopping at the bruises and scratches which still littered her young body after the chase through the woods.

"Oh, you poor dear. You really have been in the wars.

Now I'm going to do some scans, don't worry, it won't hurt. Please lie down flat."

She wheeled over a large device which looked more like something she'd expect to see assembling car parts in a factory and parked it at the foot of the bed. It whirred into life and started to traverse her body one inch at a time. A laser flashed from one side of the bed to the other. It seemed a lot fancier than the equipment back at the Medicentre in London, a million years in the past.

The doctor put on some spectacles and turned to a monitor on the desk beside her. "What a horrible time you've been through, Hope, but you're safe now. Are you looking forward to starting school again?"

Her tongue probed the inside of her mouth while she pondered the question. "Yes, I think so. I kind of miss it, except all the hardcore religious stuff."

"None of that here, except the usual boring R.E. class."

"Do they even teach about Islam and other banned faiths here, then?"

"Yes, they're all treated the same. No faiths are outlawed in Scotland."

The revelation made Hope gasp. "Wow! How long have you lived here then, Miss—"

Her face wrinkled into a smile, and she took off her glasses. "Linda, please."

"How long have you been here, Linda?"

"Well, I came about five years ago, when they started all the nonsense with the birthing schools. My sister and I, we came up from Manchester. My parents joined us just before they closed the borders."

"Do you have children?"

Linda laughed and grinned. "Yes, I'm one of the lucky

ones. I have a son, Steven. He's three now, and a right little terror."

Hope giggled, before realising she'd never met a child that age, not properly.

"Not long now, then we can…" Linda's face scrunched up, and she leaned closer to the monitor. "Oh, this can't be right."

Something was wrong. Her heart started pounding in her chest. "What is it? Am I sick?"

Her attention fixed on the screen, Linda ignored her question and shoved her glasses back on. Once she'd absorbed the picture, the doctor swiveled around to face her with a canyon-sized frown etched on her face.

She inhaled through her nose, held the breath, and released it. "No, nothing like that, Hope. You're pregnant. Two weeks gone, by the looks of it."

CHAPTER: SEVENTEEN

Michael paced the front room. They'd been gone nearly four hours already. Maybe the authorities would never release his daughter.

"What's going on, do you think? Can you call?"

Andrea had stayed behind to keep him company. They got on well enough, but he sensed an impenetrable gulf between them. What he'd been through had no parallel in her world. Ray would've told her about the mistakes he'd made in his younger days, no doubt. What must she think of him, underneath her polite exterior?

She fingered a gold crucifix around her neck. "I'm sure it's just a lot of silly bureaucracy, but of course I'll call Raymond if they're not back soon."

Five hours after their departure, his daughter and brother returned. Hope marched straight up to her room, unable to meet his eye. The colour had drained from her face. Whatever had gone down, it didn't look good.

"What's going on?"

"Michael, we need to have a serious talk, mate." Ray knitted his wrists, looking like he had the weight of a thousand bricks stacked upon him. He took a deep, bracing breath and tensed his churning stomach. Was his fragile world about to be shattered yet again?

"I'll get straight to the point, Mike. Hope can get asylum,

no problem. It won't take more than a few days and she can stay here with us indefinitely. You don't have to worry about that."

His face lifted. "That's great!" But surely there was more.

"The bad news is about you, Mike. They won't sign the papers until you hand yourself over to the cops. They know you're wanted in England on the murder charge. Relations between the countries are strained enough. They want to send you back across to stand trial, at least on trafficking charges and possibly even murder."

"I didn't kill that Hassan guy."

"If it's like you say, then their case won't hold up. But consider it from anyone else's perspective. It sounds far-fetched, does it not? Don't forget your record, too."

He had to agree, but it was more than far-fetched. It sounded crazy. His eyes lit up for a second. "Hope can verify what happened."

"Of course, if it goes to trial, she'll testify in your defence. We'll get you a hot lawyer and if the wounds are consistent with a dog attack, there's no way you'll go down for it. But it all takes time. The legal process down south is glacial. You'll probably get the mandatory twelve months for the border offences, and they'll make sure you stew while you await trial. Then they'll probably drop it."

"Fuck, Ray. You know how I feel about being caged up, man. You know what I went through. There's got to be another option."

Ray shook his head. "You were a kid then, Mike. You can cope with twelve months, for her sake. Look what you've survived already."

Could he handle another stretch? The prospect of that cold, brutal place again filled him with dread. There would be no Willy to save his soul this time. How much worse had prison got since then? The mass jail building program of the previous decade, to house the thousands of religious prisoners, refugees and illegal immigrants, along with the common-or-garden criminals, had ground to a halt when the money dried up. Everyone knew the prisons were more crowded than ever. Even with their slick spin-doctors and puppet media outlets, they couldn't hide the fact. No, it would be a miserable, soul-crushing experience.

He had to find something to look forward to. A sliver of hope crept into his voice as he asked, "Can I come back here after?"

"Sure, if they'll let you. They may do because of her, but with such a recent criminal record, you're unlikely to get a passport, maybe not even a holiday visa. As a Scottish citizen, she'll be able to visit you whenever she likes, though."

He hung his head. "I guess I could move to Penrith or something. It wasn't so bad."

Ray sat next to him and placed an arm around his shoulder, rubbing his back and giving his shoulder a gentle squeeze. "Michael, there's one more thing."

He groaned, lifting his head to look his brother in the eye. What the fuck would he say next? Didn't they usually save the worst for last? "More? Come on, man, give me a break."

"When they did Hope's examination, something came up. The hormone checks confirmed she's fertile, but there's more… Long story short, your daughter is two weeks pregnant."

Ray was a little out of shape, with a spare tyre around that once flat-iron stomach, but he had a few inches on his younger brother. In his still-weakened state, Michael was easily restrained. Ray refused to let him see his daughter until he'd calmed down, outwardly at least. Inside, his stomach swirled. Once he'd promised to go easy on her and taken a seat on the sofa, his brother dashed off to fetch Hope. A minute later, she entered the room with that familiar sheepish look of trepidation hanging off her face.

"I'm sorry, da—" He jumped up, cutting her off.

"How the hell did this happen? You're only thirteen, for fuck's sake!" His voice rose to a strained pitch, but not quite screaming. "Was it Kevin's kid?" He searched his memory for the name. *Christ, what if it wasn't him?*

"Johannes? Yes, it was him. We only did it one time, and I never meant for it to happen."

His voice rose another semi-tone. "Did the bastard force you?"

"No Dad, of course not!" She was telling the truth; she was never that great of a liar, at least not when asked a direct question.

"OK. Well, that's something, at least." He flopped onto the sofa, immediately regretting it. Why couldn't these people get a decent sofa? They could clearly afford it.

An elongated sigh, one which had been building in him ever since Ray had given him the first piece of bad news, released itself like a trapped ghost. "Fuck, what an utter shit-show."

Hope sat down beside him and hugged him tightly, tears cascading down her cheeks. For the first time since he'd sat by his exhausted wife's side in the hospital while she cradled their newborn daughter, he gave up trying to hold on to his own and sobbed wetly into her thick corkscrew hair. Her damp nose nuzzled deeper into his stubbled neck, still streaked with bruises from Miko's thick hands. She smelled of coconut scented shampoo. The hot tears poured from him, a decade's worth of emotional blockage. He couldn't stop them, but he no longer wanted to. Release was a one-way street, and with each second the dull pain which had throbbed behind his eyes for weeks, maybe even years, receded further. Neither he nor his daughter seemed willing to let go. They sat like that for a long, long time.

They had so much to talk about. In fact, she couldn't remember being so interested in her father before. Instead of frightening her, like she'd expected, his emotional outpouring brought her closer to him. Knowing the feelings inside him were unquestionably real gave her the comfort she'd always needed. Now, no matter what, she could face any adversity ahead.

But first, she had to speak to her mother. Could she ever find forgiveness in her heart for the woman? Perhaps she wouldn't be able to answer the question for a long time, years even. Their shattered bond might be irreparable, but the woman at least deserved to know she was safe, and her actions hadn't ended her daughter's freedom.

"Mom?"

The voice on the other end gasped, "Hope, is that you? Are you safe?"

"Yes, Mom, I'm OK. I'm in Glasgow, with Uncle Ray. I'll be staying here now."

Her mother sobbed on the other end of the line. Hope wished she could reach through the phone and comfort her. *No, she doesn't deserve my forgiveness, not yet. Maybe never.*

"I'm sorry, Hope. How can you ever…" She broke down. The conversation had gone nearly word for word the same as the previous one, back in Wales. But, as the connection with her father had solidified in the intervening days, she'd sensed those once taut maternal bonds weaken, until they became nothing but frayed and broken strands dangling in the ether. She understood, somewhere deep within, the repair process would only begin once she discovered her ground zero—the point where thinking about her mother produced only a blank space where emotion used to be.

But, as wrenching as it'd been, the call had provided one piece of priceless information: Johannes's mobile number. Whatever happened over the coming months and years, she'd need to reach him eventually. She didn't expect anything from the boy, but he deserved to know he was going to become a father. Kevin, who seemed like what her own father might call a man's man, would be delighted about his son's virility. Despite his stoic kindness, she'd found the immense sadness and distance in the man's eyes haunting, and the man could use some good news. The prospect of one day being able to visit the community as a free Scottish citizen, and introducing Johannes to his infant child and Kevin to his grandchild, filled her heart with joy. As long as the circumstances of their pursuit hadn't ruined everything, of course.

During dinner, Hope made her usual excuses about a lack of appetite and ate as little as possible, pushing the food around until somebody took the plate away. She didn't expect any of them to understand, but what other method did she have to hold on to any kind of control? The adults could make decisions about her life and offer a multitude of their opinions like they were facts, but only *she* decided when and how much food she consumed.

Afterwards, Ray and Andrea made their excuses and left her alone with her father so they could talk at length. He wanted to know if she was scared about becoming a mother at such a young age. After what she'd been through, something as natural as childbirth didn't hold much fear. What she felt inside more than anything was excitement. The anticipation of a fresh life, with new friends and exciting experiences. Yes, it would be far tougher with a child in tow, but they'd be permanent Scottish citizens, and she could rely on the support of her auntie and uncle while her father wasn't around.

But one thing still bothered her. "Will you tell me why you and Uncle Ray lost touch?"

Her father's gaze burrowed into the floor and his shoulders drooped like a sudden weight had fallen on his shoulders. What could be so bad? Did she even want to know?

"Hope, I can't speak about it, not yet. When we're on the other side of this mess, I'll tell you. I promise."

"There's nothing you could say which would make me not love you. I've *killed* someone, Daddy. You can't have done worse than me." They hadn't before openly acknowledged her act of violence in the woods. She'd barely even recognised it herself. Somehow, it didn't feel like a bad thing. She'd saved her father's life, like he'd saved hers more than once. Had a wry smile appeared on his lips at the mention of it? Perhaps they shared a bond of killers. What a terrible thing to hold in common!

"When all this is a distant memory, you'll know everything, Hope."

A distant memory. London felt like a distant memory. Somehow, even Wales and her brief fling with Johannes did, but she couldn't imagine what happened in the woods *ever* being distant. "I miss Wolfie," she said, so suddenly she found herself frightened by the strength of the emotion.

"I know, honey. He's gone, but you'll never forget him, even if you live to be a hundred. He saved us twice. Saved you, anyway. I was just a consequence of that."

"Do you believe in God?"

He looked shocked, as if the question had been completely unexpected. She supposed it had. "I… I don't know. I've never truly decided one way or another. Why do you ask?"

"How else do you explain it?"

"I can't. Some things cannot be explained."

"I think someone above put him there to protect me." Her assertion surprised her, but now she'd voiced it, her conviction only strengthened.

He shrugged. "Maybe, who knows? Perhaps he's descended from our old dog, which I told you about back in Penrith, or the same animal soul reborn into another? Or it's just a massive sequence of random events, unconnected to a higher power."

She scrunched up her face but didn't offer a counter argument. It was unsatisfactory. Somehow, if she could put events down to the existence of God, it meant someone was tending the light at the end of the tunnel. That thought gave her renewed strength and made everything seem so much more… more *comfortable*. Perhaps God would offer the sustenance she *really* craved and provide something more filling than food ever could.

Colin Faulkner stared around his bare new office. He couldn't quite believe it, but it seemed Beauchamp, the wily old bastard, had come through for him, after all. He'd been employed by the official branch of the government's fertility tracking operation, perhaps thanks to the abundance of soft targets, softer even than himself, to pin the blame on. These were people who wouldn't protest their innocence, or point fingers of blame in anyone's direction. Kozlowski hadn't made contact since the day Hassan died. His tracking chip's signal was weak, but they'd triangulated it within a small area near the Scottish border, a few miles from where Chandler reported finding Bertram Eriksson's corpse.

A ping from his Head-Up Display told him the lab report on Eriksson's cadaver had just landed, and Colin opened the email, absorbing the information in a few greedy bites. The bullet they'd fished out of the Norwegian's shattered skull matched the calibre and type from Johnson's missing pistol. All Johnson had admitted so far was that, after they'd gathered Hassan's mutilated corpse, the crazy Polak had ordered him to hand it over before disappearing into the woods, and he'd never seen his boss again. Well, if there was more to the story, lie detection protocol would uncover it soon enough.

It was a simple job for the top brass to pin the whole charade on a rogue agent, and Kozlowski would be strung up by the balls if he ever resurfaced. The tracking chip hadn't moved in nearly a week; either Kozlowski was dead, or he'd gouged it out from under his skin and discarded it. The remnants of Eriksson's squad were already en route to begin the search, but Colin doubted he'd ever show himself again, if he'd survived whatever had gone down in the woods.

He checked his watch. It was almost time for the meeting, so he switched his display into conference mode and logged into the virtual boardroom. Piers' avatar, somewhat slenderer than his real-life counterpart, was already waiting, along with some other top brass, hovering in observation mode, signaled only by anonymous, silent symbols. Burrows soon materialised. Somehow, he'd ended up under the woman's direct command again, like some twisted game of musical chairs. Not perfect, but better than most of the other scenarios he'd imagined.

Burrows' avatar had a permanent scowl and a fuming cigarette clamped in her creased mouth. A nice touch.

"Captain Faulkner, so glad to have you on board," Piers said, his abundant smarm impossible to hide even in the virtual world. The position came with a small salary bump, and a shitload more paperwork. But the rank of Captain was almost meaningless, a ceremonial promotion, probably so Beauchamp could keep his balls in a jar for when the time came to call in the favour. That time would come eventually.

"Your first major task, after Eriksson's most unfortunate demise in the line of duty, is to begin recruitment for his replacement. The other top priority is to tie up the loose ends of the Randall case quickly and quietly."

Colin had expected this. He figured if he fulfilled these two assignments well, his new role would be secure, and he could breathe easy again. Until then, it was probation, or a stay of execution, depending on how you looked at it.

Burrows' avatar began speaking, the endless virtual cigarette flapping between her lips. "Some good news at last. Something came across our desk yesterday which could make our job a shit-tonne easier. Michael Randall's brother, Raymond, has brokered a deal with the Scottish authorities. They've agreed to fast-track the daughter's asylum application in a matter of days, but only if the father hands himself into the English Embassy for extradition. Even better, Michael Randall has already signed over custody, so we expect he'll turn up any moment."

Colin frowned, sending his own avatar into a tailspin of vexation. Did these new emotion sensors have to be so damn sensitive? He'd better learn to hold a poker face toot-suite. But his surprise at the news was significant. Had the brothers not known father and daughter could *both* claim asylum on the grounds of persecution, murder charge or not?

"That's excellent news, sir. I'm so very grateful you've chosen to share it with me." Of course, Raymond Randall knew full well. He had connections at the Robert Office, and they would have explained it to him, even if he'd somehow been ignorant of the facts. Something else was afoot, but if Colin had learned one thing, it was when to ask questions and when to shut the hell up. Luckily, Burrows and Beauchamp seemed to be in a charitable mood.

"Faulkner, you're probably wondering why," said Burrows. "A bit of digging explained it. What we hadn't known was *who* Michael Randall had killed. The victim was a close friend of his brother."

They'd known about Michael's three-year sentence for manslaughter since day one. Now everything made perfect sense. Perhaps forgiveness had been too hard to find, and Raymond wanted him out of the picture. His guess was that the man had even leaked information about his brother's earlier crime to the Robert Office, in order to make an asylum claim difficult.

It was Beauchamp's turn to fill in the blanks. "Despite our rather fractious relationship, we still share any files of Class B clearance and below with the Scottish authorities, and they continue to reciprocate. Raymond Randall and his wife, Andrea, have tried multiple times to become adoptive parents, and even made abortive attempts to find a surrogate mother from various Eastern European hellholes."

Burrows tagged back in. "It seems we want the same thing as Raymond, namely his shit-eating son of a bitch brother out of the picture, for a while at least. We get our man, and they realise their pathetic dream of having their own child. Even if it's a bratty teen." She paused, or perhaps it was lag. Just as

Colin was about to check the connection, the avatar resumed. "What do you think, Faulkner? About our chances of putting him away for murder?"

Colin concentrated on maintaining an even expression. Why the hell did they need to know what he thought? Opinions were like assholes: everybody had one and nobody wanted to hear his. "Well, sir. Of course, this is only my opinion, and forgive me if it's ill-informed, but from the evidence I've seen, it'll be a huge leap to pin Hassan's death on Michael Randall, or any *man* for that matter."

"We're inclined to agree, Faulkner. Randall will probably walk for the murder, but that gives us twelve months to find as much dirt as possible and bury him for a while longer. The material we found at his flat was minor league crap, really. Might be worth an extra six months in a re-education camp."

Perhaps his new role wasn't merely ceremonial, after all. Was he expected not just to apprehend teenage girls, but to play the role of a bent detective, too? But then, who knew what dirt Randall had on the defunct IPA? Burrows would want certainty, but the lazy bitch was never going to get her own hands dirty.

"The guy needs some extra time to cool off, and a few more years behind bars should mellow him out. I'm sure you're looking forward to meeting him. We'd like you to pick him up from the airport. Just ensure he knows we can either make his time behind bars pleasant or, let's just say, rather *less* pleasant."

His orders were perfectly clear, but how much would Michael Randall's silence cost?

CHAPTER: EIGHTEEN

In his dream, Willy was a much younger man than when they'd met. The sequence started back in that fucking cell. But, as he stared at it, unblinking, the impenetrable iron door which separated him from the outside world faded in an effervescent glow. A young Willy, much younger than the man he'd known, stood, haloed by the light, beckoning him to rise from the squalor. Without moving his feet, Michael floated from the room and found himself sitting in a meadow, with bright sunshine cascading through the trees.

The voice came from everywhere at once, like the voice of God himself. "A good boxer knows when to move forward, and when to pull his guard up. But I never met a true fighter who knew when to throw in the towel. That's why you always need someone in your corner, Michael."

He knew Willy meant himself. Now, the familiar, wrinkled smile, and warm, caring eyes which had drawn his trust the moment they'd met had returned. If his own father had been half the person Willy was, he'd never have ended up in such a mess.

In the morning half-light, where dream and memory danced together like oil and water poured into the same glass, he recalled the first time Willy spoke openly to him about his own past. "You know the man I became, Michael, but not who I was. We're two different people. Let my own kids down the way your father failed you. Ain't seen them in over a decade. They won't speak to me no more."

Did the old fighter ever make peace with his own fractured past? He wished so with all his might.

Before lunchtime, with Michael still bleary-eyed after talking with his daughter late into the night, Ray broached the subject again. Arms crossed, he said, "It's time, Michael. If you don't go today, they're going to come back in force, and if they take you involuntarily, it won't look good." He returned his brother's stare, his own face silent and blank while Ray's expression turned to one of frustration. "Am I getting through to you? I had to pull a *lot* of favours, mate. I promised them you'd go quietly, and have you forgotten that Hope's claim depends on it?"

At some point during those swirling early morning hours, as he'd dropped in and out of a strange sleep, the plan had occurred to him, probably in that wide open, semi-conscious state following the dream. Perhaps it was sheer madness, but now it'd stuck in his head, the idea was no easier to ignore than an air-raid siren blasting next to his ear. Ray would have to understand. But could a brother who'd never trusted him for one damn second put faith in him now, when he'd never done enough to earn that trust?

He summoned the most earnest expression he could muster. "Ray, I'll do it. Of course I will. Tomorrow, in fact. *Tonight*, if need be. But there's something I have to do first. Just get them off my back for today. Also, I need to borrow your car."

"My car? What are you talking about, Mike? Are you mad?"

"Look, Ray. I was a fucked-up kid. I did stupid shit and I let you and Mum down."

Ray looked around the room quickly. Hope was up in her room, presumably sleeping, but he hushed his voice. Somehow, the facts hit harder than if his brother had been screaming in his face. "Michael, you killed a man, for Christ's sake. Sheridan was one of my best fucking friends. That's more than letting us down."

Michael wrung his hands and joined them in a praying motion. "You know it was an accident. I never meant it. You've got to believe me. The courts did, so why couldn't you?"

His brother looked away and refused to meet his pleading stare. "Do the right thing by Hope now, and you can consider yourself forgiven. You've got my word."

Michael bit his lip. "Will you take care of her?"

"Like she was our own, Mike." He smiled and pointed to the certificate on the wall. "They don't give those out to just anybody. She's in safe hands."

Soft footsteps padded down the staircase, and the two brothers exchanged a glance. Still dressed in her pyjamas, Hope entered the room, rubbing sleep from her red-ringed eyes.

"What's happening? I heard something."

"Everything's fine, honey. Ray tells me they've already found you a new school, isn't that great?"

"Yes, Dad."

"You'll be able to take your GCSE's, maybe even go to university."

"What's a Jeesy Easy?"

They shared a chuckle and Ray said, "It's an exam, Hope. You do them when you're sixteen. I think they call them something else nowadays. Forgive your father and I, we're old men."

Hope's face, creased from sleep, seemed to freshen when it broke into a smile. "I'll be a year behind, but once I've finished school, I might be able to go into veterinary college. Auntie Andrea's friend promised she'd hook me up with a job, once I'm trained."

"What about the baby, darling?"

"Andrea and I will be around to look after the child as much as necessary. I haven't seen my wife this excited about anything since we got married."

"See, Dad. We've got a plan. It's not just a daydream."

"That's great, my love. Sounds like you've got it all figured out. If only your father had been as smart as you when he was your age," said Michael, shooting his brother a knowing look.

"I think everyone could use a nice cup of tea," said Ray, leaving the room to join his wife. A comfortable silence descended. Hope seated herself, switched on the television, and patted the seat next to her.

"*The centralist Liberal Alliance has taken a shock lead in the latest polls. A closely fought election is predicted. Here from Westminster with the latest update is our English political correspondent—*"

"Boring news," said Hope, flicking the channel to a cartoon and beaming at him.

He grinned back and shuffled closer to her warmth. "Don't mind me. I'm just happy here, sitting next to you."

Michael hunched over the wheel of his brother's sports car. The Jaguar was less than a year old, and electric, of course, but with ample power beneath its dark green bonnet. From Glasgow he took the M8, turning off on to the A73 a few miles outside of the city. His hands gripped the steering wheel, sweat flowing from his palms while he guided the car around roads he'd only imagined in dreams, snaking through the stunning countryside with barely any traffic to concern himself with. When an occasional slow-moving vehicle loomed, he waited behind until the opportunity presented itself to scorch past. He was at one with the powerful engine; man and machine merged into one unthinking entity, in tune with the rolling miles of tarmac beneath.

Roads merged into one another, while hulking, snow-capped mountains gave way to pretty towns and villages. He exited the A7 at a little town called Harwick and headed towards the border, turning off to avoid Whitelee. He travelled several miles along a deserted road, slowing to enjoy the last moments of what had been a most wonderful drive, before making a sharp left at Saughtree, signposted Kielder Observatory.

He parked the car as close as he could to the border without risk of being spotted by one of the stalk-like guard towers which dotted the landscape every few miles. The car door slammed behind and he jogged into the woods, travelling off-road for a mile-and-a-half along the Scottish side of the border until he reached Bell's Burn once more, near to the location where they'd originally crossed into the country.

He stopped and breathed in the sharp air, shivering when a grim thought popped into his head. Deep in that forest, somewhere, lay Miko's rotting corpse, or what remained after the local wildlife had taken their shares. At least he'd provided something useful in death, because he doubted the man ever did an ounce of good in life. Of course, a hiker, or a local dog-walker, might spot the corpse, in which case they'd work out how the agent had met his demise. He'd have to take the rap. But, more likely, the agency for which he worked would locate the remains and quietly make them disappear. They'd not want to answer questions of why their top man turned rogue and carried out an illegal pursuit into Scottish territory, any more than Michael himself wanted to.

Despite the towers, there was little appetite in stopping anyone going from north to south and he soon crossed over to English soil, near where he'd last seen Wolfie ten days previously. The area he wanted to search appeared on the map about the radius of a cricket pitch. He first looked for a canine corpse or blood and found nothing, then took out meaty thick joints of beef from a plastic bag inside his pack, holding them by the bone and wafting them in the air while calling out the dog's name. There was every chance he'd undertaken a fool's errand, but at least he could look his daughter in the eye and say he tried. The dog could be dead, hidden from view in a bush somewhere, or it could be alive and many, many miles away, perhaps even trying to nose its way back to Hope. Stranger things had happened, after all.

After three hours spent in futile search, he neared the point of giving up. He cupped his hands to call for the dog one more time and dropped the meat on the floor at his feet, intending to leave it to the crows. From the undergrowth nearby came a rustle. A mean, black creature broke from the foliage and stalked towards him, growling and baring its fearsome teeth. It circled the meat and sniffed, never taking its violent yellow eyes from him. He was no canine expert, but it looked like a Doberman, and not a friendly one.

Inching backwards, his attention fixed on the animal, he reached for the taser, charged up and within easy grasp in his back pocket. The dog moved closer and, as it seemed poised to attack, another deep canine bark echoed out through the forest. It sounded strangely familiar.

The Doberman turned its head. Wolfie's familiar shape stepped into the clearing, fifty yards away. Michael continued moving backwards, but Wolfie trotted over and seemed to share a moment with the Doberman. Its erect tail sank towards the ground, and it whined, turned around and scuffled away, nose to the floor.

Wolfie approached him cautiously, sniffed the joint of meat at his feet and tucked in. Michael dropped to his haunches and reached out to pat him on the flank.

"Good doggy," he said, feeling a trifle silly. The dog ignored him and continued tearing flesh from bone with great relish. After Wolfie had finished his meal and licked his lips clean, Michael turned to leave. Wolfie hesitated, but after a little coaxing, he took one last, longing look at the gleaming white bone and followed him towards the burn.

He found a decent sized stick to help ford the stream's slippery bed and plunged himself waist-high, back into the freezing waters for the third time. Wolfie leapt in without hesitation and reached the far bank before Michael passed halfway. The dog shook himself dry and watched him, panting impassively while he stumbled and nearly fell. Only the stick saved him from an icy bath.

He dragged himself up the bank and into Scottish territory again. The relief was palpable, but he'd soon find himself hauled back to England, and returned to a lonely cell. The receding warmth of his early morning dream filtered back into his mind, providing welcome comfort. Willy would be beside him every step, and the promises in his distant future were worth any amount of temporary discomfort. He'd stand firm, stoic in the face of all accusations and receive whatever punishment they dished out. He could trust Ray's assertions. His brother wouldn't let him rot in jail, but twelve months or twelve years, he'd do it for Hope and take it with a smile.

On the meandering stroll through the gloomy woodland, he and Wolfie held an uneasy alliance. The dog gave him no trouble, but kept its distance. Perhaps the animal somehow understood it had to suffer him so it could get back to the girl it longed to see so much. Wolfie would have her to himself for a while. He'd make a fine surrogate guardian alongside Ray and Andrea.

Despite the bracing north easterly wind, he didn't hurry. If this was his last few hours as a free man, then he should damn well treasure each precious second. The cold air whipped through his pores, reaching every cell in his body, invigorating the depths which he'd never known existed, or he'd assumed long since dead. The wheels of his mind, unblocked by the earlier outpouring of tears, now turned as freely as greased gears.

Above, as night-time began to oust its eternal foe, an effervescent full moon peeked out between parting clouds. The majesty of the bruised sky awed him. He could almost hear its voice, and it compelled him to answer. With a broad smile on his face, he turned towards the heavens and howled like a wolf.

Acknowledgments

Much love to my wife Jenny for supporting me when my head is lost in these stories, and to my mother Alex for always encouraging my creativity.

Special thanks to Trevor Hatton. Without your keen eye for detail, this book may never have reached the world.

Thanks to Tim McWhorter and the team at Manta Press for their faith in my manuscript. I'd also like to acknowledge my beta readers Chris Hansell and Jon Taylor who both provided invaluable feedback, and also Michele Rubin and Carlyn Greenwald for their editorial assistance.

About the Author

Joseph always knew he would write seriously one day. That moment arrived in 2020, when his thriving hospitality business was temporarily shuttered. With time on his hands, he quickly fell into an obsession and became a keen student of the craft. Since finding the passion, he can't imagine life without stories rattling around his head. Eager to make up for lost time, he's been fairly prolific, and his short stories have appeared in several anthologies and literary magazines.

Even better, his rejections are getting nicer by the week.

He lives in London with his wife and their Scotty dog. Mandate: THIRTEEN is his first published novel, but with another manuscript already completed and outlines for several more, it's unlikely to be his last.

You can find Joseph's short stories in the following anthologies:

Worlds Collide (Nordic Press)
Summer Bludgeon (Unsettling Reads)
Nerve Janglers (Night Terror Novels)
I Cast You Out (Pulp Cult)
Freedom (Gravestone Press)

Lightning Source UK Ltd.
Milton Keynes UK
UKHW031032181022
410673UK00010B/547